THE
FIFTH WHEEL

A NOVEL

OLIVE HIGGINS PROUTY

1st WORLD
LIBRARY
Literary Society

The Fifth Wheel

Olive Higgins Prouty

© 1st World Library, 2006
PO Box 2211
Fairfield, IA 52556
www.1stworldlibrary.com
First Edition

LCCN: 2006936236

Softcover ISBN: 978-1-4218-3101-5
Hardcover ISBN: 978-1-4218-3001-8
eBook ISBN: 978-1-4218-3201-2

Purchase *"The Fifth Wheel"*
as a traditional bound book at:
www.1stWorldLibrary.com/purchase.asp?ISBN=978-1-4218-3101-5

1st World Library Literary Society

Giving Back to the World

"If you want to work on the core problem, it's early school literacy."

- James Barksdale, former CEO of Netscape

"No skill is more crucial to the future of a child, or to a democratic and prosperous society, than literacy."

- Los Angeles Times

Literacy... means far more than learning how to read and write... The aim is to transmit... knowledge and promote social participation."

- UNESCO

"Literacy is not a luxury, it is a right and a responsibility. If our world is to meet the challenges of the twenty-first century we must harness the energy and creativity of all our citizens."

- President Bill Clinton

"Parents should be encouraged to read to their children, and teachers should be equipped with all available techniques for teaching literacy, so the varying needs and capacities of individual kids can be taken into account."

- Hugh Mackay

DEDICATED
TO
MY MOTHER

CONTENTS

CHAPTER I

RUTH VARS COMES OUT

I spend my afternoons walking alone in the country. It is sweet and clean out-of-doors, and I need purifying. My wanderings disturb Lucy. She is always on the lookout for me, in the hall or living-room or on the porch, especially if I do not come back until after dark.

She needn't worry. I am simply trying to fit together again the puzzle-picture of my life, dumped out in terrible confusion in Edith's sunken garden, underneath a full September moon one midnight three weeks ago.

Lucy looks suspiciously upon the portfolio of theme paper I carry underneath my arm. But in this corner of the world a portfolio of theme paper and a pile of books are as common a part of a girl's paraphernalia as a muff and a shopping-bag on a winter's day on Fifth Avenue. Lucy lives in a university town. The university is devoted principally to the education of men, but there is a girls' college connected with it, so if I am caught scribbling no one except Lucy needs to wonder why.

I have discovered a pretty bit of woods a mile west of Lucy's house, and an unexpected rustic seat built among a company of murmurous young pines beside a lake. Opposite the seat is an ecstatic little maple tree, at this season of the year flaunting all the pinks and reds and yellows of a fiery opal. There, sheltered by the pines, undisturbed except by a scurrying chipmunk or two or an inquisitive, gray-tailed squirrel, I sit and write.

I heard Lucy tell Will the other day (Will is my intellectual brother-in-law) that she was really anxious about me. She believed I was writing poetry! "And whenever a healthy, normal girl like Ruth begins to write poetry," she added, "after a catastrophe like hers, look out for her. Sanitariums are filled with such."

Poetry! I wish it were. Poetry indeed! Good heavens! I am writing a defense.

I am the youngest member of a large grown-up family, all married now except myself and a confirmed bachelor brother in New York. We are the Vars of Hilton, Massachusetts, cotton mill owners originally, but now a little of everything and scattered from Wisconsin to the Atlantic Ocean. I am a New England girl, not the timid, resigned type one usually thinks of when the term is used, but the kind that goes away to a fashionable boarding-school when she is sixteen, has an elaborate coming-out party two years later, and then proves herself either a success or a failure according to the number of invitations she receives and the frequency with which her dances are cut into at the balls. She is supposed to feel grateful for the sacrifices that are made for her debut, and the best way to show it is by becoming engaged when the time is right to a man one rung higher up on the social ladder than she.

I had no mother to guide me through these intricacies. My pilot was my ambitious sister-in-law, Edith, who married Alec when I was fifteen, remodeled our old 240 Main Street, Hilton, Mass., into a very grand and elegant mansion and christened it The Homestead. Hilton used to be just a nice, typical New England city. It had its social ambitions and discontents, I suppose, but no more pronounced than in any community of fifty or sixty thousand people. It was the Summer Colony with its liveried servants, expensive automobiles, and elaborate entertaining that caused such discontent in Hilton.

I've seen perfectly happy and good-natured babies made cross and irritable by putting them into a four-foot-square nursery yard. The wall of wealth and aristocracy around Hilton has had somewhat the same effect upon the people that it confines. If a social barrier of any sort appears upon the horizon of my sister-in-law Edith, she is never happy until she has climbed over it. She was in the very midst of scaling that high and difficult barrier built up about Hilton by the Summer Colonists, when she married Alec.

It didn't seem to me a mean or contemptible object. To endeavor to place our name—sunk into unjust oblivion since the reverses of our fortune—in the front ranks of social distinction, where it belonged, impressed me as a worthy ambition. I was glad to be used in Edith's operations. Even as a little girl something had rankled in my heart, too, when our once unrestricted fields and hills gradually became posted with signs such as, "Idlewold, Private Grounds," "Cedarcrest, No Picnickers Allowed," "Grassmere, No Trespassing."

I wasn't eighteen when I had my coming-out party. It was decided, and fully discussed in my presence, that, as young as I was, chance for social success would be greater this fall than a year hence, when the list of debutantes among our summer friends promised to be less distinguished. It happened that many of these debutantes lived in Boston in the winter, which isn't very far from Hilton, and Edith had already laid out before me her plan of campaign in that city, where she was going to give me a few luncheons and dinners during the month of December, and possibly a Ball if I proved a success.

If I proved a success! No young man ever started out in business with more exalted determination to make good than I. I used to lie awake nights and worry for fear the next morning's mail would not contain some cherished invitation or other. And when it did, and Edith came bearing it triumphantly up to my room, where I was being combed, brushed and polished by her maid, and kissed me ecstatically on the brow and whispered, "You little winner, you!" I could have run up a flag for relief and joy.

I kept those invitations stuck into the mirror of my dressing-table as if they were badges of honor. Edith used to make a point of having her luncheon and dinner guests take off their things in my room. I knew it was because of the invitations stuck in the mirror, and I was proud to be able to return something for all the money and effort she had expended.

It appeared incumbent upon me as a kind of holy duty to prove myself a remunerative investment. The long hours spent in the preparation of my toilette; the money paid out for my folderols; the deceptions we had to resort to for the sake of expediency; everything—schemes, plans and devices—all appeared to me as simply necessary parts of a big and difficult contest I had entered and must win. It never occurred to me then that my efforts were unadmirable. When at the end of my first season Edith and I discovered to our delight, when the Summer Colony returned to our hills, that our names had become fixtures on their exclusive list of invitations, I felt as much exaltation as any runner who ever entered a Marathon and crossed the white tape among the first six.

There! That's the kind of New England girl I am. I offer no excuses. I lay no blame upon my sister-in-law. There are many New England girls just like me who have the advantage of mothers—tender and solicitous mothers too. But even mothers cannot keep their children from catching measles if there's an epidemic—not unless they move away. The social fever in my community was simply raging when I was sixteen, and of course I caught it.

Even my education was governed by the demands of society. The boarding-school I went to was selected because of its reputation for wealth and exclusiveness. I practised two hours a day on the piano, had my voice trained, and sat at the conversation-French table at school, because Edith impressed upon me that such accomplishments would be found convenient and convincing. I learned to swim and dive, play

Olive Higgins Prouty

tennis and golf, ride horseback, dance and skate, simply because if I was efficient in sports I would prove popular at summer hotels, country clubs and winter resorts. Edith and I attended symphony concerts in Boston every Friday afternoon, and opera occasionally, not because of any special passion for music, but to be able to converse intelligently at dinner parties and teas.

It was not until I had been out two seasons that I met Breckenridge Sewall. When Edith introduced me to society I was younger than the other girls of my set, and to cover up my deficiency in years I affected a veneer of worldly knowledge and sophistication that was misleading. It almost deceived myself. At eighteen I had accepted as a sad truth the wickedness of the world, and especially that of men. I was very blase, very resigned—at least the two top layers of me were. Down underneath, way down, I know now I was young and innocent and hopeful. I know now that my first meeting with Breckenridge Sewall was simply one of the stratagems that the contest I had entered required of me. I am convinced that there was no thought of anything but harmless sport in my encounter.

Breckenridge Sewall's mother was the owner of Grassmere, the largest and most pretentious estate that crowns our hills. Everybody bowed down to Mrs. Sewall. She was the royalty of the Hilton Summer Colony. Edith's operations had not succeeded in piercing the fifty thousand dollar wrought-iron fence that surrounded the acres of Grassmere. We had never been honored by one of Mrs. F. Rockridge Sewall's heavily crested invitations. We had drunk tea in the same drawing-room with her; we had been formally introduced on one occasion; but that was all. She imported most of her guests from New York and Newport. Even the Summer Colonists considered an invitation from Mrs. Sewall a high mark of distinction.

Her only son Breckenridge was seldom seen in Hilton. He preferred Newport, Aix les Bains, or Paris. It was reported among us girls that he considered Hilton provincial and was distinctly bored at any attempt to inveigle him into its society. Most of us had never met him, but we all knew him by sight. Frequently during the summer months he might be seen speeding along the wide state road that leads out into the region of Grassmere, seated in his great, gray, deep-purring monster, hatless, head ducked down, hair blown straight back and eyes half-closed to combat the wind.

One afternoon Edith and I were invited to a late afternoon tea at Idlewold, the summer residence of Mrs. Leonard Jackson. I was wearing a new gown which Edith had given me. It had been made at an expensive dressmaker's of hers in Boston. I remember my sister-in-law exclaimed as we strolled up the cedar-lined walk together, "My, but you're stunning in that wistaria gown. It's a joy to buy things for you, Ruth. You set them off so. I just wonder who you'll slaughter *this* afternoon."

It was that afternoon that I met Breckenridge Sewall.

It was a week from that afternoon that two dozen American Beauties formed an enormous and fragrant center-piece on the dining-room table at old 240 Main Street. Suspended on a narrow white ribbon above the roses Edith had hung from the center light a tiny square of pasteboard. It bore in engraved letters the name of Breckenridge Sewall.

The family were deeply impressed when they came in for dinner. The twins, Oliver and Malcolm, who were in college at the time, were spending part of their vacation in Hilton; and my sister Lucy was there too. There was quite a tableful. I can hear now the Oh's and Ah's as I sat nonchalantly nibbling a cracker.

"Not too fast, Ruth, not too fast!" anxious Alec had cautioned.

"For the love o' Mike! Hully G!" had ejaculated Oliver and Malcolm, examining the card.

"O Ruth, tell us about it," my sister Lucy in awed tones had exclaimed.

I shrugged. "There's nothing to tell," I said. "I met Mr. Sewall at a tea not long ago, as one is apt to meet people at teas, that's all."

Edith from the head of the table, sparkling, too joyous even to attempt her soup, had sung out, "I'm proud of you, rascal! You're a wonder, you are! Listen, people, little sister here is going to do something splendid one of these days—she is!"

CHAPTER II

BRECKENRIDGE SEWALL

When I was a little girl, Idlewold, the estate of Mrs. Leonard Jackson where I first met Breckenridge Sewall, was a region of rough pasture lands. Thither we children used to go forth on Saturday afternoons on marauding expeditions. It was covered in those days with a network of mysteriously winding cow-paths leading from shadow into sunshine, from dark groves through underbrush and berry-bushes to bubbling brooks. Many a thrilling adventure did I pursue with my brothers through those alluring paths, never knowing what treasure or surprise lay around the next curve. Sometimes it would be a cave appearing in the dense growth of wild grape and blackberry vines; sometimes a woodchuck's hole; a snake sunning himself; a branch of black thimble-berries; a baby calf beside its mother, possibly; or perhaps even a wild rabbit or partridge.

Mrs. Leonard Jackson's elaborate brick mansion stood where more than once bands of young vandals were guilty of stealing an ear or two of corn for roasting purposes, to be blackened over a forbidden fire in the corner of an old stone wall; and her famous wistaria-and-grape arbor followed for nearly a quarter of a mile the wandering path laid out years ago by cows on their way to water. What I discovered around one of the curves of that path the day of Mrs. Jackson's garden tea was as thrilling as anything I had ever chanced upon as a little girl. It was Mr. Breckenridge Sewall sitting on the corner of a rustic seat smoking a cigarette!

I had seen Mr. Sewall enter that arbor at the end near the house, a long way off beyond lawns and flower beds. I was standing at the time with a fragrant cup of tea in my hand beside the wistaria arch that forms the entrance of the arbor near the orchard. I happened to be alone for a moment. I finished my tea without haste, and then placing the cup and saucer on a cedar table near-by, I decided it would be pleasant to escape for a little while the chatter and conversation of the two or three dozen women and a handful of men. Unobserved I strolled down underneath the grape-vines.

I walked leisurely along the sun-dappled path, stopped a moment to reach up and pick a solitary, late wistaria blossom, and then went on again smiling a little to myself and wondering just what my plan was. I know now that I intended to waylay Breckenridge Sewall. His attitude toward Hilton had had somewhat the same effect upon me as the No Trespassing and Keep Off signs when I was younger. However, I hadn't gone very far when I lost my superb courage. A little path branching off at the right offered me an opportunity for escape. I took it, and a moment later fell to berating myself for not having been bolder and played my game to a finish. My impulses always fluctuate and flicker for a moment or two before they settle down to a steady resolve.

I did not think that Mr. Sewall had had time to reach the little path, or if so, it did not occur to me that he would select it. It was grass-grown and quite indistinct. So my surprise was not feigned when, coming around a curve, I saw him seated on a rustic bench immediately in front of me. It would have been awkward if I had exclaimed, "Oh!" and turned around and run away. Besides, when I saw Breckenridge Sewall sitting there before me and myself complete mistress of the situation, it appeared almost like a duty to play my cards as well as I knew how. I had been brought up to take advantage of opportunities, remember.

I glanced at the occupied bench impersonally, and then coolly strolled on toward it as if there was no one there. Mr. Sewall got up as I approached.

"Don't rise," I said, and then as if I had dismissed all thought of him, I turned away and fell to contemplating the panorama of stream and meadow. Mr. Sewall could have withdrawn if he had desired. I made it easy for him to pass unheeded behind me while I was contemplating the view. However, he remained standing, looking at me.

"Don't let me disturb you," I repeated after a moment. "I've simply come to see the view of the meadows."

"Oh, no disturbance," he exclaimed, "and say, if it's the view you're keen on, take the seat."

"No, thank you," I replied.

"Go on, I've had enough. Take it. I don't want it."

"Oh, no," I repeated. "It's very kind, but no, thank you."

"Why not? I've had my fill of view. Upon my word, I was just going to clear out anyway."

"Oh, were you?" That altered matters.

"Sure thing."

Then, "Thank you," I said, and went over and sat down.

Often under the cloak of just such innocent and ordinary phrases is carried on a private code of rapid signs and signals as easily understood by those who have been taught as dots and dashes by a telegraphic operator. I couldn't honestly say whether it was Mr. Sewall or I who gave the first signal, but at any rate the eyes of both of us had said what convention would never allow to pass our lips. So I wasn't surprised, as perhaps an outsider will be, when Mr. Sewall didn't raise his hat, excuse himself, and leave me alone on the rustic seat, as he should have done according to all rules of good form and etiquette. Instead he remarked, "I beg your pardon, but haven't I met you before somewhere?"

"Not that I know of," I replied icily, the manner of my glance, however, belying the tone of my voice. "I don't recall you, that is. I'm not in Hilton long at a time, so I doubt it."

"Oh, not in Hilton!" He scoffed at the idea. "Good Lord, no. Perhaps I'm mistaken though. I suppose," he broke off, "you've been having tea up there in the garden."

"I suppose so," I confessed, as if even the thought of it bored me.

He came over toward the bench. I knew it was his cool and audacious intention to sit down. So I laid my parasol lengthwise beside me, leaving the extreme corner vacant, by which I meant to say, "I'm perfectly game, as you see, but I'm perfectly nice too, remember."

He smiled understandingly, and sat down four feet away from me. He leaned back nonchalantly and proceeded to test my gameness by a prolonged and undisguised gaze, which he directed toward me through half-closed lids. I showed no uneasiness. I kept right on looking steadily meadow-ward, as if green fields and winding streams were much more engrossing to me than the presence of a mere stranger. I enjoyed the game I was playing as innocently, upon my word, as I would any contest of endurance. And it was in the same spirit that I took the next dare that was offered me.

I do not know how long it was that Breckenridge Sewall continued to gaze at me, how long I sat undisturbed beneath the fire of his eyes. At any rate it was he who broke the tension first. He leaned forward and drew from his waistcoat pocket a gold cigarette case.

"Do you object?" he asked.

"Certainly not," I replied, with a tiny shrug. And then abruptly, just as he was to return the case to his pocket, he leaned forward again.

"I beg your pardon—won't *you*?" And he offered *me* the cigarettes, his eyes narrowed upon me.

It was not the custom for young girls of my age to smoke cigarettes. It was not considered good form for a debutante to do anything of that sort. I had so far refused all cocktails and wines at dinners. However, I knew how to manage a cigarette. As a lark at boarding-school I had consumed a quarter of an inch of as many as a half-dozen cigarettes. In some amateur theatricals the winter before, in which I took the part of a young man, I had bravely smoked through half of one, and made my speeches too. What this man had said of Hilton and its provincialism was in my mind now. I meant no wickedness, no harm. I took one of the proffered cigarettes with the grand indifference of having done it many times before. Mr. Sewall watched me closely, and when he produced a match, lit it, and stretched it out toward me in the hollow of his hand. I leaned forward and simply played over again my well-learned act of the winter before. Instead of the clapping of many hands and a curtain-call, which had pleased me very much last winter, my applause today came in a less noisy way, but was quite as satisfying.

"Look here," softly exclaimed Breckenridge Sewall. "Say, who are you, anyway?"

Of course I wasn't stupid enough to tell him, and when I saw that he was on the verge of announcing his identity, I exclaimed:

"Oh, don't, please. I'd much rather not know."

"Oh, you don't know then?"

"Are you Mr. Jackson?" I essayed innocently.

"No, I'm not Buck Jackson, but he's a pal of mine. I'm—"

"Oh, please," I exclaimed again. "Don't spoil it!"

"Spoil it!" he repeated a little dazed. "Say, will you talk English?"

"I mean," I explained, carelessly tossing away now into the grass the nasty little thing that was making my throat smart, "I mean, don't spoil my adventure. Life has so few. To walk down a little path for the purpose of looking at a view, and instead to run across a stranger who may be anything from a bandit to an Italian Count is so—so romantic."

"Romantic!" he repeated. He wasn't a bit good at repartee. "Who are you, anyway?"

"Why, I'm any one from a peasant to an heiress."

"You're a darned attractive girl, anyhow!" he ejaculated, and as lacking in subtlety as this speech was, I prized it as sign of my adversary's surrender.

Five minutes later Mr. Sewall suggested that we walk back together to the people gathered on the lawn. But I had no intention of appearing in public with a celebrated person like Breckenridge Sewall, without having first been properly introduced. Besides, my over-eager sister-in-law would be sure to pounce upon us. I remembered my scarf. I had left it by my empty cup on the cedar table. It seemed quite natural for me to suggest to this stranger that before rejoining the party I would appreciate my wrap. It had grown a little chilly. He willingly went to get it. When he returned he discovered that the owner of the bit of lavender silk that he carried in his hand had mysteriously disappeared. Thick, close-growing vines and bushes surrounded the bench, bound in on both sides the shaded path. Through a network of thorns and tangled branches, somehow the owner of that scarf had managed to break her way. The very moment that Mr. Sewall stood blankly surveying the empty bench, she, hidden by a row of young firs, was eagerly skirting the west wall of her hostess's estate.

CHAPTER III

EPISODE OF A SMALL DOG

During the following week Miss Vars often caught a fleeting glimpse of Mr. Sewall on his way in or out of town. She heard that he attended a Country Club dance the following Saturday night, at which she chanced not to be present. She was told he had actually partaken of refreshment in the dining-room of the Country Club and had allowed himself to be introduced to several of her friends.

It was very assuming of this modest young girl, was it not, to imagine that Mr. Sewall's activities had anything to do with her? It was rather audacious of her to don a smart lavender linen suit one afternoon and stroll out toward the Country Club. Her little dog Dandy might just as well have exercised in the opposite direction, and his mistress avoided certain dangerous possibilities. But fate was on her side. She didn't think so at first when, in the course of his constitutional, Dandy suddenly bristled and growled at a terrier twice his weight and size, and then with a pull and a dash fell to in a mighty encounter, rolling over and over in the dirt and dust. Afterward, with the yelping terrier disappearing down the road, Dandy held up a bleeding paw to his mistress. She didn't have the heart to scold the triumphant little warrior. Besides he was sadly injured. She tied her handkerchief about the paw, gathered the dog up in her arms, turned her back on the Country Club a quarter of a mile further on, and started home. It was just then that a gray, low, deep-purring automobile appeared out of a cloud of dust in the distance. As it approached it slowed down and came to a full stop three feet in front of her. She looked up. The occupant of the car was smiling broadly.

"Well!" he ejaculated. "At last! Where did you drop from?"

"How do you do," she replied loftily.

"Where did you drop from?" he repeated. "I've been hanging around for a week, looking for you."

"For *me*?" She was surprised. "Why, what for?"

"Say," he broke out. "That was a mean trick you played. I was mad clean through at first. What did you run off that way for? What was the game?"

"Previous engagement," she replied primly.

"Previous engagement! Well, you haven't any previous engagement now, have you? Because, if you have, get in, and I'll waft you to it."

"Oh, I wouldn't think of it!" she said. He opened the door to the car and sprang out beside her.

"Come, get in," he urged. "I'll take you anywhere you're going. I'd be delighted."

"Why," she exclaimed, "we haven't been introduced. How do I know who you are?" She was a well brought-up young person, you see.

"I'll tell you who I am fast enough. Glad to. Get in, and we will run up to the Club and get introduced, if that's what you want."

"Oh, it isn't!" she assured him. "I just prefer to walk—that's

　　　　　　　Olive Higgins Prouty

all. Thank you very much."

"Well, walk then. But you don't give me the slip this time, young lady. Savvy that? Walk, and I'll come along behind on low speed."

She contemplated the situation for a moment, looking away across fields and green pastures. Then she glanced down at Dandy. Her name in full appeared staring at her from the nickel plate of the dog's collar. She smiled.

"I'll tell you what you can do," she said brightly. "I'd be so grateful! My little dog has had an accident, you see, and if you would be so kind—I hate to ask so much of a stranger—it seems a great deal—but if you would leave him at the veterinary's, Dr. Jenkins, just behind the Court House! He's so heavy! I'd be awfully grateful."

"No, you don't," replied Mr. Sewall. "No more of those scarf games on me! Sorry. But I'm not so easy as all that!"

The girl shifted her dog to her other arm.

"He weighs fifteen pounds," she remarked. And then abruptly for no apparent reason Mr. Sewall inquired:

"Is it yours? Your own? The dog, I mean?"

"My own?" she repeated. "Why do you ask?" Innocence was stamped upon her. For nothing in the world would she have glanced down upon the collar.

"Oh, nothing—nice little rat, that's all. And I'm game. Stuff him in, if you want. I'll deliver him to your vet."

"You will? Really? Why, how kind you are! I do appreciate it. You mean it?"

"Of course I do. Stuff him in. Delighted to be of any little service. Come on, Towzer. Make it clear to your little pet, pray, before starting that I'm no abductor. Good-by—and say," he added, as the car began to purr, "Say, please remember you aren't the only clever little guy in the world, Miss Who-ever-you-are!"

"Why, what do you mean?" She looked abused.

"That's all right. Good-by." And off he sped down the road.

Miss "Who-ever-you-are" walked the three miles home slowly, smiling almost all the way. When she arrived, there was a huge box of flowers waiting on the hall-table directed to:

> "Miss Ruth Chenery Vars
> The Homestead, Hilton, Mass.
> License No. 668."

Inside were two dozen American Beauty roses. Tied to the stem of one was an envelope, and inside the envelope was a card which bore the name of Breckenridge Sewall.

*   *   *   *   *

"So *that's* who he is!" Miss Vars said out loud.

I saw a great deal of the young millionaire during the remainder of the summer. Hardly a day passed but that I heard the approaching purr of his car. And never a week but that flowers and candy, and more flowers and candy, filled the rejoicing Homestead.

I was a canny young person. I allowed Mr. Sewall very little of my time in private. I refused to go off alone with him anywhere, and the result was that he was forced to attend teas and social functions if he wanted to indulge in his latest fancy. The affair, carried on as it was before the eyes of the whole community, soon became the main topic of conversation. I felt myself being pointed out everywhere I went as the girl distinguished by the young millionaire, Breckenridge Sewall. My friends regarded me with wonder.

Before a month had passed a paragraph appeared in a certain periodical in regard to the exciting affair. I burst into flattering notoriety. What had before been slow and difficult sailing for Edith and me now became as swift and easy as if we had added an auxiliary engine to our little boat. We found ourselves receiving invitations from hostesses who before had been impregnable. Extended hands greeted us—kindness, cordiality.

Finally the proud day arrived when I was invited to Grassmere as a guest. One afternoon Breck came rushing in upon me and eagerly explained that his mother sent her apologies, and would I be good enough to fill in a vacancy at a week-end house-party. Of course I would! Proudly I rode away beside Breck in his automobile, out of the gates of the Homestead along the state road a mile or two, and swiftly swerved inside the fifty thousand dollar wrought-iron fence around the cherished grounds of Grassmere. My trunks followed, and Edith's hopes followed too!

It was an exciting three days. I had never spent a night in quite such splendid surroundings; I had never mingled with quite such smart and fashionable people. It was like a play to me. I hoped I would not forget my lines, fail to observe cues, or perform the necessary business awkwardly. I wanted to do credit to my host. And I believe I did. Within two hours I felt at ease in the grand and luxurious house. The men were older, the women more experienced, but I wasn't uncomfortable. As I wandered through the beautiful rooms, conversed with what to me stood for American aristocracy, basked in the hourly attention of butlers and French maids, it occurred to me that I was peculiarly fitted for such a life as this. It became me. It didn't seem as if I could be the little girl who not so very long ago lived in the old French-roofed house with the cracked walls, stained ceilings and worn Brussels carpets, at 240 Main Street, Hilton, Mass. But the day Breck asked me to marry him I discovered I was that girl, with the same untainted ideal of marriage, too, hidden away safe and sound under my play-acting.

"Why, Breck!" I exclaimed. "Don't be absurd. I wouldn't *marry* you for anything in the world."

And I wouldn't! My marriage was dim and indistinct to me then. I had placed it in a very faraway future. My ideal of love was such, that beside it all my friends' love affairs and many of those in fiction seemed commonplace and mediocre. I prized highly the distinction of Breckenridge Sewall's attentions, but marry him—of course I wouldn't!

Breck's attentions continued spasmodically for over two years. It took some skill to be seen with him frequently, to accept just the right portion of his tokens of regard, to keep him interested, and yet remain absolutely free and uninvolved. I couldn't manage it indefinitely; the time would come when all the finesse in the world would avail nothing. And come it did in the middle of the third summer.

Breck refused to be cool and temperate that third summer. He insisted on all sorts of extravagances. He allowed me to monopolize him to the exclusion of every one else. He wouldn't be civil even to his mother's guests at Grassmere. He deserted them night after night for Edith's sunken garden, and me, though I begged him to be reasonable, urging him to stay away. I didn't blame his mother, midsummer though it was, for closing Grassmere, barring the windows, locking the gates and abruptly packing off with her son to an old English estate of theirs near London. I only hoped Mrs. Sewall didn't think me heartless. I had always been perfectly honest with Breck. I had always, from the first, said I couldn't marry him.

Not until I was convinced that the end must come between Breck and me, did I tell the family that he had ever proposed marriage. There exists, I believe, some sort of unwritten law that once a man proposes and a girl refuses, attentions should cease. I came in on Sunday afternoon from an automobile ride

Olive Higgins Prouty

with Breck just before he sailed for England and dramatically announced his proposal to the family—just as if he hadn't been urging the same thing ever since I knew him.

I expected Edith would be displeased when she learned that I wasn't going to marry Breck, so I didn't tell her my decision immediately. I dreaded to undertake to explain to her what a slaughter to my ideals such a marriage would be. Oh, I was young then, you see, young and hopeful. Everything was ahead of me. There was a splendid chance for happiness.

"I can't marry Breck Sewall, Edith," I attempted at last. "I can't marry any one—yet."

"And what do you intend to do with yourself?" she inquired in that cold, unsympathetic way she assumes when she is angry.

"I don't know, yet. There's a chance for all sorts of good things to come true," I replied lightly.

"You've been out three years, you know," she reminded me icily.

The Sewalls occupied their English estate for several seasons. Grassmere remained closed and barred. I did not see my young millionaire again until I was an older girl, and my ideals had undergone extensive alterations.

CHAPTER IV

A BACK-SEASON DEBUTANTE

Debutantes are a good deal like first novels—advertised and introduced at a great expenditure of money and effort, and presented to the public with fear and trembling. But the greatest likeness comes later. The best-sellers of one spring must be put up on the high shelves to make room for new merchandise the next. At the end of several years the once besought and discussed book can be found by the dozens on bargain counters in department stores, marked down to fifty cents a copy.

The first best-seller I happened to observe in this ignominious position was a novel that came out the same fall that I did. It was six years old to the world, and so was I. I stopped a moment at the counter and opened the book. It had been strikingly popular, with scores of reviews and press notices, and hundreds of admirers. It had made a pretty little pile of money for its exploiters. Perhaps, too, it had won a few friends. But its day of intoxicating popularity had passed. And so had mine. And so must every debutante's. By the fourth or fifth season, cards for occasional luncheons and invitations to fill in vacancies at married people's dinner parties must take the place of those feverish all-night balls, preceded by brilliantly lighted tables-full of debutantes, as excited as yourself, with a lot of gay young lords for partners and all the older people looking on, admiring and taking mental notes. Such excitement was all over with me by the time I was twenty-two. I had been a success, too, I suppose. Any girl whom Breckenridge Sewall had launched couldn't help being a success.

During the two or three years that Breck was in Europe I passed through the usual routine of back-season debutantes. They always resort to travel sooner or later; visit boarding-school friends one winter; California, Bermuda or Europe the next; eagerly patronize winter resorts; and fill in various spaces acting as bridesmaids. When they have the chance they take part in pageants and amateur theatricals, periodically devote themselves to some fashionable charity or other, read novels, and attend current event courses if very desperate.

I used to think when I was fifteen that I should like to be an author, more specifically, a poet. I used to write verses that were often read out loud in my English course at the Hilton High School. And I designed book plates, too, and modeled a little in clay. The more important business of establishing ourselves socially interrupted all that sort of thing, however. But I often wish I might have specialized in some line of art. Perhaps now when I have so much time on my hands it would prove my staunchest friend. For a girl who has no established income it might result in an enjoyable means of support.

I have an established income, you see. Father kindly left me a little stock in some mines out West, stock or bonds—I'm not very clear on business terms. Anyhow I have an income of about eight hundred dollars a year, paid over to me by my brother Tom, who has my affairs in charge. It isn't sufficient for me to live on at present, of course. What with the traveling, clothes—one thing and another—Edith has had to help out with generous Christmas and birthday gifts. This she does lavishly. She's enormously rich herself, and very generous. My last Christmas present from her was a set of furs and a luxurious coon-skin motor coat. Perhaps I wouldn't feel quite so hopeless if my father and mother were living, and I felt that my idleness in some way was making them happy. But I haven't such an excuse. I am not necessary to the happiness of any household. I am what is known as a fifth wheel—a useless piece of paraphernalia carried along as necessary impedimenta on other people's journeys.

There are lots of fifth wheels in the world. Some are old and rusty and out of repair, and down in their inmost hubs they long to roll off into the gutter and lie there quiet and undisturbed. These are the old people—silver-haired, self-effacing—who go upstairs to bed early when guests are invited for dinner. Some are emergency fifth wheels, such as are carried on automobiles, always ready to take their place on the road, if one of the regular wheels breaks down and needs to be sent away for repairs. These are the middle-aged, unmarried aunts and cousins—staunch, reliable—who are sent for to take care of the children while mother runs over to Europe for a holiday. And some are fifth wheels like myself—neither old nor self-effacing, neither middle-aged nor useful, but simply expensive to keep painted, and very hungry for the road. It may be only a matter of time, however, when I shall be middle-aged and useful, and later old and self-effacing; when I shall stay and take care of the children, and go upstairs early when the young people are having a party.

A young technical college graduate told me once, to comfort me, I suppose, that a fifth wheel is considered by a carriage-maker a very important part of a wagon. He tried to explain to me just what part of a wagon it was. You can't see it. It's underneath somewhere, and has to be kept well oiled. I am not very mechanical, but it sounded ignominious to me. I told that young man that I wanted to be one of the four wheels that held the coach up and made it speed, not tucked out of sight, smothered in carriage-grease.

It came as a shock to me when I first realized my superfluous position in this world. The result of that shock was what led me to abandon my ideals on love in an attempt to avoid the possibility of going upstairs early and having dinners off a tray.

When my brother Alec married Edith Campbell, and Edith came over to our house and remodeled it, I didn't feel supplanted. There was a room built especially for me with a little bath-room of its own, a big closet, a window-box filled with flowers in the summer, and cretonne hangings that I picked out myself. My sister Lucy had a room too—for she wasn't married then—and the entire attic was finished up as barracks for my brothers, the twins, who were in college at the time. They were invited to bring home all the friends they wanted to. Edith was a big-hearted sister-in-law. To me her coming was like the advent of a fairy godmother. I had chafed terribly under the economies of my earlier years. It wasn't until Alec married Edith that fortune began to smile.

One by one the family left the Homestead—Lucy, when she married Dr. William Maynard and went away to live near the university with which Will was connected, and Oliver and Malcolm when they graduated from college and went into business. I alone was left living with Alec and Edith. I was so busy coming-out and making a social success of myself that it never occurred to me but that I was as important a member in that household as Edith herself. I wasn't far from wrong either. When I was a debutante and admired by Breckenridge Sewall, I was petted and pampered and kept in sight. When I became a back-season number of some four or five years' staleness, any old north room would do for me!

I used to dread Hilton in the winter, with nothing more exciting going on than a few horrible thimble parties with girls who were beginning to discuss how to keep thin, the importance of custom-made corsets, and various other topics of advancing years. I soon acquired the habit of interrupting these long seasons. I was frequently absent two months at a time, visiting boarding-school friends, running out to California, up to Alaska, or down to Mexico with some girl friend or other, with her mother or aunt for a chaperon. Traveling is pleasant enough, but everybody likes to feel a tie pulling gently at his heartstrings when he steps up to a hotel register to write down the name of that little haven that means home. It is like one of those toy return-balls. If the ball is attached by an elastic string to some little girl's middle finger how joyfully it springs forth from her hand, how eagerly returns again! When suddenly on one of its trips the elastic snaps, the ball becomes lifeless and rolls listlessly away in the gutter. When my home ties broke, I, too, abandoned myself.

I had been on a visiting-trip made up of two-week stands in various cities between Massachusetts and the Great Lakes, whither I had set out to visit my oldest brother, Tom, and his wife, Elise, who live on the edge of one of the Lakes in Wisconsin. I had been gone about six weeks and had planned not to return to Hilton until the arrival of Hilton's real society in May.

When I reached Henrietta Morgan's, just outside New York, on the return trip, I fully expected to remain with her for two weeks and stop off another week with the Harts in New Haven. But after about three days at Henrietta's, I suddenly decided I couldn't stand it any longer. My clothes all needed pressing—they had a peculiar trunky odor—even the tissue paper which I used in such abundance in my old-fashioned tray trunk had lost its life and crispness; I had gotten down to my last clean pair of long white gloves; everything I owned needed some sort of attention—I simply must go home!

I woke up possessed with the idea, and after putting on my last really respectable waist and inquiring of myself in the mirror how in the world I expected to visit Henrietta Morgan with such a dreary trunkful of travel-worn articles, anyhow, I went down to the breakfast table with my mind made up.

Henrietta left me after breakfast for a hurried trip to town. I didn't go with her. I had waked up with a kind of cottony feeling in my throat, and as hot coffee and toast didn't seem to help it, I made an examination with a hand-mirror after breakfast. I discovered three white spots! I wasn't alarmed. They never mean anything serious with me, and they offered an excellent excuse for my sudden departure. It didn't come to my mind that the white spots might have been the cause of my sudden longing for my own little pink room. I simply knew I wanted to go home; and wake up in the morning cross and disagreeable; and grumble about the bacon and coffee at the breakfast table if I wanted to.

While Henrietta and her mother were out in the morning, I clinched my decision by engaging a section on the night train and telegraphing Edith. Although I was convinced that my departure wouldn't seriously upset any of the small informal affairs so far planned for my entertainment, I was acquainted with Mrs. Morgan's tenacious form of hospitality. By the time she returned my packing was finished, and I was lying down underneath a down comforter on the couch. I told Mrs. Morgan about the white spots and my decision to return home.

She would scarcely hear me through. She announced emphatically that she wouldn't think of allowing me to travel if I was ill. I was to undress immediately, crawl in between the sheets, and she would call a doctor. I wasn't rude to Mrs. Morgan, simply firm—that was all—quite as persistent in my resolve as she in hers.

When finally she became convinced that nothing under heaven could dissuade me, she flushed slightly and said icily, "Oh, very well, very well. If that is the way you feel about it, very well, my dear," and sailed out of the room, hurt. Even Henrietta, though very solicitous, shared her mother's indignation, and I longed for the comfort and relief of the Pullman, the friendly porters, and my own understanding people at the other end.

So, you see, when in the middle of the afternoon I was summoned to the telephone to receive a telegram from Hilton, I wasn't prepared for the slap in the face that Edith's message was to me.

"Sorry," it was repeated. "Can't conveniently have you until next week. House packed with company. Better stay with the Morgans." Signed, "Edith."

CHAPTER V

THE UNIMPORTANT FIFTH WHEEL

Better stay with the Morgans! Who was I to be bandied about in such fashion? Couldn't have me! I wasn't a seamstress who went out by the day. House packed with company! Well— what of that? Hadn't I more right there? Wasn't I Alec's own sister? Wasn't I born under the very roof to which I was now asked not to come? Weren't all my things there—my bed, my bureau, my little old white enameled desk I used when I was a child? Where was I to go, I'd like to ask? Couldn't have me! Very well, then, I wouldn't go!

I called up my brother Malcolm's office in New York. Perhaps he would be kind enough to engage a room in a hospital somewhere, or at least find a bed in a public ward. "Sorry, Miss Vars," came the answer finally to me over the long distance wire, "but Mr. Vars has gone up to Hilton, Massachusetts, for the week-end. Not returning until Monday."

I sat dumbly gazing into the receiver. Where could I go? Lucy, I was sure, would squeeze me in somewhere if I applied to her—she always can—but a letter received from Lucy two days before had contained a glowing description of some celebrated doctor of science and his wife, who were to be her guests during this very week. She has but one guest room. I couldn't turn around and go back to Wisconsin. I couldn't go to Oliver, now married to Madge. They live in a tiny apartment

Olive Higgins Prouty

outside Boston. There is nothing for me to sleep on except a lumpy couch in the living-room. Besides there is a baby, and to carry germs into any household with a baby in it is nothing less than criminal.

Never before had I felt so ignominious as when, half an hour later, I meekly passed my telegram to Mrs. Morgan and asked if it would be terribly inconvenient if I did stay after all.

"Not at all. Of course not," she replied coldly. "I shall not turn you out into the street, my dear. But you stated your wish to go so decidedly that I have telephoned Henrietta's friends in Orange to come over to take your place. We had not told you that tickets for the theater tonight and matinee tomorrow had already been bought. The friends are coming this evening. So I shall be obliged to ask you to move your things into the sewing-room."

I moved them. A mean little room it was on the north side of the house. Piles of clothes to be mended, laundry to be put away, a mop and a carpet sweeper greeted me as I went in. The floor was untidy with scraps of cloth pushed into a corner behind the sewing machine. The mantel was decorated with spools of thread, cards of hooks and eyes, and a pin-cushion with threaded needles stuck in it. The bed was uncomfortable. I crawled into it, and lay very still. My heart was filled with bitterness. My eyes rested on the skeleton of a dressmaker's form. A man's shirt ripped up the back hung over a chair. I staid for three days in that room! Mrs. Morgan's family physician called the first night, and announced to Mrs. Morgan that probably I was coming down with a slight attack of tonsilitis. I thought at least it was diphtheria or double pneumonia. There were pains in my back. When I tried to look at the dressmaker's skeleton it jiggled uncomfortably before my eyes.

I didn't see the new guests once. Even Henrietta was allowed to speak to me only from across the hall.

"Tonsilitis *is* catching, you know, my dear," Mrs. Morgan sweetly purred from heights above me, "and I'd never forgive myself if the other two girls caught anything here. I've forbidden Henrietta to see you. She's so susceptible to germs." I felt I was an unholy creature, teeming with microbes.

The room was warm; they fed me; they cared for me; but I begged the doctor for an early deliverance on Monday morning. I longed for home. I cried for it a little. Edith couldn't have known that I was ill; she would have opened her arms wide if she had guessed—of course she would. I ought to have gone in the beginning. I poured out my story into that old doctor's understanding ears, and he opened the way for me finally. He let me escape. Very weak and wobbly I took an early train on Monday morning for Hilton. At the same time I sent the following telegram to my sister-in-law: "Arrive Hilton 6:15 tonight. Have been ill. Still some fever, but doctor finally consents to let me come."

Six fearful hours later I found myself, weak-kneed and trembling, on the old home station platform. I was on the verge of tears. I looked up and down for Edith's anxious face, or for Alec's—they would be disturbed when they heard I had a fever, they might be alarmed—but I couldn't find them. The motor was not at the curb either. I stepped into a telephone-booth and called the house. Edith answered herself. I recognized her quick staccato "Hello."

I replied, "Hello, that you, Edith?"

"Yes. Who is this?" she called.

"Ruth," I answered feebly.

"Ruth! Where in the world are you?" she answered.

"Oh, I'm all right. I'm down here at the station. Just arrived. I'm perfectly all right," I assured her.

Olive Higgins Prouty

"Well, well," she exclaimed. "That's fine. Awfully glad you're back! I do wish I could send the limousine down for you, Ruth. But I just can't. We're going out to dinner—to the Mortimers, and we've just *got* to have it. I'm awfully sorry, but do you mind taking the car, or a carriage? I'm right in the midst of dressing. I've got to hurry like mad. It's almost half-past six now. Jump into a taxi, and we can have a nice little chat before I have to go. Got lots to tell you. It's fine you're back. Good-by. Don't mind if I hurry now, do you?"

I arrived at the house ten minutes later in a hired taxicab. I rang the bell, and after a long wait a maid I had never seen before let me in. Edith resplendent in a brand new bright green satin gown was just coming down the stairs. She had on all her diamonds.

"Hello, Toots," she said. "Did you get homesick, dearie? Welcome. Wish I could kiss you, Honey, but I can't. I've just finished my lips. Why didn't you telegraph, Rascal? It's a shame not to have you met."

"I did," I began.

"Oh, well, our telephone has been out of order all day. It makes me tired the way they persist in telephoning telegrams. We do get the worst service! I had no idea you were coming. Why, I sent off a perfect bunch of mail to you this very morning. You weren't peeved, were you, Toots, about my telegram, I mean? I was right in the midst of the most important house-party I've ever had. As it was I had too many girls, and at the last minute had to telegraph Malcolm to come and help me out. And he did, the lamb! The house-party was a screaming success. I'm going to have a regular series of them all summer. How do you like my gown? Eighty-five, my dear, marked down from a hundred and fifty."

"Stunning," I replied, mingled emotions in my heart.

"There!" exclaimed Edith abruptly. "There's your telegram

now. Did you ever? Getting here at this hour!"

A telegraph boy was coming up the steps. I was fortunately near the door, and I opened it before he rang, received my needless message myself, and tore open the envelope.

"You're right," I said. "It is my telegram. It just said I was coming. That's all. It didn't matter much. Guess I'll go up to my room now, if you don't mind."

"Do, dear. Do," said Edith, "and I'll come along too. I want to show you something, anyhow. I've picked up the stunningest high-boy you ever saw in your life. A real old one, worth two hundred and fifty, but I got it for a hundred. I've put it right outside your room, and very carefully—oh, *most* carefully— with my own hands, Honey, I just laid your things in it. I simply couldn't have the bureau drawers in that room filled up, you know, with all the house-parties I'm having, and you not here half the time. I knew *you* wouldn't mind, and the high-boy is so stunning!" We had gone upstairs and were approaching it now. "I put all your underclothes in those long shallow drawers; and your ribbons and gloves and things in these deep, low ones. And then up here in the top I've laid carefully all the truck you had stowed away in that little old white enameled desk of yours. The desk I put up in the store-room. It wasn't decent for guests. I've bought a new one to take its place. I do hope you'll like it. It's a spinet desk, and stunning. Oh, dear—there it is now ten minutes of seven, and I've simply got to go. I promised to pick up Alec at the Club on the way. I don't believe I've told you I've had your room redecorated. I wish I could wait and see if you're pleased. But I can't—simply can't! You understand, don't you, dear? But make yourself comfy."

She kissed me then very lightly on the cheek, and turned and tripped away downstairs. When I caught the purr of the vanishing limousine as it sped away down the winding drive, I opened the door of my room. It was very pretty, very elegant, as perfectly appointed as any hotel room I had ever gazed upon, but mine no more. This one little sacred precinct had been entered in my absence and robbed of every vestige of me. Instead of my single four-poster were two mahogany sleigh beds, spread with expensively embroidered linen. Instead of my magazine cut of Robert Louis Stevenson pinned beside the east window was a signed etching. Instead of my own familiar desk welcoming me with bulging packets of old letters, waiting for some rainy morning to be read and sentimentally destroyed, appeared the spinet desk, furnished with brand new blotters, chaste pens, and a fresh book of two-cent stamps. All but my mere flesh and bones had been conveniently stuffed into a two-hundred and fifty dollar high-boy!

I could have burst into tears if I had dared to fling myself down upon the embroidered spreads. And then suddenly from below I heard the scramble of four little feet on the hardwood floor, the eager, anxious pant of a wheezy little dog hurrying up the stairs. It was Dandy—my Boston terrier. Somehow, down behind the kitchen stove he had sensed me, and his little dog heart was bursting with welcome. Only Dandy had really missed me, sitting long, patient hours at a time at the living-room window, watching for me to come up the drive; and finally starting out on mysterious night searches of his own, as he always does when days pass and I do not return. I heard the thud of his soft body as he slipped and fell, in his haste, on the slippery hall floor. And then a moment later he was upon me—paws and tongue and half-human little yelps and cries pouring out their eloquence.

I held the wriggling, ecstatic little body close to me, and wondered what it would be like if some human being was as glad to see me as Dandy.

CHAPTER VI

BRECK SEWALL AGAIN

As I stood there in my devastated room, hugging to me a little scrap of a dog, a desire to conceal my present poverty swept over me, just as I had always wanted to hide the tell-tale economies of our household years ago from my more affluent friends. I did not want pity. I was Ruth, of whom my family had predicted great things—vague great things, I confess. Never had I been quite certain what they were to be—but something rather splendid anyhow.

We become what those nearest to us make us. The family made out of my oldest brother Tom counselor and wise judge; out of my sister Lucy chief cook and general-manager; out of me butterfly and ornament. In the eyes of the family I have always been frivolous and worldly, and though they criticize these qualities of mine, underneath their righteous veneer I discover them marveling. They disparage my extravagance in dressing, and then admire my frocks. In one breath they ridicule social ambition, and in the next inquire into my encounters and triumphs. A desire to remain in my old position I offer now as the least contemptible excuse of any that I can think of for the following events of my life. I didn't want to resign my place like an actress who can no longer take ingenue parts because of wrinkles and gray hairs. When I came home that day and discovered how unimportant I was, how weak had become my applause, instead of trying to play a new part by making myself useful and necessary—helping with the housework, putting away laundry, mending, and so on—I went about concocting ways and methods of filling more dazzlingly my old role.

Although my fever had practically disappeared by the time I went to bed that night, I lolled down to the breakfast table the next morning later than ever, making an impression in a shell-pink tea-gown; luxuriously dawdled over a late egg and coffee; and then lazily borrowed a maid about eleven o'clock and allowed her to unpack for me. Meanwhile I lay back on the couch, criticized to Edith the tone of gray of the paper in my room, carelessly suggested that there were too many articles on the shelf from an artistic point of view, and then suffered myself to be consulted on an invitation list for a party Edith was planning to give. The description of my past two months' gaieties, recited in rather a bored and blase manner, lacked none of the usual color. My references to attentions from various would-be suitors proved to Edith and Alec that I was keeping up my record.

One Saturday afternoon not long after my return to Hilton, Edith and I attended a tea at the Country Club. The terrace, open to the sky and covered with a dozen small round tables, made a pretty sight—girls in light-colored gowns and flowery hats predominating early in the afternoon, but gradually, from mysterious regions of lockers and shower-baths below, joined by men in white flannels and tennis-shoes.

Edith's and my table was popular that day. I had been away from Hilton for so long that a lot of our friends gathered about us to welcome me home. I was chatting away to a half dozen of them, when I saw two men strolling up from the seventeenth green. One of the men was Breckenridge Sewall. I glanced over the rim of my cup the second time to make certain. Yes, it was Breck—the same old blase, dissipated-looking Breck. I had thought he was still in Europe. To reach the eighteenth tee the men had to pass within ten feet of the terrace. My back would be toward them. I didn't know if a second opportunity would be offered me. Grassmere, the Sewall estate, was not open this year. Breck might be gone by the next day. I happened at the time to be talking about a certain tennis tournament with a man who had been an eye-witness. I rose and put down my cup of tea.

"Come over and tell me about it, please," I said, smiling upon him. "I've finished. Take my chair, Phyllis," I added sweetly to a young girl standing near. "Do, dear. Mr. Call and I are going to decorate the balustrade."

I selected a prominent position beside a huge earthen pot of flowering geraniums. It was a low balustrade with a flat top, designed to sit upon. I leaned back against the earthen jar and proceeded to appear engrossed in tennis. Really, though, I was wondering if Breck would see me after all, and what I should say if he did.

What I did say was conventional enough—simply, "Why, how do you do," to his eager, "Hello, Miss Vars!" while I shook hands with him as he stood beneath me on the ground.

"Saw you on Fifth Avenue a week ago," he went on, "hiking for some place in a taxi. Lost you in the crowd at Forty-second. Thought you might be rounding up here before long. So decided I'd run up and say howdy. Look here, wait for me, will you? I've got only one hole more to play. Do. Wait for me. I'll see that you get home all right."

Edith returned alone in the automobile that afternoon.

"I'll come along later," I explained mysteriously.

She hadn't seen Breck, thank heaven! She would have been sure to have blundered into a dinner invitation, or some such form of effusion. But she surmised that something unusual was in the air, and was watching for me from behind lace curtains in the living-room when I returned two hours later. She saw a foreign-made car whirl into the drive and stop at the door. She saw me get out of it and run up the front steps. The features of the man behind the big mahogany steering-wheel could be discerned easily. When I opened the front door my sister-in-law was in the vestibule. She grasped me by both my arms just above my elbows.

"Breck Sewall!" she ejaculated. "My dear! Breck Sewall again!"

The ecstasy of her voice, the enthusiasm of those hands of hers grasping my arms soothed my hurt feelings of a week ago. I was led tenderly—almost worshipfully—upstairs to my room.

"I believe he is as crazy as ever about you," Edith exclaimed, once behind closed doors. "I honestly think"—she stopped abruptly—"What if—" she began again, then excitedly kissed me. "You little wonder!" she said. "There's no one in the whole family to match you. I'll wager you could become a veritable gateway for us all to pass into New York society if you wanted to. You're a marvel—you are! Tell me about it." Her eyes sparkled as she gazed upon me. I realized in a flash just what the splendid thing was that I might do. Of course! How simple! I might marry Breck!

"Well," I said languidly, gazing at my reflection in the mirror and replacing a stray lock, "I suppose I'd rather be a gateway than a fifth wheel."

The next time that Breck asked me to marry him, I didn't call him absurd. I was older now. I must put away my dolls and air-castles. The time had come, it appeared, for me to assume a woman's burdens, among which often is an expedient marriage. I could no longer offer my tender years as an excuse for side-stepping a big opportunity. I musn't falter. The moment had arrived. I accepted Breck, and down underneath a pile of stockings in the back of my lowest bureau drawer I hid a little velvet-lined jewel-box, inside of which there lay an enormous diamond solitaire—promise of my brilliant return to the footlights.

CHAPTER VII

THE MILLIONS WIN

Some people cannot understand how a girl can marry a man she doesn't love. She can do it more easily than she can stay at home, watch half her friends marry, and feel herself slowly ossifying into something worthless and unessential. It takes more courage to sit quietly, wait for what may never come, and observe without misgiving the man you might have had making some other woman's life happy and complete.

I couldn't go on living in guest-rooms forever. I was tired of traveling, and sick to death of leading a life that meant nothing to anybody but Dandy. As a debutante I had had a distinct mission—whether worthy or unworthy isn't the point in question—worked for it hard, schemed, devised, and succeeded. As Mrs. Breckenridge Sewall I could again accomplish results. Many women marry simply because they cannot endure an arid and purposeless future.

Some people think that a girl who marries for position is hard and calculating. Why, I entered into my engagement in the exalted mood of a martyr! I didn't feel hard—I felt self-sacrificing, like a girl in royal circles whose marriage may distinguish herself and her people to such an extent that the mere question of her own personal feelings is of small importance. The more I considered marrying Breck the more convinced I became that it was the best thing I could do. With my position placed upon my brow, like a crown on a king,

Olive Higgins Prouty

freed at last from all the mean and besmirching tricks of acquiring social distinction, I could grow and expand. When I looked ahead and saw myself one day mistress of Grassmere, the London house, the grand mansion in New York; wise and careful monitor of the Sewall millions; gracious hostess; kind ruler; I felt as nearly religious as ever before in my life. I meant to do good with my wealth and position and influence. Is that hard and calculating?

I accepted Breck's character and morals as a candidate chosen for the honorable office of governor of a state must accept the condition of politics, whether they are clean or rotten. Clean politics are the exception. So also are clean morals. I knew enough for that. Way back in boarding-school days, we girls had resigned ourselves to the acceptance of the deplorable state of the world's morals. We had statistics. I had dimly hoped that one of the exceptions to the rule might fall to my lot, but if not, I wasn't going to be prudish. Breck's early career could neither surprise nor alarm me. I, like most girls in this frank and open age, had been prepared for it. So when Lucy, who is anything but worldly wise, and Will, her husband, who is a scientist and all brains, came bearing frenzied tales of Breck's indiscretions during his one year at the university where Will is now located, I simply smiled. Some people are so terribly naive and unsophisticated!

The family's attitude toward my engagement was consistent— deeply impressed, but tainted with disapproval. Tom came way on from Wisconsin to tell me how contemptible it was for a girl to marry for position, even for so amazingly a distinguished one. Elise, his wife, penned me a long letter on the emptiness of power and wealth. Malcolm wrote he hoped I knew what I was getting into, and supposed after I became Mrs. Breckenridge Sewall I'd feel too fine to recognize him, should we meet on Fifth Avenue. Oliver was absolutely "flabbergasted" at first, he wrote, but must confess it would save a lot of expense for the family, if they could stop with Brother Breck when they came down to New York. "How'd you pull it off, Toots?" he added. "Hope little Cupid had something to do with it."

Alec waited until Edith had gone to Boston for a day's shopping, and took me for a long automobile ride. Alec, by the way, is one of this world's saints. He has always been the member of the Vars family who has resigned himself to circumstances. It was Tom who went West and made a brilliant future for himself; Alec who remained in Hilton to stand by father's dying business. It was the twins who were helped to graduate from college in spite of difficulties; Alec who cheerfully gave up his diploma to offer a helping hand at home. When Alec married Edith Campbell it appeared that at last he had come into his own. She was immensely wealthy. Father's business took a new lease of life. At last Alec was prosperous, but he had to go on adapting and resigning just the same. With the arrival of the Summer Colony Edith's ambitions burst into life, and of course he couldn't be a drag on her future—and mine—any more than on Tom's or the twins'. He acquiesced; he fitted in without reproach. Today in regard to my engagement he complained but gently.

"We're simple New England people after all," he said. "A girl is usually happier married to a man of her own sort. You weren't born into the kind of life the Sewalls lead. You weren't born into even the kind of life you're leading now. Edith— Edith's fine, of course, and I've always been glad you two were so congenial—but she does exaggerate the importance of the social game. She plays it too hard. I don't want you to marry Sewall. I'm afraid you won't be happy."

When Edith came home that night I asked her if she knew how Alec felt.

"Of course I do. The dear old fogey! But this is the way I look at it, Ruth. Some people *not* born into a high place get there just the same through sheer nerve and determination, and others spend their whole worthless lives at home on the farm. It isn't what a person is born into, but what he is equal to, that decides his success. Mercy, child, don't let a dear, silly, older brother bother you. Sweet old Al doesn't know what he's talking about. I'd like to know what he *would* advise doing with his little sister, if, after all the talk there is about her and Breck, he could succeed in breaking off her engagement. She'd be just an old glove kicking around. That's what she'd be. Al is simply crazy. I'll have to talk to him!"

"Don't bother," I said, "I'm safe. I have no intention of becoming an old glove."

Possibly in the privacy of my own bed at night, where so often now I lay wide-awake waiting for the dawn, I did experience a few misgivings. But by the time I was ready to go down to breakfast I had usually persuaded myself into sanity again. I used to reiterate all the desirable points about Breck I could think of and calm my fears by dwelling upon the many demands of my nature that he could supply—influence, power, delight in environment, travel, excitement.

When I was a child I was instructed by my drawing-teacher to sketch with my stick of charcoal a vase, a book, and a red rose, which he arranged in a group on a table before me. I had a great deal of difficulty with the rose; so after struggling for about half an hour I got up and, unobserved, put the rose behind the vase, so that only its stem was visible to me. Then I took a fresh page and began again. The result was a very fair portrayal of the articles as they then appeared. So with my ideal of marriage—when I found its arrangement impossible to portray in my life—I simply slipped out of sight that for which the red rose is sometimes the symbol (I mean love) and went ahead sketching in the other things.

I explained all this to Breck one day, I wanted to be honest with him.

"Say, what are you driving at? Red roses! Drawing lessons! What's that got to do with whether you'll run down to Boston for dinner with me tonight? You do talk the greatest lot of stuff! But have it your own way. I'm satisfied. Just jump in beside me! Will you? Darn it! I haven't the patience of a saint!"

Olive Higgins Prouty

CHAPTER VIII

THE HORSE SHOW

Conventions may sometimes appear silly and absurd, but most of them are made for practical purposes. Ignore them and you'll discover yourself in difficulty. Leave your spoon in your cup and your arm will unexpectedly hit it sometime, and over will go everything on to the tablecloth. If I had not ignored certain conventions I wouldn't be crying over spilled milk now.

I allowed myself to become engaged to Breck; accepted his ring and hid it in my lowest bureau drawer; told my family my intentions; let the world see me dining, dancing, theater-ing and motoring like mad with Breck and draw its conclusions; and all this, mind you, before I had received a word of any sort whatsoever from my prospective family-in-law. This, as everybody knows, is irregular, and as bad form as leaving your spoon in your cup. No wonder I got into difficulty!

My prospective family-in-law consisted simply of Breck's mother, Mrs. F. Rockridge Sewall—a very elegant and perfectly poised woman she seemed to me the one time I had seen her at close range, as she sat at the head of the sumptuous table in the tapestry-hung dining-room at Grassmere. I admired Mrs. Sewall. I used to think that I could succeed in living up to her grand manners with better success than the other rather hoidenish young ladies who chanced to be the guests at Grassmere the time I was there. Mrs. Sewall is a small woman, always dressed in black, with a superb string of pearls invariably about her neck, and lots of brilliant diamonds on her slender fingers. Breck with his heavy features, black hair brushed straight back, eyes half-closed as if he was always riding in a fifty-mile gale, deep guffaw of a laugh, and inelegant speech does not resemble his mother. It is strange, but the picture that I most enjoyed dwelling upon, when I contemplated my future life, was one of myself creeping up Fifth Avenue on late afternoons in the Sewalls' crested automobile, seated, not beside Breck, but in intimate conversation beside my aristocratic mother-in-law.

As humiliating as it was to me to continue engaged to a man from whose mother there had been made no sign of welcome or approval, I did so because Breck plead that Mrs. Sewall was on the edge of a nervous break-down, and to announce any startling piece of news to her at such a time would be unwise. I was foolish enough to believe him. I deceived myself into thinking that my course was allowable and self-respecting.

Breck used to run up from New York to Hilton in his car for Sunday; and sometimes during the week, in his absurd eagerness, he would dash up to our door and ring the bell as late as eleven o'clock, simply because he had been seized with a desire to bid me good-night.

When Edith and I went to New York for a week's shopping we were simply deluged with attentions from Breck—theater every night, luncheons, dinners and even breakfasts occasionally squeezed in between. All this, I supposed, was carried on without Mrs. Sewall's knowledge. I ought to have known better than to have excused it. It was my fault. I blame myself. Such an unconventional affair deserved to end in catastrophe. But to Edith it ended not in spilled milk, but in a spilled pint of her life's blood.

One night in midsummer when I was just dropping off to sleep, Edith knocked gently on my door, and then opened it and came in. She was all ready for bed with her hair braided down her back.

"Asleep?"

"No," I replied. "What's the matter?"

"Did you know Grassmere was open?"

"Why?" I demanded.

"Because, just as I was fixing the curtain in my room I happened to look up there. It's all lit up, upstairs and down. Even the ball-room. Did you know about it?"

I had to confess that I didn't. Breck had told me that his mother would remain in the rented palace at Newport for the remainder of the season, under the care of a specialist.

"Looks as if they were having a big affair of some sort up there. I guess Mrs. F. Rockridge has recovered from her nervous break-down! Come, get up and see."

"Oh, I'll take your word for it," I replied indifferently. But I won't say what my next act was after Edith had gone out of the room. You may be sure I didn't immediately drop off to sleep.

I looked for one of Breck's ill-penned letters the next morning, but none came. No wire or telephone message either. Not until five o'clock in the afternoon did I receive any explanation of the lights at Grassmere. Edith had been to her bridge club, and came rushing up on the veranda, eager and excited. There were little bright spots in the center of each cheek. Edith's a handsome woman, thirty-five or eight, I think, and very smart in appearance. She has dark brilliant eyes, and a quality in her voice and manner that makes you feel as if there were about eight cylinders and all in perfect order, too, chugging away underneath her shiny exterior.

"Where's the mail?" she asked of me. I was lying on the

wicker couch.

"Oh, inside, I guess, on the hall table. I don't know. Why?"

"Wait a minute," she said, and disappeared. She rejoined me an instant later, with two circulars and a printed post-card.

"Is this all there is?" Edith demanded again, and I could see the red spots on her cheeks grow deeper.

"That's all," I assured her. "Expecting something?"

"Have you had any trouble with Breck?" she flashed out at me next.

"What are you driving at, Edith?" I inquired. "What's the matter?"

"Mrs. Sewall is giving a perfectly enormous ball at Grassmere on the twenty-fourth, and we're left out. That's the matter!" She tossed the mail on the table.

"Oh," I said, "our invitations will come in the morning probably. There are often delays."

"No, sir, I know better. The bridge club girls said their invitations came yesterday afternoon. I can't understand it. We certainly were on Mrs. Sewall's list when she gave that buffet-luncheon three years ago. And now we're not! That's the bald truth of it. It was terribly embarrassing this afternoon—all of them telling about what they were going to wear—it's going to be a masquerade—and I sitting there like a dummy! Helene McClellan broke the news to me. She blurted right out, 'Oh, do tell us, Edith,' she said to me, 'is Mrs. Sewall's ball to announce your sister's engagement to her son? We're crazy to know!' Of course I didn't let on at first that we weren't even invited, but it had to leak out later. Oh, it is simply humiliating!"

"Is she at Grassmere now—Mrs. Sewall, I mean?" I asked quietly.

"Yes, she is. There's a big house-party going on there this very minute. The club girls knew all about it. Mrs. Sewall has got a niece or somebody or other with her, for the rest of the summer, and the ball is being given in her honor. Gale Oliphant, I believe the girl's name is. But look here, it seems very queer to me that *I'm* the one to be giving you this information instead of Breck. What does it all mean anyhow? Come, confess. You must have had a tiff or something with Breck."

"I don't have tiffs, Edith," I said, annoyed.

"Well, you needn't get mad about it. There must be some reason for our being slighted in this fashion. I'm sure *I've* done nothing. It's not my fault. I wouldn't care if it was small, but everybody who isn't absolutely beyond the pale is invited."

"There's no use losing your nerve, Edith," I said in an exasperatingly calm manner.

"Good heavens!" Edith exclaimed. "You seem to enjoy slights, but if I were in your place I shouldn't enjoy slights from my prospective mother-in-law, anyhow!"

"You needn't be insulting," I remarked, arranging a sofa-pillow with care underneath my head and turning my attention to my magazine.

Edith went into the house. The screen door slammed behind her. I didn't stir, just kept right on staring at the printed page before me and turning a leaf now and again, as if I were really reading.

Gale Oliphant! I knew all about her. I had met her first at the house-party at Grassmere—a silly little thing, I had thought her, rather pretty, and a tremendous flirt. Breck had said she was worth a million in her own name. I remembered that, because he explained that he had been rather keen about her before he met me. "That makes my eight hundred dollars a year look rather sickly, doesn't it?" I replied. "Yes," he said, "it sure does! But let me tell you that *you* make *her* look like a last year's straw hat." However, the last year's straw hat possessed some attraction for Breck, because during the three years that Grassmere was closed and the Sewalls were in Europe, Breck and Gale Oliphant saw a lot of each other. Breck told me that she really was better than nothing, and his mater was terribly keen about having her around.

I tried in every way I could to explain away my fears. I mustn't be hasty. Well-mannered thoughts didn't jump to foolish conclusions. Breck would probably explain the situation to me. I must wait with calmness and composure. And I did, all the next day, and the next, and the third, until finally there arrived one of Breck's infrequent scrawls.

The envelope was post-marked Maine. I opened it, and read:

"DEAR RUTH:

"I am crazy to see you. It seems like a week of Sundays. The mater got a notion she wanted me to come up to Bar Harbor and bring down the yacht. I brought three fellows with me. Some spree! But we're good little boys. The captain struck. Waiting for another. Won't round up at your place for another week. I'm yours and don't forget it. It seems like a week of Sundays. Mater popped the news she's going to open up old Grassmere pretty soon. Then it will be like a week of holidays for yours truly, if you're at home to sit in that pergola effect with. Savvy? Showed the fellows the snapshots tonight but didn't tell them. Haven't touched a drop for four weeks and three days. Never did that stunt for any queen before. Goodnight, you little fish. Don't worry about that though. I'll warm you up O.K. Trust Willie."

Olive Higgins Prouty

I used to feel apologetic for Breck's letters, and tear them up as quickly as possible, before any one could see how crude and ill-spelled they were. But I wasn't troubled about such details in this letter. It brought immense relief. Breck was so natural and so obviously unaware of trouble brewing at home. Surely, I needn't be alarmed. The invitation for the masquerade might have been misdirected or have slipped down behind something. Accidents do take place. Of course it was most unfortunate, but fate performs unfortunate feats sometimes.

In my eagerness to dispel my fears it never crossed my mind that Breck's absence was planned, so that Mrs. Sewall could start her attack without interference. She was a very clever woman, an old and experienced hand at social maneuvers. I am only a beginner. It was an uneven, one-sided fight—for fight it was after all. She won. She bore away the laurels. I bore away simply the tattered remnants of my self-respect.

*   *   *   *   *

Every year at the Hilton Country Club a local horse show is held in mid-August, and many of the summer colonists—women as well as men—exhibit and take part in the different events.

Edith always has liked horses, and when she married Alec she rebuilt our run-down stable along with the house, and filled the empty old box stalls with two or three valuable thorough-breds. Edith's Arrow, Pierre, and Blue-grass had won some sort of a ribbon for the last half-dozen years. I usually rode Blue-grass for Edith in the jumping event. I was to do so on the afternoon that Breck's letter arrived.

It was a perfect day. The grand-stand with its temporary boxes that always sell at absurdly high prices was filled with the summer society, dressed in its gayest and best. The brass band was striking up gala airs now and again, and the big bell in the tower clanged at intervals. Between events horses were being led to and fro, and in front of the grand-stand important individuals wearing white badges leaned over the sides of the lowest tier of boxes, chatting familiarly with the ladies above. A lot of outsiders, anybody who could pay a dollar admission, wandered at large, staring openly at the boxes, leveling opera-glasses, and telling each other who the celebrities were.

Alec was West on a business trip, but Edith had a box, of course, as she always does. All around us were gathered in their various stalls our friends and acquaintances. It is the custom to visit back and forth from box to box, and the owner of each box is as much a host in his own reservation as in his own reception-room at home. Our box is usually very popular, but this year there was a marked difference. Of course some of our best friends did stop for a minute or two, but those who sat down and stayed long enough to be observed were only men. I was surprised and unpleasantly disturbed.

Mrs. Sewall's box was not far away. We could see her seated prominently in a corner of it, surrounded by a very smart bevy—strangers mostly, New Yorkers I supposed—with Miss Gale Oliphant, strikingly costumed in scarlet, in their midst. A vigilant group of summer colonists hovered near-by, now and again becoming one of the party. Edith and I sat quite alone in our box for an hour fully; I in my severe black habit, with my elbow on the railing, my chin in my hand, steadily gazing at the track; Edith erect, sharp-eyed, and nervously looking about in search of some one desirable to bow to and invite to join us.

Finally she leaned forward and said to me, "Isn't this simply terrible? I can't stand it. Come, let's get out."

"Where to?" I asked. "My event comes very soon."

"Oh, let's go over and see Mrs. Jackson. I'm sick of sitting here stark alone. Come on—the girls are all over there."

I glanced toward the Jackson box and saw a group of our most intimate friends—Edith's bridge club members and several of the girls in my set, too.

"All right," I said, and we got up and strolled along the aisle.

As we approached I observed one of the women nudge another. I saw Helene McClellan open her mouth to speak and then close it quickly as she caught sight of us. I felt under Mrs. Jackson's over-effusive greeting the effort it was for her to appear easy and cordial. The group must have been talking about the masquerade, for as we joined it there ensued an uncomfortable silence. I would have withdrawn, but Edith pinched my arm and boldly went over and sat down in one of the empty chairs.

We couldn't have been there five minutes when Mrs. Sewall came strolling along the aisle, accompanied by Miss Oliphant. She, who usually held herself so aloof, was very gracious this afternoon, smiling cordially at left and right, and stopping now and again to present her niece. I saw her recognize Mrs. Jackson and then smilingly approach her. We all rose as our hostess got up and beamingly put her hand into Mrs. Sewall's extended one.

"How do you do, Mrs. Jackson," said Mrs. Sewall. "I've been enjoying your lovely boxful of young ladies all the afternoon. Charming, really! Delightful! I hope you are all planning to come to my masquerade," she went on, addressing the whole group now. "I want it to be a success. I am giving it for my little guest here—and my son also," she added with a significant smile, as if to imply that the coupling of Miss Oliphant's and her son's names was not accidental. "Oh, how do you do, Mrs. McClellan!" she interrupted herself, smiling across the group to Helene who stood next to me, "I haven't caught your eye before today. I hope you're well—and oh, Miss McDowell!" She bowed to Leslie McDowell on my other side.

It was just about at this juncture that I observed Edith threading her way around back of several chairs toward Mrs. Sewall. I wish I could have stopped her, but it was too late. I heard her clear voice suddenly exclaiming from easy speaking distance,

"How do you do, Mrs. Sewall."

"Ah! how do you do!" the lady condescended to reply. There was chilliness in the voice. Edith continued.

"We're so delighted," she went on bravely, "to have Grassmere occupied again. The lights are very pretty on your hilltop from The Homestead, our place, you know."

"Ah, The Homestead!" The chilliness was frosty now. Edith blushed.

"Perhaps you do not recall me, Mrs. Sewall—I am Mrs. Alexander Vars—you know. My sister—"

"Oh, yes—Mrs. Alexander Vars. I recall you quite well, Mrs. Vars. Perfectly, in fact," she said. Then stopped short. There was a terrible silence. It continued like a long-drawn out note on a violin.

"Oh," nervously piped out some one in the group, at last, "look at that lovely horse! I just adore black ones!"

Mrs. Sewall raised her lorgnette and gazed at the track.

"By the way, Mrs. Jackson," she resumed, as if she had not just slaughtered poor Edith. "By the way, can you tell me the participants in the next event? I've left my program. So careless!" she purred. And afterwards she smilingly accepted a proffered armchair in the midst of the scene of her successful encounter.

It would have been thoughtful, I think, and more humane to have waited until the wounded had been carried away—or crawled away. For there was no one to offer a helping hand to Edith and me. I didn't expect it. In social encounters the vanquished must look out for themselves. With what dignity I could, I advanced towards Mrs. Jackson.

"Well, I must trot along," I said lightly. "My turn at the hurdles will be coming soon. Come, Edith, let's go and have a look at Blue-grass. Good-by." And leisurely, although I longed to cast down my eyes and hasten quickly away from the staring faces, I strolled out of the box, followed by Edith; walked without haste along the aisle, even stopping twice to exchange a word or two with friends; and finally escaped.

CHAPTER IX

CATASTROPHE

The incident at the horse show was simply the beginning. I couldn't go anywhere—to a tea, to the Country Club, or even down town for a morning's shopping—and feel sure of escaping a fresh cut or insult of some kind. Mrs. Sewall went out of her way to make occasion to meet and ignore me. It was necessary for her to go out of her way, for we didn't meet often by chance. I was omitted from the many dinners and dances which all the hostesses in Hilton began to give in Miss Oliphant's honor. I was omitted from the more intimate afternoon tea and sewing parties. Gale attended them now, and of course it would have been awkward.

I didn't blame my girl friends for leaving me out. I might have done the same to one of them. It isn't contrary to the rules. In fact the few times I did encounter the old associates it was far from pleasant. There was a feeling of constraint. There was nothing to talk about, either. Even my manicurist and hairdresser, usually so conversational about all the social events of the community, felt embarrassed and ill at ease, with the parties at Grassmere, the costumes for the masquerade, Miss Oliphant, and the Vars scandal barred from the conversation.

I was glad that Alec was away on a western trip. He, at least, was spared the unbeautifying effect of the ordeal upon his wife and sister. Alec hardly ever finds fault or criticizes, but underneath his silence and his kindness I often wonder if there

Olive Higgins Prouty

are not hidden, wounded illusions and bleeding ideals. Edith and I were both in the same boat, and we weren't pleasant traveling companions. I had never sailed with Edith under such baffling winds as we now encountered. Squalls, calms, and occasional storms we had experienced, but she had always kept a firm hand on the rudder. Now she seemed to lose her nerve and forget all the rules of successful navigation that she ever had learned. She threw the charts to the winds, and burst into uncontrolled passions of disappointment and rage.

I couldn't believe that Edith was the same woman who but six months ago had nursed her only little daughter, whom she loves passionately, through an alarming sickness. There had been trained nurses, but every night Edith had taken her place in the low chair by the little girl's crib, there to remain hour after hour, waiting, watching, noting with complete control the changes for better or for worse; sleeping scarcely at all; and always smiling quiet encouragement to Alec or to me when we would steal in upon her. Every one said she was marvelous— even the nurses and the doctor. It was as if she actually willed her daughter to pass through her terrific crisis, speaking firmly now and again to the little sufferer, holding her spirit steady as it crossed the yawning abyss. She had seemed superb to me. I had asked myself if I could ever summon to my support such unswerving strength and courage.

I didn't hear from Breck again until he arrived at the front door unexpectedly one night at ten o'clock. I led the way down into the shaded pergola, and there we remained until nearly midnight. When I finally stole back to my room, I found Edith waiting for me, sitting bolt upright on the foot of my bed, wide-awake, alert, eyes bright and hard as steel.

"Well?" she asked the instant I came in, "tell me, is he as keen as ever?"

A wave of something like sickness swept over me.

"Yes," I said shortly.

"Is he *really*?" she pursued. "Oh, isn't that splendid! Really? He still wants you to marry him?"

"Yes," I said.

Edith flung her arm about me and squeezed me hard.

"We'll make that old cat of a mother of his sing another song one of these days," she said. "You're a wonderful little kiddie, after all. You'll save the day! Trust you! You'll pull it off yet! Oh, I have been horrid, Ruth, this last fortnight. Really I have. I was so afraid we were ruined, and we would be if it wasn't for you. Wait a jiffy."

Fifteen minutes later, just as, very wearily, I was putting out my light, Edith pushed open my door again with a cup of something steaming hot in her hand.

"Here," she said. "Malted milk, good and hot, with just a dash of sherry in it. 'Twill make you sleep. You drink it, poor child—wonderful child too! You jump in and drink it! I'll fix the windows and the lights."

I tried to be Edith's idea of wonderful. For a week I endured the ignominy of receiving calls from Breck in secret, late at night when he was able to steal away from the gaieties at Grassmere. For a week I spent long idle days in the garden, in my room, on the veranda—anywhere at all where I could best kill the galling, unoccupied hours until night, and Breck was free to come to me.

I did not annoy him with demands for explanation of a situation already painfully clear to me. I knew that he spoke truth when he assured me he could not alter his mother's opposition at present, and I did not disturb our evening talks by reproaches. I assumed a grand air of indifference toward Mrs. Sewall and her attacks, as if I was some invulnerable creature beyond and above her. I didn't even cheapen myself by appearing to observe that Breck's invitations to appear in

Olive Higgins Prouty

public with him had suddenly been replaced by demands for private and stolen interviews.

Of course his duties as host were many and consumed most of his time. His clever mother saw to that. He said that there were twenty guests at Grassmere. Naturally, I told myself, he couldn't take all-day motor trips with me. I was convinced that my strength lay in whatever charm I possessed for him, and I had no intention of injuring it by ill-timed complaints. I was attractive, alluring to him—more so than ever. I tried to be! Oh, I tried to be diplomatic, wise, to bide my time; by quiet and determined endurance to withstand the siege of Mrs. Sewall's disapproval; to hold her son's affection; and to marry him some day, with her sanction, too, just exactly as I had planned. I tried and I failed.

The very fact that I could hold Breck's affection hastened my defeat—that and my lacerated pride.

I met him one day when I was out walking with Dandy, not far from the very spot where once he had begged me to ride with him in his automobile. Today in the seat beside him, which had been of late so often mine, sat Gale Oliphant, her head almost upon his shoulder, and Breck leaning toward her laughing as they sped by.

He saw me, I was sure he saw me, but he did not raise his hat. His signal of recognition had been without Miss Oliphant's knowledge. After they had passed he had stretched out his arm as a sign to turn to the left, and had waved his hand without looking around. My face grew scarlet. What had I become? Why, I might have been a picked-up acquaintance, somebody to be ashamed of! Ruth Chenery Vars—where had disappeared that once proud and self-respecting girl?

Insignificant as the event really was, it stood as a symbol of the whole miserable situation to me. It was just enough to startle me into contempt for myself. That night Breck came stealing down to me along the dark roads in his quiet car about eleven-thirty. I knew he had been to the Jackson dinner and was surprised to find he had changed into street clothes. He was more eager than ever in his greeting.

"Come down into the sunken garden," he pleaded. "I've got something to say to you."

It was light in the garden. There was a full September moon. I stood beside the bird-bath and put a forefinger in it. I could hear Breck breathing hard beside me. I was sure he had broken his pledge and had been drinking.

"Well?" I said at last, calmly, looking up.

He answered me silently, vehemently.

"Don't, please, *here*. It's so fearfully light. Don't, Breck," I said.

"I've got the car," he whispered. "It will take us two hours. I've got it all planned. It's a peach of a night. You've got to come. I'm not for waiting any longer. You've got to marry me tonight, you little fish! I'll wake you up. Do you hear me? Tonight in two hours. I'm not going to hang around any longer. You've got to come!"

I managed to struggle away.

"Don't talk like that to me. It's insulting! Don't!" I said.

"Insulting! Say, ring off on that—will you? Insulting to ask a girl to marry you! Say, that's good! Well, insulting or not, I've made up my mind not to hang around any longer. I'll marry you tonight or not at all! You needn't be afraid. I've got it all fixed up—license and everything." He whipped a paper out of his pocket. "We'll surprise 'em, we will—you and I. I'm mad about you, and always have been. The mater—huh! Be a shock to her—but she'll survive."

"I wouldn't elope with the king of England!" I said hotly. "What do you think I am? Understand this, Breck. I require all the honors and high ceremonies that exist."

"Damn it," he said, "you've been letting me come here without much ceremony every night, late, on the quiet. What have you got to say to that? I'm tired of seeing you pose on that high horse of yours. Come down. You know as well as I you've been leading me along as hard as you could for the last week. Good Lord—what for? Say, what's the game? I don't know. But listen—if you don't marry me *now*, then you never will. There's a limit to a man's endurance. Come, come, you can't do better for yourself. You aren't so much. The mater will never come around. She's got her teeth set. The car's ready. I shan't come again."

"Wait a minute," I said. "I'll be back in a minute." And I went straight into the house and upstairs to my room, knelt down before my bureau and drew out a blue velvet box. Breck's ring was inside.

Just as I was stealing down the stairs again, ever-on-the-guard, Edith appeared in the hall in her nightdress.

"What are you after?" she asked.

For answer I held out the box toward her. She came down two or three of the stairs.

"What you going to do with it?" she demanded.

"Give it back to Breck."

She grasped my wrist. "You little fool!" she exclaimed.

"But he wants me to run off with him. He wants me to elope."

"He does!" she ejaculated, her eyes large. "Well?" she inquired.

I stared up at Edith on the step above me in silence.

"Well?" she repeated.

"You don't mean—" I began.

"His mother is sure to come around in time. They always do. *My* mother eloped," she said.

"Edith Campbell Vars," I exclaimed, "do you actually mean—" I stopped. Even in the dim light of the hall I saw her flush before my blank astonishment. "Do you mean—"

"Well, if you don't," she interrupted in defense, "everybody will think he threw *you* over. You'll simply become an old glove. There's not much choice."

"But my pride, my own self-respect! Edith Vars, you'd sell your soul for society; and you'd sell me too! But you can't— you can't! Let go my wrist. I'm sick of the whole miserable game. I'm sick of it. Let me go."

"And I'm sick of it too," flung back Edith. "But *I've* got a daughter's future to think about, I'd have you know, as well as yours. I've worked hard to establish ourselves in this place, and I've succeeded too. And now you come along, and look at the mess we're in! Humiliated! Ignored! Insulted! It isn't my fault, is it? If I'd paddled my own canoe, I'd be all right today."

"You can paddle it hereafter," I flashed out. "I shan't trouble you any more."

"Yes, that's pleasant, after you've jabbed it full of holes!"

"Let me go, Edith," I said and pulled away my wrist with a jerk.

"Are you going to give it back to him?"

"Yes, I am!" I retorted and fled down the stairs, out of the door, across the porch, and into the moonlit garden as fast as I could go.

"Here, Breck—here's your ring! Take it. You're free. You don't need to hang around, as you say, any more. And I'm free, too, thank heaven! I would have borne the glory and the honor of your name with pride. Your mother's friendship would have been a happiness, but for no name, and for no woman's favor will I descend to a stolen marriage. You're mistaken in me. Everybody seems to be. I'm mistaken in myself. I don't want to marry you after all. I don't love you, and I don't want to marry you. I'm tired. Please go."

He stared at me. "You little fool!" he exclaimed, just like Edith. Then he slipped the box into his pocket, shrugged his shoulders, and in truly chivalrous fashion added, "Don't imagine I'm going to commit suicide or anything tragic like that, young lady, because I'm not."

"I didn't imagine it," I replied.

"I'm going to marry Gale Oliphant," he informed me coolly. "I'm going to give her a ring in a little box—and she'll wear hers. You'll see." He produced a cigarette and lit it. "She's no fish," he added. "She's a pippin, she is. Good night," he finished, and turned and walked out of the garden.

Three days later I went away from Hilton. Edith's tirades became unendurable. I didn't want even to eat her food. The spinet desk, the bureau, the chiffonier, the closet, I cleared of every trace of me. I stripped the bed of its linen and left the mattress rolled over the foot-board in eloquent abandonment. The waste-basket bulged with discarded odds and ends. One had only to look into that room to feel convinced that its occupant had disappeared, like a spirit from a dead body, never to return.

I went to my sister Lucy's. I did not write her. I simply took a morning train to Boston and called her up on the 'phone in her not far distant university town. She came trotting cheerfully in to meet me. I told her my news; she tenderly gathered what was left of me together, and carried the bits out here to her little white house on the hill.

Olive Higgins Prouty

CHAPTER X

A UNIVERSITY TOWN

I did not think I would be seated here on my rustic bench writing so soon again. I finished the history of my catastrophe a week ago. But something almost pleasant has occurred, and I'd like to try my pencil at recording a pleasant story. Scarcely a story yet, though. Just a bit of a conversation—that's all— fragmentary. It refers to this very bench where I am sitting as I write, to the hills I am seeing out beyond the little maple tree stripped now of all its glory. I cannot see a dash of color anywhere. The world is brown. The sky is gray. It is rather chilly for writing out-of-doors.

The conversation I refer to began in an ugly little room in a professor's house. There was a roll-top desk in the room, and a map, yellow with age, hanging on the wall. The conversation ended underneath a lamp-post on a street curbing, and it was rainy and dark and cold. And yet when I think of that conversation, sitting here in the brown chill dusk, I see color, I feel warmth.

When I first came here to Lucy's three weeks ago, she assumed that I was suffering from a broken heart. I had been exposed and showed symptoms—going off alone for long walks and consuming reams of theme paper as if I was half mad. I told Lucy that my heart was too hard to break, but I couldn't convince her. There wasn't a day passed but that she planned some form of amusement or diversion. Even Will, her husband, cooperated and spent long evenings playing rum or three-handed auction, so I might not sit idle. I tried to fall in with Lucy's plans.

"But, please, no men! I don't want to see another man for years. If any man I know finds out I'm here, tell him I won't see him, absolutely," I warned. "I want to be alone. I want to think things out undisturbed. Sometimes I almost wish I could enter a convent."

"Oh, I'm so sorry!" Lucy would exclaim.

"You needn't be. You didn't break my engagement. For heaven's sake, Lucy, *you* needn't take it so hard."

But she did. She simply brooded over me. She read to me, smiled for me, and initiated every sally that I made into public. In conversation she picked her way with me with the precaution of a cat walking across a table covered with delicate china. She made wide detours to avoid a reference or remark that might reflect upon my engagement. Will did likewise. I lived in daily surprise and wonder. As a family we are brutally frank. This was a new phase, and one of the indirect results, I suppose, of my broken engagement.

What I am trying to arrive at is the change of attitude in me toward Lucy. Usually when I visit Lucy I do just about as I please; refuse to attend a lot of stupid student-teas and brain-fagging lectures, or to exert myself to appear engrossed in the conversation of her intellectual dinner guests.

I used to scorn Lucy's dinners. They are very different from Edith's, where, when the last guest in her stunning new gown has arrived and swept into the drawing-room, followed by her husband, a maid enters, balancing on her tray a dozen little glasses, amber filled; everybody takes one, daintily, between a thumb and forefinger and drains it; puts it nonchalantly aside on shelf or table; offers or accepts an arm and floats toward the dining-room. At Edith's dinners the table is long, flower-laden, candle-lighted. Your partner's face smiles at you dimly. His voice is almost drowned by the chatter and the laughter all about, but you hear him—just barely—and you laugh—he is immensely droll—and then reply. And he laughs, too, contagiously, and you know that you are going to get on!

Incidentally at Edith's dinners silent-footed servants pass you things; you take them; you eat a little, too—delicious morsels if you stopped to consider them; but you and your partner are having far too good a time (he is actually audacious, and so, if you please, are you) to bother about the food.

There's a little group of glasses beside your water, and once in a while there appears in your field of vision a hand grasping a white napkin folded like a cornucopia, out of which flows delicious nectar. You sip a little of it occasionally, a very little—you are careful of course—and waves of elation sweep over you because you are alive and happy and good to look upon; waves of keen delight that such a big and splendid life (there are orchids in the center of the table, there are pearls and diamonds everywhere)—that such a life as this is yours to grasp and to enjoy.

At Lucy's dinners the women do not wear diamonds and pearls. Lucy seldom entertains more than six at a time. "Shall we go out?" she says when her Delia mumbles something from the door. You straggle across the hall into the dining-room, where thirteen carnations—you count them later, there's time enough—where thirteen stiff carnations are doing duty in the center of the prim table. At each place there is a soup plate sending forth a cloud of steam. You wait until Lucy points out your place to you, and then sit down at last. There is a terrible pause—you wonder if they say grace—and then finally Lucy picks up her soup-spoon for signal and you're off! The conversation is general. That is because Lucy's guests are usually intellectuals, and whatever any one of them says is supposed to be so important that every one else must keep still and listen. You can't help but notice the food, because there's nothing to soften the effect of it upon your nerves, as it were.

There are usually four courses, with chicken or ducks for the main dish, accompanied by potatoes cut in balls, the invariable rubber stamp of a party at Lucy's. Afterward there's coffee in the living-room, and you feel fearfully discouraged when you look at the clock and find it's only eight-thirty. You're surprised after the guests have gone to find that Lucy considers her party a success.

"Why," she exclaims, cheeks aglow, "Dr. Van Breeze gave us the entire resume of his new book. He seldom thinks anybody clever enough to talk to. It was a perfect combination!"

As I said, I usually visit Lucy in rather a critical state of mind and hold myself aloof from her learned old doctors and professors. On this visit, though, she is so obviously careful of me and my feelings, that I find myself going out of my way to consider hers a little. One day last week when she so brightly suggested that we go to a tea given by the wife of a member of the faculty, instead of exclaiming, "Oh, dear! it would bore me to extinction," I replied sweetly, "All right, if you want to, I'll go."

I wasn't feeling happy. I didn't want to go. I had been roaming the woods and country roads round about for a month in search of an excuse for existence. I had been autobiographing for days in the faint hope that I might run across something worth while in my life. But no. It was hopeless. I had lost all initiative. I couldn't see what reason there was for me to eat three meals a day. It seemed as foolish as stoking the furnaces of an ocean liner when it is in port. In such a mood, and through the drifting mist of a complaining October afternoon, in rubbers and a raincoat, I started out with Lucy for her afternoon tea.

The other guests wore raincoats, too—we met a few on the way—with dull-colored suits underneath, and tailored hats. There wasn't a single bright, frivolous thing about that tea. Even the house was dismal—rows of black walnut bookcases with busts of great men on top, steel engravings framed in oak

Olive Higgins Prouty

on the walls, and a Boston fern or two in red pots sitting about on plates. When I looked up from my weak tea, served in a common stock-pattern willow cup, and saw Lucy sparkling with pleasure, talking away for dear life with a white-haired old man who wore a string tie and had had two fingers shot off in the Civil War (I always hated to shake hands with him) a wave of intolerance for age and learning swept over me. I told Lucy if she didn't mind I'd run along home, and stepped across the hall into a little stupid room with a roll-top desk in it, where we had left our raincoats, and rubbers. I put on my things and then stood staring a moment at a picture on the wall. I didn't know what the picture was. I simply looked at it blindly while I fought a sudden desire to cry. I hadn't wept before. But this dreadful house, these dry, drab people were such a contrast to my all-but-realized ambitions that it brought bitter tears to my eyes. Life at Grassmere—*that* was living! This was mere existence.

Just as I was groping for a handkerchief some little fool of a woman exclaimed, "Oh, there she is—in the study! I thought she hadn't gone. O Miss Vars, there's somebody I want you to meet, and meet you. Here she is, Mr. Jennings. Come in. Miss Vars," I was still facing the wall, "Miss Vars, I want to introduce Mr. Jennings." I turned finally, and as I did so she added, "Now, I must go back to Dr. Fuller. I was afraid you'd gone," and out she darted. I could have shot her.

Mr. Jennings came straight across the room. Through a blur I caught an impression of height, breadth and energy. His sudden hand-grasp was firm and decisive. "How do you do?" he said, and then abruptly observed my tears.

"You've caught me with my sails all down," I explained.

"Have I?" he replied pleasantly. "Well, I like sails down."

"Please do not think," I continued, "that I am often guilty of such a thing as this. I'm not. Who was that woman anyhow?"

"Oh, don't blame her," he laughed, and he stepped forward to look at the picture which I had been staring at. I was busy putting away my handkerchief. "Who was that woman?" Mr. Jennings repeated, abruptly turning away from the picture back to me, "Who was she? I'll tell you who she was—a good angel. Why," he went on, "I'd got into the way of thinking that sympathy as expressed by tears had gone out of style with the modern girl. They never shed any at the theater nowadays, I notice. I'm glad to know there is one who hasn't forgotten how."

I stepped forward then to find out what manner of picture it was to cause such a tribute to be paid me. It was called "The Doctor." A crude bare room was depicted. The light from a lamp on an old kitchen table threw its rays on the turned-aside, face of a little girl, who lay asleep—or unconscious—on an improvised bed made of two chairs drawn together. Beyond the narrow confines of the cot the little girl's hand extended, wistfully upturned. Seated beside her, watching, sat the big kind doctor. Anxiety, doubt were in his intelligent face. Near an east window, through which a streak of dawn was creeping, sat a woman, her face buried in the curve of her arms folded on the table. Beside her stood a bearded man, brow furrowed, his pleading eyes upon the doctor, while his hand, big, comforting, rested on the woman's bowed shoulders. A cup with a spoon in it, a collection of bottles near-by—all the poor, human, useless tools of defense were there, eloquent of a long and losing struggle. Every one who recalls the familiar picture knows what a dreary, hopeless scene it is—the room stamped with poverty, the window stark and curtainless, the woman meagerly clad, the man bearing the marks of hardship.

Suddenly in the face of all that, Mr. Jennings softly exclaimed, "That's living."

Only five minutes ago I had said the same thing of life at Grassmere.

"Is it?" I replied. "Is that living? I've been wondering lately. I

Olive Higgins Prouty

thought—I thought—it's so poor and sad!" I remonstrated.

"Poor! Oh, no, it's rich," he replied quickly, "rich in everything worth while. Anyhow, only lives that are vacuums are free from sadness."

"Are lives that are vacuums free from happiness, too?" I enquired.

He took my question as if it was a statement. "That's true, too, I suppose," he agreed.

"How hopeless," I murmured, still gazing at the picture, but in reality contemplating my own empty life. He misunderstood.

"See here," he said. "I believe this little girl here is going to pull through after all. Don't worry. I insist she is. That artist ought to paint a sequel—just for you," he added, and abruptly he unfolded his arms and looked at me squarely for the first time. "I didn't in the least get your name," he broke off. "The good angel flew away so soon."

I told him.

"Oh, yes, Miss Vars. Thank you. Mine's Jennings. People mumble names so in introductions." He glanced around at the piles of raincoats and racks of umbrellas. I already had my coat on. "You weren't just going, were you?" he inquired brightly. "For if you were, so was I, too. Perhaps you will let me walk along—unless you're riding."

I forgot just for a minute that I didn't want to see another man for years and years. He wasn't a man just then, but a bright and colorful illumination. He stood before me full of life and vigor. He was tall and straight. His close-cropped hair shone like gold in the pale gas-light, and there was a tan or glow upon his face that made me think of out-of-doors. His smile, his straightforward gaze, his crisp voice, had brightened that dull little room for me. I went with him. Of course I did—out into the rainy darkness of the late October afternoon, drawn as a child towards the glow of red fire.

Olive Higgins Prouty

CHAPTER XI

A WALK IN THE RAIN

Once on the side-walk Mr. Jennings said, "I'm glad to know your name, for I know you by sight already. Shall we have any umbrella?"

"Let's not," I replied. "I like the mist. But how do you know me?"

"I thought you would—like the mist, I mean—because you seem to like my woods so well."

"Your woods! Why—what woods?"

"The ones you walk in every day," he cheerfully replied; "they're mine. I discovered them, and to whom else should they belong?"

"I've been trespassing, then."

"Oh, no! I'm delighted to lend my woods to you. If you wear blinders and keep your eyes straight ahead and stuff your ears with cotton so you can't hear the trolleys, you can almost cheat yourself into thinking they're real woods with a mountain to climb at the end of them. Do you like that little rustic seat I made beside the lake?"

"Did you make it?"

"Yes, Saturdays, for recreation last year. I'm afraid it doesn't fit very well." He smiled from out of the light of a sudden lamp-post. "You'll find a birch footstool some day pretty soon. I noticed your feet didn't reach. By the way," he broke off, "pardon me for quoting from you, but *I* don't think back-season debutantes are like out-of-demand best-sellers—not all of them. Anyhow, all best-sellers do not deteriorate. And tell me, is this chap with the deep-purring car the villain or the hero in your novel—the dark one with the hair blown straight back?"

I almost stopped in my amazement. He was quoting from my life history.

"I don't understand," I began. I could feel the color in my cheeks. "I dislike mystery. Tell me. Please. How did you—I dislike mystery," I repeated.

"Are you angry? It's so dark I can't see. Don't be angry. It was written on theme paper, in pencil, and in a university town theme paper is public property. I found them there one day— just two loose leaves behind the seat—and I read them. Afterwards I saw you—not until afterwards," he assured me, "writing there every day. I asked to be introduced to you when I saw you tucked away in a corner there this afternoon drinking tea behind a fern, so that I could return your property."

"Oh, you've kept the leaves! Where are they?" I demanded.

"Right here. Wait a minute." And underneath an arc-light we stopped, and from out of his breast-pocket this surprising man drew a leather case, and from out of that two crumpled pages of my life. "If any one should ask me to guess," he went on, "I should say that the author of these fragments is a student at Shirley" (the girls' college connected with the University) "and that she had strolled out to my woods for inspiration to write a story for an English course. Am I right?" He passed me the leaves. "It sounds promising," he added, "the story, I mean."

I took the leaves and glanced through them. There wasn't a name mentioned on either. "A student at Shirley!" I exclaimed. "How perfectly ridiculous! A school girl! Well, how old do you think I am?" and out of sheer relief I rippled into a laugh.

"I don't know," he replied. "How old are you?" And he laughed, too. The sound of our merriment mixing so rhythmically was music to my ears. I thought I had forgotten how to be foolish, and inconsequential.

"I don't know why it strikes me so funny," I tried to explain—for really I felt fairly elated—"I don't know why, but a story for an English course! A college girl!" And I burst into peals of mirth.

"That's right. Go ahead. I deserve it," urged Mr. Jennings self-depreciatively. "How I blunder! Anyhow I've found you can laugh as well as cry, and that's something. Perhaps now," he continued, "seeing I'm such a failure as a Sherlock Holmes, you will be so kind as to tell me yourself who you are. Do you live here? I never saw you before. I'm sure you're a stranger. Where is your home, Miss Vars?"

"Where is my home?" I repeated, and then paused an instant. Where indeed? "A wardrobe-trunk is my home, Mr. Jennings," I replied.

"Oh!" he took it up. "A wardrobe-trunk. Rather a small house for you to develop your individuality in, very freely, I should say!"

"Yes, but at least nothing hangs within its walls but of my own choosing."

"And it's convenient for house-cleaning, too," he followed it up. "But see here, is there room for two in it, because I was just going to ask to call."

"I usually entertain my callers in the garden," I

primly announced.

"How delightful! I much prefer gardens." And we laughed again. "Which way?" he abruptly inquired. "Which way to your garden, please?" We had come to a crossing. I stopped, and he beside me.

"Why, I'm sure I don't know!" Nothing about me looked familiar. "These winding streets of yours! I'm afraid I'm lost," I confessed. "You'll have to put me on a car—a Greene Hill Avenue car. I know my way alone then. At least I believe it's a Greene Hill Avenue car. They've just moved there—my sister. Perhaps you know her—Mrs. William Maynard."

"Lucy Maynard!" he exclaimed. "I should say I did! Are you— why, are you her sister?"

He had heard about me then! Of course. How cruel!

"Yes. Why?" I managed to inquire.

"Oh, nothing. Only I've met you," he brought out triumphantly. "I met you at dinner, two or three years ago—at your sister's house. We're old friends," he said.

"Are we?" I asked in wonder. "Are we old friends?" I wanted to add, "How nice!"

He looked so steady and substantial, standing there—so kind and understanding. Any one would prize him for an old friend. I gazed up at him. The drifting mist had covered his broad chest and shoulders with a glistening veil of white. It shone like frost on the nap of his soft felt hat. It sparkled on his eyebrows and the lashes of his fine eyes. "How nice," I wanted to add. But a desire not to flirt with this man honestly possessed me. Besides I must remember I was tired of men. I wanted nothing of any of them. So instead I said, "Well, then, you know what car I need to take."

He ignored my remark.

"You had on a yellow dress—let's walk along—and wore purple pansies, fresh ones, although it was mid-winter. I remember it distinctly. But a hat and a raincoat today make you look different, and I couldn't get near enough to you in the woods. I remember there was a medical friend of your sister's husband there that night, and Will and he monopolized the conversation. I hardly spoke to you; but tell me, didn't you wear pansies with a yellow dress one night at your sister's?"

"Jennings? Are you Bob Jennings?" (Lucy's Bob Jennings! I remembered now—a teacher of English at the University.) "Of course," I exclaimed, "I recall you now. I remember that night perfectly. When you came into my sister's living-room, looking so—so unprofessor-like—I thought to myself, 'How nice for me; Professor Jennings couldn't come; she's got one of the students to take his place—some one nice and easy and my size.' I wondered if you were on the football team or crew, and it crossed my mind what a perfect shame it was to drag a man like you away from a dance in town, perhaps, to a stupid dinner with one of the faculty. And then you began to talk with Will about—what was it—Chaucer? Anyhow something terrifying, and I knew then that you *were* Professor Jennings after all."

"Oh, but I wasn't. I was just an assistant. I'm not a professor even yet. Never shall be either—the gods willing. I'm trying hard to be a lawyer. Circuitous route, I confess. But you know automobile guide-books often advise the longer and smoother road. Do you mind walking? It isn't far, and the cars are crowded."

We walked.

"I suppose," I remarked a little later, "trying hard to become a lawyer is what keeps your life from being a vacuum."

"Yes , that, and a little white-haired lady I call my mother," he added gallantly.

"Do you want to know what keeps my life from being a vacuum?" I abruptly asked.

"Of course I do!"

"Well, then—a little brown Boston terrier whom I call Dandy," I announced.

He laughed as if it was a joke. "What nonsense! Your sister has told me quite a lot about you, Miss Vars, one time and another; that you write verse a little, for instance. Any one who can create is able to fill all the empty corners of his life. You know that as well as I do."

I considered this new idea in silence for a moment. We turned in at Lucy's street.

"How long shall you be here, Miss Vars?" asked Mr. Jennings. "And, seriously, may I call some evening?"

How could I refuse such a friendly and straightforward request?

"Why, yes," I heard myself saying, man though he was, "I suppose so. I should be glad, only—"

"Only what?"

"Only—well—" We were at Lucy's gate. I stopped beneath the lamp-post. "I don't believe my sister has told you all about me, Mr. Jennings."

"Of course not!" He laughed. "I don't want her to. I don't want to know all that's in a new book I am about to read. It's pleasanter to discover the delights myself."

I felt conscience-stricken. There were no delights left in me. I ought to tell him. However, all I replied was, "How nicely you put things!"

And he: "Do I? Well—when may I come?"

"Why—any night. Only I'm not a very bright book—rather dreary. Truly. I warn you. You found me in tears, remember."

"Don't think again about that," he said to me. "Please. Listen. I always try to take home to the little white-haired lady something pleasant every night—a rose or a couple of pinks, or an incident of some sort to please her, never anything dreary. *You*, looking at the picture of the little sick girl, are to be the gift tonight." And then suddenly embarrassed, he added hastily, "I'm afraid you're awfully wet. I ought to be shot. Perhaps you preferred to ride. You're covered with mist. And perhaps it's spoiled something." He glanced at my hat.

"No, it hasn't," I assured him, "and good night. I can get in all right."

"Oh, let me—"

"No, please," I insisted.

"Very well," he acquiesced. And I gave him my hand and sped up the walk.

He waited until the door was opened to me, and then, "Good night," came his clear, pleasant voice to me from out of the rainy dark.

I went straight upstairs to my room. I felt as if I had just drunk long and deep of pure cold water. Tired and travel-worn I had been, uncertain of my way, disheartened, spent; and then suddenly across my path had appeared an unexpected brook, crystal clear, soul-refreshing. I had rested by it a moment, listened to its cheerful murmur, lifted up a little of its coolness in the hollow of my hand, and drunk. I went up to my room with a lighter heart than I had known for months, walked over to the window, raised it, and let in a little of the precious mistiness that had enshrouded me for the last half hour.

Standing there looking out into the darkness, I was interrupted by a knock on my door.

"I was just turning down the beds, Miss," explained Lucy's Delia, "and so brought up your letter." And she passed me the missive I had not noticed on the table as I came in, so blind a cheerful "good night" called from out of the rain had made me.

"A letter? Thank you, Delia. Isn't it rainy!" I added impulsively.

"It is, Miss. It is indeed, Miss Ruth!"

"Come," I went on, "let me help you turn down the beds. I haven't another thing to do." The letter could wait. Benevolence possessed my soul.

Later alone in my room I opened my note. It was from Edith. I had recognized her handwriting instantly. She seldom harbors ill-feeling for any length of time.

"Three cheers!" the letter jubilantly began. "Run up a flag. We win!" it shouted. "Prepare yourself, Toots. We have been bidden to Grassmere! Also I have received a personal note from the great Mogul herself. You were right, I guess, as always. Let's forgive and forget. Mrs. Sewall writes to know if we will honor her by our presence at a luncheon at Grassmere. What do you say to that? With pleasure, kind lady, say I! I enclose your invitation. You'll be ravishing in a new gown which I want you to go right in and order at Madame's—*on me*, understand, dearie. I'm going to blow myself to a new one, too. Won't the girls be surprised when they hear of this? The joke will be on them, I'm thinking. Probably you and Breck will be patching up your little difference, too. I don't pretend to fathom Mrs. S.'s change of front, but it's changed anyhow! That's all I care about. Good-by. Must hurry to catch mail. Hustle home, rascal. Love, Edith."

Two weeks later on the morning after the luncheon, to which it is unnecessary to say I sent my immediate regrets, the morning paper could not be found at Lucy's house. Will went off to the University berating the paper-boy soundly. After I had finished my coffee and toast and moved over to the front window, Lucy opened the wood-box.

"I stuffed it in here," she said, "just as you and Will were coming downstairs. I thought you'd rather see it first." And she put the lost paper into my hands and left me.

On the front page there appeared the following announcement:

"Breckenridge Sewall Engaged to be Married to Miss Gale Oliphant of New York and Newport. Announcement of Engagement Occasion for Brilliant Luncheon Given by Mrs. F. Rockridge Sewall at her Beautiful Estate in Hilton. Wedding Set for Early December."

I read the announcement two or three times, and afterward the fine print below, containing a long list of the luncheon guests with Edith's name proudly in its midst. The scene of my shame and the actors flashed before me. Ignominy and defeat were no part of the new creature I had become since Lucy's tea. I read the announcement again. It was as if a dark cloud passed high over my head and cast a shadow on the sparkling beauty of the brook beside which I had been lingering for nearly two weeks.

CHAPTER XII

A DINNER PARTY

Robert Jennings sees the plainest and commonest things of life through the eyes of an artist. He never goes anywhere without a volume of poetry stuffed into his pocket, and if he runs across anything that no one else has endowed with beauty, then straightway he will endow it himself. Crowded trolleys, railroad stations, a muddy road—all have some hidden appeal. Even greed and discord he manages to ignore as such by looking beneath their exteriors for hidden significance. The simpler a pleasure, the greater to him its joy.

He is tall, broad; of light complexion; vigorous in every movement that he makes. Upon his face there is a perpetual glow, whether due to mere color, or to expression, I cannot make up my mind. He enters the house and brings with him a feeling of out-of-doors. His smile is like sunshine on white snow, his seriousness like a quiet pool hidden among trees, his enthusiasm like mad whitecaps on a lake stirred by a gale, his tenderness like the kind warmth of Indian summer caressing drooping flowers. I have never known any one just like him before. Instead of inviting me in town to luncheon and the matinee, or to dinner and the opera, he takes me out with him to drink draughts of cold November air, and to share the glory of an autumn sunset.

The first time he called he mentioned a course at Shirley offered to special students. I told him if he would use his influence and persuade the authorities to accept me, I believed I should like to take a course in college. I thought it would help to kill time while I was making up my mind how better to dispose of myself. I have therefore become what Mr. Jennings thought I was in the beginning—a student at Shirley; not a full-fledged one but a "special" in English. I attend class twice a week and in between times write compositions that are read out loud in class and criticized. Also in between times I occasionally see Mr. Jennings.

Last week each member of the class was required to submit an original sonnet. Mine is not finished yet. I am trying a rhapsody on the autumn woods. This is the way I work. Pencil, pad, low rocking-chair by the window. First line:

"I see the saffron woods of yesterday!" Then fixedly I gaze at the rubber on the end of my pencil. "I see the saffron woods of yesterday!" (What a young god he looked the day he called for me to go chestnutting! How his eyes laughed and his voice sang, and as we scuffled noisily through the leaf-strewn forest, how his long, easy stride put me in mind of the swinging meter of Longfellow's Hiawatha!)

"I see the saffron woods of yesterday!" (I see, too, the setting sun shining on the yellow leaves, clinging frailly. I see myself standing beneath a tree holding up an overcoat—his overcoat, thrown across my outstretched arms to catch the pelting burrs that he is shaking off. I see his eyes looking down from the tree into mine. Later as we lean over a rock to crack open the prickly burrs, I feel our shoulders touch! Did he feel them, too, I wonder? If he were any other man I would say that he meant that our eyes should meet too long, our shoulders lean too near, and our silence, as we walked home in the dark, continue too tense. But he is different. He is not a lover. He is a friend—a comrade.) "I see the saffron woods of yesterday!"

Abruptly I lay aside my pad and pencil. I put on my coat and hat, pull on my gloves, and in self-defense plunge out into the cold November afternoon. I avoid the country, and try to keep my recreant thoughts on such practical subjects as trolley cars, motor-trucks and delivery wagons, rumbling noisily beside me along the street. A sudden "To Let" card appears in a new apartment. I wonder how much the rent is. I wonder how much the salary of an assistant professor is. Probably something under five thousand a year. The income from the investments left me by my father amounts to almost eight hundred dollars. Clothes alone cost me more than a thousand. Of course one wouldn't need so many, but what with rent, and food, and service, and—what am I thinking of? Why, I've known the man only four weeks, and considering my recent relations with Breckenridge Sewall such mad air-castling is lacking in good taste. Besides, a teacher—a professor! I've always scorned professors. I was predestined to fill a high and influential place. A professor's wife? It is unthinkable! And then abruptly appears a street vender beside me. I smell his roasting chestnuts. And again—again, "I see the saffron woods of yesterday!"

About two days after I went chestnutting with Mr. Jennings, I went picnicking. We built a fire in the corner of two stones and cooked chops and bacon. Two days after that we tramped to an old farm-house, five miles straight-away north, and drank sweet cider—rather warm—from a jelly tumbler with a rough rim. Once we had some tea and thick slabs of bread in a country hotel by the roadside. Often we pillage orchards for apples. Day before yesterday we stopped in a dismantled vegetable garden and pulled a raw turnip from out of the frosty ground. Mr. Jennings scraped the dirt away and pared off a little morsel with his pocket knife. He offered it to me, then took a piece himself.

"Same old taste," I laughed.

"Same old taste," he laughed back. And we looked into each other's eyes in sympathetic appreciation of raw turnip. As he wiped the blade of his knife he added, "If I didn't know it wasn't so, I would swear we played together as children. Most young ladies, of this age, do not care for raw turnips."

A thrill passed through me. I blessed my brothers who had enriched my childhood with the lore of out-of-doors. I blessed even the difficult circumstances of my father's finances, which had forced me as a little girl to seek my pleasures in fields and woods and tilled gardens. Had I once said that my nature required a luxurious environment? I had been mistaken. I gazed upon Robert Jennings standing there before me in the forlorn garden. Bare brown hills were his background. The wind swept down bleakly from the east, bearing with it the dank odor of frostbitten cauliflower. Swift, sharp memories of my childhood swept over me. Smothered traditions stirred in my heart. All the young sweet impulses of my youth took sudden possession of me, and through a mist that blurred my eyes I recognized with a little stab in my breast—that was half joy, half fear—I recognized before me my perfect comrade!

Last night Lucy had one of her dinners and one of the men invited was Robert Jennings. She had increased the usual number of six to eight. "A real party," she explained to me, "with a fish course!"

For no other dinner party in my life did I dress with more care or trembling expectation. Lucy's dinners are always at seven o'clock. I was ready at quarter of, with cold hands and hot cheeks. I knew the very instant that Mr. Jennings entered the room that evening. I was standing at the far end with my back toward the door, talking to the war veteran. At the first sound of Mr. Jennings' greeting as he met Lucy, I became deaf to all else. I heard him speaking to the others near her—such a trained and cultured voice—but I didn't turn around. I kept my eyes riveted on the veteran. It was enough, at that instant, to be in the same room with Robert Jennings. And when Lucy finally said, "Shall we go out?" I wondered if I could bear the ordeal of turning around and meeting his eyes. I needn't have been afraid. He spared me that. There was no greeting of any kind between us until we sat down.

Lucy had placed him at the end of the table farthest away from me, and after the guests were all settled, I dared at last to look up. A swift, sweeping glance I meant it to be, but his eyes were waiting for mine, and secretly, concealed by the noise and chatter all around, somewhere among Lucy's carnations in the center of the table, we met. Only for an instant. He returned immediately to his partner, and I to mine. He answered her, we both selected a piece of silver—and then, abruptly, ran away to each other again. Frequently, during that dinner, as we gained confidence and learned the way, we met among the carnations.

Never before was I so glad of what good looks heaven had bestowed upon me as when I saw this man's eyes examine and approve. Never before did I feel so elated at a dinner, so glad to be alive. My pulse ran high. My spirits fairly danced. And all without cocktails, too! Not only did our eyes meet in stolen interviews, but our voices, too. He couldn't speak but what I heard him, nor did I laugh but what it was meant for him.

During the hour occasions occurred when Mr. Jennings alone did the talking, while the rest listened. I could observe him then without fear of discovery. He sat there opposite me in his perfect evening clothes, as much at home and at ease as in Scotch tweeds in the woods. As he leaned forward a little, one cuffed wrist resting on the table's edge, his fine head held erect, expressing his ideas in clear and well-turned phrases, confident in himself, and listened to with attention, I glowed with pride at the thought of my intimacy with him. A professor's wife? That was a mere name—but *his*, this young aristocrat's—what a privilege!

We didn't speak to each other until late in the evening, when the ladies rose from their chairs about the fire in the living-room and began to talk about the hour. I was standing alone by the mantel when I became conscious that Mr. Jennings had moved away from beside Mrs. Van Breeze, and was making his way toward me. Everybody was saying good night to Lucy. We were quite alone for a minute. He didn't shake hands—just stood before me smiling.

"Well, who are *you*?" he asked.

"Don't you recognize me?" I replied.

He looked me up and down deliberately.

"It is very pretty," he said quietly.

I felt my cheeks grow warm. I blushed. Somebody told me my dress was pretty, and I blushed! I might have been sixteen.

"Your sister said I could stay a little after the others go if I wanted to," Mr. Jennings went on. "Of course I want to. Shall I?"

"Yes," I said, with my cheeks still on fire. "Yes. Stay." And he went away in a moment. I heard him laughing with the others.

I strolled over to the pile of music on the back of Lucy's piano and became engrossed in looking it over. I felt weak and suddenly incompetent. I felt frightened and unprepared. I was still there with the pile of music when, fifteen minutes later, Lucy and Will, with effusive apologies, excused themselves and went upstairs. Mr. Jennings approached me. We were alone at last, and each keenly conscious of it.

"Any music here you know?" he asked indifferently, and drew a sheet towards him.

"Not a great deal."

"It looks pretty much worn," he attempted.

"Doesn't it?" I agreed.

"I hardly know you tonight!" he exclaimed, suddenly personal.

"Don't you? I wore a yellow dress and purple pansies on purpose," I replied as lightly as I could, touching the flowers at my waist.

"Yes, but you didn't wear the same look in your eyes," he remarked.

"No, I didn't," I acknowledged.

A silence enfolded us—sweet, significant.

Mr. Jennings broke it. "I think I had better go," he remarked.

"Had you?" I almost whispered. "Well—" and acquiesced.

"Unless," he added, "you'll sing me something. Do you sing—or play?"

"A little," I confessed.

"Well, *will* you then?"

"Why, yes, if you want me to." And I went over and sat down before the familiar keys.

It was at that moment that I knew at last why I had taken lessons for so many years; why so much money had been put into expensive instruction, and so many hours devoted to daily practise. It was for this—for this particular night—for this particular man. I saw it in a flash. I sang a song in English. "In a Garden," it was called. Softly I played the opening phrases, and then raised my chin a little and began. My voice isn't strong, but it can't help but behave nicely. It can't help but take its high notes truly, like a child who has been taught pretty manners ever since he could walk.

After I had finished Mr. Jennings said nothing for an instant. Then, "Sing something else," he murmured, and afterward he exclaimed, "I didn't know! I had no idea! Your sister never told me *this*!" Then, "I have come to a very lovely part in the beautiful book I discovered," he said to me. "It makes me want

Olive Higgins Prouty

never to finish the book. Sing something else." His eyes admired; his voice caressed; his tenderness placed me high in the sacred precincts of his soul.

"Listen, please," I said impulsively. "You mustn't go on thinking well of me. It isn't right. I shall not let you. I'm not what you think. Listen. When I first met you, I had just broken my engagement—just barely. I never said a word about it. I let you go on thinking that I—you see it was this way— my pride was hurt more than my heart. I'm that sort of girl. His mother is Mrs. F. Rockridge Sewall. They have a summer place in Hilton, and—and—"

"Don't bother to go into that. I've known it all from the beginning," Mr. Jennings interrupted gently.

"Oh, have you? You've known then, all along, that I'm just a frivolous society girl who can't do anything but perform a few parlor tricks—and things like that? I was afraid—I was so afraid I had misled you."

"You've misled only yourself," he smiled, and suddenly he put his hand over mine as it rested beside the music rack. I met his steady eyes. Just for an instant. Abruptly he took his hand away, went over to the fireplace, and began poking the logs. When he spoke next he did not turn around.

"This is an evening of confessions," he said. "There are some things about me you might as well know, too. I am an instructor, with a salary of two thousand five hundred dollars a year. I hope to make a lawyer out of myself some day, I don't know when. I've hoped to for a long while. Circumstances made it necessary after I graduated from college to find something to do that was immediately remunerative. I discovered that my mother was entirely dependent upon me. My ambitions had to be postponed for a while. I had tutored enough during my college course to make it evident that I could teach, and I grasped this opportunity as a fortunate one. There are hours each day when I can read law. There are even opportunities to attend lectures. It's a long way around to my goal, I know that, and a steep way. Everything that I can save is laid aside for the time when, finally admitted to the bar, I dare throw off the security of a salary. My mother is quite alone. I must always look out for her. I am all she has. I shall inherit little or nothing. If there is any one who has allowed a possible delusion to continue about himself it is I—not you, Miss Vars. Hello," he interrupted himself, "it's getting late. Quarter of twelve! I ought to be shot." He turned about and came over toward me. "Your sister will be turning me out next," he said glibly. He was quite formal now. We might have been just introduced.

His manner forbade me to speak. He gave me no opportunity to tell him that his circumstances made no difference. Salary or no salary I did not care—nothing made any difference now. He simply wanted me to keep still. He eagerly desired it.

"Good night," he said cheerfully. In matter-of-fact fashion we shook hands. "Forgive me for the disgraceful hour. Good night."

CHAPTER XIII

LUCY TAKES UP THE NARRATIVE

It was an afternoon in late February. A feeling of spring had been in the air all day. In the living-room a lingering sun cast a path of light upon the mahogany surface of a grand piano. In *my* living-room, I should say. For I am Mrs. Maynard, wife of Doctor William Ford Maynard of international guinea-pig fame; sister of Ruth Chenery Vars; one-time confidante of Robert Hopkinson Jennings. I haven't any identity of my own. I'm simply one of the audience, an onlooker—an anxious and worried one, just at present, who wishes somebody would assure me that the play has a happy ending. I don't like sad plays. I don't like being harrowed for nothing. I've taken to paper simply because I'm all of a tremble for fear the play I've been watching for the last month or two won't come out right. Sometimes I feel as if I'd like to dash across the footlights and tell the actors what to say.

Ruth is engaged to be married to Robert Jennings. At first it seemed to me too good to be true. After the sort of bringing up my sister has had, culminating in that miserable affair of hers with Breckenridge Sewall, I was afraid that happiness would slip by her altogether.

Robert Jennings is the salt of the earth. I believe I was as happy as Ruth the first four weeks of her engagement, and then these clouds began to gather. The first time I was conscious of them was the afternoon I have just referred to, in late February.

I went into my living-room that day just to see that it was in order in case of callers. It is difficult to keep a living-room in order when your spoiled young society-sister is visiting you. Today in the middle of one of the large cushions on the sofa appeared an indentation. From beneath one corner of the cushion escaped the edge of a crushed handkerchief. Open, face down, upon the floor lay an abandoned book. I straightened the pillow and then picked up the book.

"Oh!" I exclaimed, actually out loud as my eyes fell on the title. "This!"

It was a modern novel much under discussion, an unpleasant book, reviewers pronounced it, and unnecessarily bold. I opened it. Certain passages were marked with wriggling lines made with a soft pencil. I read a marked paragraph or two, standing just where I was in the middle of the room.

Suddenly the door-bell rang, twice, sharply, and almost immediately afterward I heard some one shove open the front door.

I slipped the book behind the pillow which I had just straightened, walked over to a geranium in the window, and nonchalantly snipped off a leaf.

"Hello!" a man's cheerful voice called out. "Any one at home?"

"Yes, in here, Bob," I called back. "Come in."

Robert Jennings entered. He glowed as if he had just been walking up hill briskly. He shook hands with me.

"Hello," he said, his gray eyes smiling pleasantly. "Been out today? Ought to! Like spring. Where's Ruth?"

"Just gone to the Square. She'll be right back. Run out of cotton for your breakfast-napkins."

"Breakfast-napkins!" he exclaimed, and laughed boyishly. I laughed, too. "It doesn't seem quite possible, does it? Breakfast-napkins, and four months ago I didn't even know her! Mind?" he asked abruptly, holding up a silver case. He selected and lit a cigarette, flipping the charred match straight as an arrow into the fireplace. He smoked in silence a moment, smiling meditatively. "Mother's making some napkins, too!" he broke out. "They're going to get on—Ruth and mother—beautifully. 'She's a dear!' That's what mother says of Ruth half a dozen times a day. 'She's a dear!' And somehow the triteness of the phrase from mother is ridiculously pleasing to me. May I sit down?"

"Of course. Do."

He approached the sofa, but before throwing himself into one of its inviting corners, manlike he placed one of the large sofa pillows rather gingerly on the floor against a table-leg. Behind the pillow appeared the book.

"Hello," he exclaimed, "what's this?" And he held it up.

I put out my hand. "I'll take it, thank you," I said.

"Whose is this, anyhow?" he asked, opening the book instead of passing it over to me. "Looks like Ruth's marks." Then after a pause, "*Is* it Ruth's?"

"I don't know. Perhaps."

"She shouldn't read stuff like this!" pronounced the young judge.

"Oh, Ruth has always read everything she wanted to."

"Yes, I suppose so—more's the pity—best-sellers, anything that's going. But *this*—*this!* It's not decent for her, for any girl. I don't believe in this modern idea of exposure, anyhow. But here she comes." His face lighted. He put aside the book.

"Here Ruth comes!" And he went out into the hall to meet her.

I heard the front door open, the rustle of a greeting, and a moment later my sister and Robert Jennings both came in.

Ruth had become a shining roseate creature. Always beautiful, always exquisite—flawless features, perfect poise, now she pulsated with life. A new brightness glowed in her eyes. Of late across her cheeks color was wont to come and go like the shadow of clouds on a hillside on a windy day. Even her voice, usually steady and controlled, now and again trembled and broke with sudden emotion. She came into the room smiling, very pretty, very lovely (could we really be children of the same parents?), with a pink rose slipped into the opening of her coat. She drew out her rose and came over and passed it to me.

"There," she said, "it's for you, Lucy. I bought it especially!" Such a strange new Ruth! Once so worldly, so selfish; now so sweet and full of queer tenderness. I hardly recognized her. "It's heavenly out-doors," she went on. "I'll be back in a minute." And she went out into the hall to take off her hat and coat.

Robert went over to the book he had laid on the table and picked it up. When Ruth joined us he inquired pleasantly, "Where in the world did you run across this, Ruth?"

"That?" she smiled. "Oh, I bought it. Everybody is talking about it, and I bought it. It isn't so bad. Some parts are really very nice. I've marked a few I liked."

"Why, Ruth," he said solicitously, "it isn't a book for you to read."

"That's very sweet and protective, Bob," she laughed gently, "but after all I'm not—what do you call it—early Victorian. I'm twentieth century, and an American at that. Every book printed is for me to read."

"Oh, no! I should hope not! Too much of this sort of stuff would rob a girl of every illusion she ever had."

"Illusions! Oh, well," she shrugged her shoulders, "who wants illusions? I don't. I want truth, Bob. I want to know everything there is to know in this world, good, bad or indifferent. And you needn't be afraid. It won't hurt me. Truth is good for any one, whether it's pleasant truth or not. It makes one's opinions of more value, if nothing else. And of course you want my opinions to be worth something, don't you?" she wheedled.

"But, my dear," complained Bob, "this book represents more lies than it does truth."

"Do you think so?" she asked earnestly. "Now I thought it was a wonderfully true portrayal of just how a man and woman would feel under those circumstances."

Bob looked actually pained. "O Ruth, how can you judge of such circumstances? Of such feelings? Why, I don't like even to discuss such rottenness with you as *this*."

"How absurd, Bob," Ruth deprecated lightly. "I'm not a Jane Austen sort of girl. I've always read things. I've always read everything I wanted to." Bob was still standing with the book in his hands, looking at it. He didn't reply for a moment. Something especially obnoxious must have met his eyes, for abruptly he threw the book down upon the table.

"Well," he said, "I'm going to ask you not to finish reading *this*."

"You aren't serious!"

"Yes, I am, Ruth," replied Bob. "Let me be the judge about this. Trust it to me. You've read only a little of the book. It's worse later—unpleasant, distorted. There are other avenues to truth—not this one, please. Yes, I am serious."

He smiled disarmingly. For the first time since their engagement I saw Ruth fail to smile back. There was a perceptible pause. Then in a low voice Ruth asked, "Do you mean you ask me to stop reading a book right in the middle of it? Don't ask me to do a childish thing like that, Bob."

"But Ruth," he persisted, "it's to guard you, to protect you."

"But I don't want to be protected, not that way," she protested. Her gray eyes were almost black. Her voice, though low and quiet enough, trembled. They must have forgotten I was in the room.

"Is it such a lot to ask?" pleaded Bob.

"You *do* ask it then?" repeated Ruth uncomprehendingly.

"Why, Ruth, yes, I do. If a doctor told you not to eat a certain thing," Bob began trying to be playful, "that he knew was bad for you and—"

"But you're not my doctor," interrupted Ruth. "That's just it. You're—It seems all wrong somehow," she broke off, "as if I was a child, or an ignorant patient of yours, and I'm not. I'm not. Will you pass it to me, please—the book?"

Bob gave it to her immediately. "You're going to finish it then?" he asked, alarmed.

"I don't know," said Ruth, wide-eyed, a little alarmed herself, I think. "I don't know. I must think it over." She crossed the room to the secretary, opened the glass door, and placed the book on one of the high shelves. "There," she said, "there it is." Then turning around she added, "I'll let you know when I decide, Bob. And now I guess I'll go upstairs, if you don't mind. These walking-shoes are so heavy. Good-by." And she fled, on the verge of what I feared was tears.

Both Bob and Ruth were so surprised at the appearance of this sudden and unlooked-for issue that I felt convinced it was their first difference of opinion. I was worried. I couldn't foretell how it would come out. Their friendship had been brief—perhaps too brief. Their engagement was only four weeks old. They loved—I was sure of that—but they didn't know each other very well. Old friend of Will's and mine as Robert Jennings is, I knew him to be conservative, steeped in traditions since childhood. Robert idealizes everything mellowed by age, from pictures and literature to laws and institutions. Ruth, on the other hand, is a pronounced modernist. It doesn't make much difference whether it's a hat or a novel, if it's new and up to date Ruth delights in it.

I poured out my misgivings to Will that night behind closed doors. Will had never had a high opinion of Ruth.

"Modernism isn't her difficulty, my dear," he remarked. "Selfishness, with a big S. That's the trouble with Ruth. Society too. Big S. And a pinch of stubbornness also. She never would take any advice from any one—self-satisfied little Ruth wouldn't—and poor Bob is the salt of the earth too. It's a shame. Whoever would have thought fine old Bob would have fallen into calculating young Ruth's net anyhow!"

"O Will, please. You do misjudge her," I pleaded. "It isn't so. She isn't calculating. You've said it before, and she isn't—not always. Not this time."

"You ruffle like a protecting mother hen!" laughed Will. "Don't worry that young head of yours too much, dear. It isn't *your* love affair, remember."

It *is* my love affair. That's the difficulty. In all sorts of quiet and covered ways have I tried to help and urge the friendship along. Always, even before Ruth was engaged to Breckenridge Sewall, have I secretly nursed the hope that Robert Jennings and my sister might discover each other some day—each so beautiful to look upon, each so distinguished in poise and speech and manner; Ruth so clever; Bob such a scholar; both of them clean, young New Englanders, born under not dissimilar circumstances, and both much beloved by me. It *is* my love affair, and it simply mustn't have quarrels.

I didn't refer to the book the next day, nor did I let Ruth know by look or word that I noticed her silence at table or her preoccupied manner. I made no observation upon Robert's failure to make his daily call the next afternoon. She may have written and told him to stay away. I did not know. In mute suspense I awaited the announcement of her decision. It was made at last, sweetly, exquisitely, I thought.

On the second afternoon Robert called as usual. I was in the living-room when he came in. When Ruth appeared in the doorway, I got up to go.

"No, please," she said. "Stay, Lucy, you were here before. Hello, Bob," she smiled, then very quietly she added, "I've made my decision."

"Ruth!" Robert began.

"Wait a minute, please," she said.

She went over to the secretary, opened the door and took down the book. Then she crossed to the table, got a match, approached the fireplace, leaned down, and set fire to my cherished selected birch-logs. She held up the book then and smiled radiantly at Robert. "This is my decision!" she said, and laid the book in the flames.

"Good heavens," I wanted to exclaim, "that's worth a dollar thirty-five!"

"I've thought it all over," Ruth said simply, beautiful in the dignity of her new-born self-abnegation. "A book is only paper and print, after all. I was making a mountain out of it. It's as you wish, Bob. I won't finish reading it."

We were very happy that night. Robert stayed to dinner. Will chanced to be absent and there were only the three of us at table. There was a mellow sort of stillness. A softness of voice possessed us all, even when we asked for bread or salt. Our conversation was trivial, unimportant, but kind and gentle. Between Ruth and Robert there glowed adoration for each other, which words and commonplaces could not conceal.

Robert stayed late. Upstairs in Will's study the clock struck eleven-thirty when I heard the front door close, and peeked out and saw Robert walking down over our flag-stones.

A moment later Ruth came upstairs softly. She went straight to her own room. She closed the door without a sound. My sister, I knew, was filled with the kind of exaltation that made her gentle even to stairs and door-knobs.

Next morning she was singing as usual over her initialing. We went into town at eleven-thirty to look up table linen. Edith met us for lunch. One of the summer colonists had told Edith about Robert's "connections" (he has several in Boston in the Back Bay and he himself was born in a house with violet-colored panes) and Edith had become remarkably enthusiastic. She was going to present Ruth with all her lingerie.

"After all," she said one day in way of reassurance to Ruth, "you would have been in a pretty mess if you'd married Breck Sewall. Some gay lady in Breck's dark and shady past sprang up with a spicy little law suit two weeks before he was to be married to that Oliphant girl. Perhaps you saw it in the paper. Wedding all off, and Breck evading the law nobody knows where. This Bob of yours is as poor as Job's turkey, I suppose, but anyhow, he's *decent*. An uncle of his is president of a bank in Boston and belongs to all sorts of exclusive clubs and things. I'm going to give you your wedding, you know, Toots. I've always wanted a good excuse for a hack at Boston."

CHAPTER XIV

BOB TURNS OUT A CONSERVATIVE

But Edith didn't give Ruth her wedding. There was no wedding. Ruth didn't marry Robert Jennings!

I cannot feel the pain that is Ruth's, the daily loss of Bob's eyes that worshiped, voice that caressed—no, not that hurt—but I do feel bitterness and disappointment. They loved each other. I thought that love always could rescue. I was mistaken. Love is not the most important thing in marriage. No. They tell me ideals should be considered first. And yet as I sit here in my room and listen to the emptiness of the house—Ruth's song gone out of it, Ruth fled with her wound, I know not where— and see Bob, a new, quiet, subdued Bob, walking along by the house to the University, looking up to my window and smiling (a queer smile that hurts every time), the sparkle and joy gone out like a flame, I whisper to myself fiercely, "It's all wrong. Ideals to the winds. They loved each other, and it is all wrong."

They were engaged about three months in all. They were so jubilant at first that they wanted the engagement announced immediately. The college paper triumphantly blazoned the news, and of course the daily papers too. Everybody was interested. Everybody congratulated them. Ruth has hosts of friends, Robert too. Ruth's mail for a month was enormous. The house was sweet with flowers for days. Her presents rivaled a bride's. And yet she gave it all up—even loving Bob. She chose to face disapproval and distrust. Will called her heartless for it; Tom, fickle; Edith, a fool; but I call her courageous.

There was no doubt of the sincerity of Ruth's love for Robert Jennings. No other man before had got beneath the veneer of her worldliness. Robert laid bare secret expanses of her nature, and then, like warm sunlight on a hillside from which the snow has melted away, persuaded the expanses into bloom and beauty. Timid generosities sprang forth in Ruth. Tolerance, gratitude, appreciation blossomed frailly; and over all there spread, like those hosts of four-petaled flowers we used to call bluets, which grew in such abundance among rarer violets or wild strawberry—there spread through Ruth's awakened nature a thousand and one little kindly impulses that had to do with smiles for servants, kind words for old people, and courtesy to clerks in shops. I don't believe that anything but love could work such a miracle with Ruth. If only she had waited, perhaps it would have performed more wonderful feats.

The book incident was the first indication of trouble. The second was more trivial. It happened one Sunday noon. We had been to church that morning together—Ruth, Will and I—and Robert Jennings was expected for our mid-day dinner at one-thirty. He hadn't arrived when we returned at one, and after Ruth had taken off her church clothes and changed to something soft and filmy, she sat down at the piano and played a little while—five minutes or so—then rose and strolled over toward the front window. She seated herself, humming softly, by a table there. "Bob's late," she remarked and lazily reached across the table, opened my auction-bridge box, selected a pack of cards, and still humming began to play solitaire.

The cards were all laid out before her when Robert finally did arrive. Ruth gave him one of her long, sweet glances, then demurely began laying out more cards. "Good morning, Bob," she said richly.

Bob said good morning, too, but I discerned something forced and peremptory in his voice. I felt that that pack of playing cards laid out before Ruth on the Sabbath-day affected him just as it had me when first Ruth came to live with us. I had been brought up to look upon card-playing on Sunday as forbidden. In Hilton I could remember when policemen searched vacant lots and fields on Sunday for crowds of bad boys engaged in the shocking pastime beneath secreted shade trees. Ruth had traveled so widely and spent so many months visiting in various communities where card-playing on Sunday was the custom that I knew it didn't occur to her as anything out of the ordinary. I tried to listen to what Will was reading out loud to me from the paper, but the fascination of the argument going on behind my back by the window held me.

"But, Bob dear," I heard Ruth's surprised voice expostulate pleasantly, "you play golf occasionally on Sunday. What's the difference? Both a game, one played with sticks and a ball, and the other with black and red cards. I was allowed to play Bible authors when I was a child, and it's terribly narrow, when you look at it squarely, to say that one pack of cards is any more wicked than another."

"It's not a matter of wickedness," Bob replied in a low, disturbed voice. "It's a matter of taste, and reverence for pervading custom."

"But—" put in Ruth.

"Irreverence for pervading custom," went on Bob, "is shown by certain men when they smoke, with no word of apology, in a lady's reception-room, or track mud in on their boots, as if it was a country club. Some people enjoy having their Sundays observed as Sunday, just as they do their reception-rooms as reception-rooms."

"But, Bob—"

"I think of you as such an exquisite person," he pursued, "so fine, so sensitive, I cannot associate you with any form of offense or vulgarity, like this," he must have pointed to the cards, "or extreme fashions, or cigarette smoking. Do you see what I mean?"

"Vulgarity! Cigarette smoking! Why, Bob, some of the most refined women in the world smoke cigarettes—clever, intelligent women, too. And I never could see any justice at all in the idea some people have that it's any worse, or more vulgar, as you say, for women to smoke cigarettes than for men."

"Irreverence for custom again, I suppose," sighed Bob.

"Well, then, if it's a custom that's unjust and based on prejudice, why keep on observing it? It used to be the custom for men to wear satin knickerbockers and lace ruffles over their wrists, but some one was sensible enough—or irreverent enough—" she tucked in good-naturedly, "to object—and you're the gainer. There! How's that for an answer? Doesn't solitaire win?"

"Custom and tradition," replied Bob earnestly, anxiously, "is the work of the conservative and thoughtful majority, and to custom and tradition every civilization must look for a solid foundation. Ignore them and we wouldn't be much of a people."

"Then how shall we ever progress?" eagerly took up Ruth, "if we just keep blindly following old-fogey laws and fashions? It seems to me that the only way people ever get ahead is by breaking traditions. Father broke a few in his generation—he had to to keep up with the game—and so must I."

"Oh, well," said Bob, almost wearily, "let's not argue, you and I."

"Why not?" inquired Ruth, and I heard her dealing out more cards as she went on talking gaily. "I love a good argument. It wakes me up intellectually. My mind's been so lazy. It *needs* to be waked up. It feels good, like the first spring plunge in a pond of cold water to a sleepy old bear who's been rolled up in a ball in some dark hole all winter. That's what it feels like. I never knew what fun it was to think and argue till I began taking the English course at Shirley. We argue by the hour there. It's great fun. But I suppose I'm terribly illogical and no fun to argue with. That's the way with most women. It isn't our fault. Men seem to want to make just nice soft pussy-cats out of us, with ribbons round our necks," she laughed, "and hear us purr. There! wait a minute. I'm going to get this. Come and see." Then abruptly, "Why, Bob, do the cards shock *you*?"

"No, no—not a bit," he assured her.

"They do," she affirmed. "How funny. They do." There was a pause. "Well," she said at last (Will was still reading out loud and I could barely catch her answer). "Well, I suppose they're only pasteboard, just as the book was only paper and print. I can give them up."

"I don't want you to—not for me. No, don't. Go right ahead. Please," urged Bob. But it was too late.

"Of course not," replied Ruth, and I heard the cards going back into the box. "If I offend—and I see I do—of course not." And she rose and came over and sat on the sofa beside me.

From that time on I noticed a change in Robert and Ruth— nothing very perceptible. Robert came as often, stayed as late—later. That was what disturbed me. Ruth rose in the morning, after some of those protracted sessions, suspiciously quiet and subdued. In place of the radiance that so lately had shone upon her face, often I perceived a puzzled and troubled expression. In place of her almost hilarious joy, a wistfulness stole into her bearing toward Bob.

"Of course," she said to me one day, "I have been living a sort of—well, broad life you might call it for a daughter of father's, I suppose. He was so straightlaced. But all the modes and codes I've been adopting for the last several years I adopted only to be polite, to do as other people did, simply not to offend—as Bob said the other day. I thought if I ever wanted to go back to the strict laws of my childhood again, I could easily enough. In fact I intended to, after I had had my little fling. But I've outgrown them. They don't seem reasonable to me now. I can't go back to them. Convictions stand in my way."

"Women ought not to have convictions," I said shortly.

"Don't you think so?" queried Ruth.

"Men," I replied, "have so much more knowledge and experience of the world. Convictions have foundations with men."

"How unfair somehow," said Ruth, looking away into space.

"Just you take my advice, Ruth," I went on, "and don't you let any convictions you may think you have get in the way of your happiness. Just you let them lie for a while. When you and Bob are hanging up curtains in your new apartment, and pictures and things, you won't care a straw about your convictions, then."

"I don't suppose so," replied Ruth, still meditative. "No, I suppose you're right. I'll let Bob have the convictions for both of us. I'm younger. I can re-adjust easier than he, I guess."

A few days later Ruth went to a suffrage meeting in town; not because she was especially interested, but because a friend she had made in a course she was taking at Shirley College invited her to go.

It was the winter that everybody was discussing suffrage at teas and dinner parties; fairs and balls and parades were being given in various cities in its interest; and anti-organizations being formed to fight it and lend it zest. It was the winter that the term Feminism first reached the United States, and books on the greater freedom of women and their liberalization burst into print and popularity.

On the suffrage question Ruth had always been prettily "on the fence," and "Oh, dear, do let's talk of something else," she would laugh, while her eyes invited. Her dinner partners were always willing.

"On the fence, Kidlet," Edith had once remonstrated to Ruth, "that's stupid!" Edith herself was strongly anti. "Of course I'm anti," she maintained proudly. "Anybody who *is* anybody in Hilton is anti. The suffragists—dear me! Perfect freaks—most of them. People you never heard of! I peeked in at a suffrage tea the other day and mercy, such sights! I wouldn't be one of them for money. We're to give an anti-ball here in Hilton. I'm a patroness. Name to be printed alongside Mrs. ex-Governor Vaile's. How's that? 'On the fence,' Ruth! Why, good heavens, there's simply no two sides to the question. You come along to this anti-ball and you'll see, Kiddie!"

Well, as I said, Ruth went one day to a suffrage meeting in town. She had never heard the question discussed from a platform. When she came into the house about six o'clock, she was so full of enthusiasm that she didn't stop to go upstairs. She came right into the room where Will and I were reading by the cretonne-shaded lamp.

"I've just been to the most wonderful lecture!" she burst out, "on suffrage! I never cared a thing about the vote one way or the other, but I do now. I'm *for* it. Heart and soul, I'm for it! Oh, the most wonderful woman spoke. Every word she said applied straight to me. I didn't know I had such ideas until that woman got up and put them into words for me. They've been growing and ripening in me all these years, and I didn't know it—not until today. That woman said that sacrifices are made again and again to send boys to college and prepare them to earn a living, but that girls are brought up simply to be pretty and attractive, so as to capture a man who will provide them with food and clothes. Why, Lucy, don't you see that that's just what happened in *our* family? We slaved to send Oliver and Malcolm through college—but for *you* and for *me*—what slaving was there done to prepare us to earn a living? Just think what I might be had *I* been prepared for life like Malcolm or Oliver, instead of wasting all my years frivoling. Why, don't you see I could have convictions with a foundation then? I feel so helpless and ignorant with a really educated person now. Oh, dear, I wish this movement had been begun when I was a baby, so I could have profited by it! That woman said that when laws are equal for men and women, *then* advantages will be, and that every step we can make toward equalization is a step in the direction toward a fairer deal for women. Suffrage? Well, I should say I was for it! I think it's wonderful. I went straight up to that woman and said I wanted to join the League; and I did. It cost me a dollar."

"Good heavens, Ruth," exclaimed Will sleepily, from behind his paper. "Don't you go and get rabid on suffrage—Ease up, old girl. Steady."

"I don't see how any one can help but get rabid, Will, as you say, any more than a person could keep calm if he was a slave, when he first heard what Abraham Lincoln was trying to do."

"Steady there, old girl," jibed Will. "Is Bob such a terrific master as all that?"

"That's not the point, Will. Convention is the master—that's what the woman said. It isn't free of men we're trying to be."

"We! we! Come, Ruth. You aren't one of them in an hour, are you? Better wait and consult Bob first."

"Oh, Bob will agree with me. I know he will. It's such a progressive idea. And I *am* one of them. I'm proud to be. I'm going to march in the parade next week."

I came to life at that. "Oh, Ruth, not really—not in Boston!"

"What? Up the center of Washington Street in French heels and a shadow veil?" scoffed Will.

"Up the center of Washington Street in something," announced Ruth, "if that's the line of march. Remember, Will, French heels and shadow veils have been my stock in trade, and not through any choice of mine, either. So don't throw them at me, please."

Will subsided. "Well, well, what next? A raring, tearing little suffragette, in one afternoon, too!"

Ruth went upstairs.

"Poor old Bob," remarked Will to me when we were alone.

CHAPTER XV

ANOTHER CATASTROPHE

I didn't know whether it was more "poor old Bob" or "poor old Ruth." Ruth was so arduous at first, so in earnest—like a child with a new and engrossing plaything for a day or two, and then, I suppose, she showed her new toy to Bob, and he took it away from her. Anyway, she put it by. It seemed rather a shame to me. The new would have worn off after a while.

"And after all, Will," I maintained to my husband, "Robert Jennings is terribly old-school, sweet and chivalrous as can be toward women, but he can't treat Ruth in the way he does that helpless little miniature of a mother of his. He simply lives to protect her from anything practical or disagreeable. She adores it, but Ruth's a different proposition. The trouble with Robert is, he's about ten years behind the times."

"And Ruth," commented Will, "is about ten years ahead of the times."

"That is true of the different members of lots of households, in these times, but they don't need to come to blows because of it. Everybody ought to be patient and wait. Ruth has a pronounced individuality, for all you think she is nothing but a society butterfly. I can see it hurts to cram it into Robert Jennings' ideal of what a woman should be. It makes me feel badly to see Ruth so quiet and resigned, like a little beaten thing, so pitiably anxious to please. Self-confidence became her more. She hasn't mentioned suffrage since Robert called and stayed so late Wednesday, except to say briefly, 'I'm not going to march in the parade.' 'Why not?' I asked. 'Doesn't Bob want you to?' 'Oh, certainly. He leaves it to me,' she pretended proudly. 'But, you see, women in parades do offend some people. It isn't according to tradition, and I think it's only courteous to Bob, just before we are to be married, not to do anything offensive. After all, I must bear in mind,' she said, 'that this parade is only a matter of walking—putting one foot in front of the other. I'm bound to be happy, and I don't intend to allow suffrage to stand in my way either. Even convictions are only a certain condition of gray matter.' Oh, it was just pitiful to hear her trying to convince herself. I'm just afraid, Will, afraid for the future."

Not long after that outburst of mine to Will, my fears came true. One late afternoon, white-faced, wide-eyed, Ruth came in to me. She closed the door behind her. Her outside things were still on. I saw Robert Jennings out the window going slowly down the walk. Before Ruth spoke I knew exactly what she had to say.

"We aren't going to be married," she half whispered to me.

"Oh, Ruth—"

"No. Please. Don't, don't talk about it," she said. "And don't tell Will. Don't tell any one. Promise me. I've tried so hard— so hard. But my life has spoiled me for a man like Bob. Don't talk of it, please."

"I won't, Ruth," I assured her.

"I can do it. I thought I couldn't at first. But I *can*!" she said fiercely, "I *can*! I'll be misunderstood, I know. But I can't help that. We've decided it together. It isn't I alone. Bob has decided it, too. We both prefer to be unhappy alone, rather than unhappy together."

"In every marriage, readjustments are necessary," I commented.

"Don't argue," she burst out at me. "Don't! Don't you suppose Bob and I have thought of every argument that exists to save our happiness? For heaven's sake, Lucy, don't argue. I can't quite bear it." She turned away and went upstairs.

She didn't want any dinner. "I'm going to bed early," she told me an hour later when I knocked at her door. "No, not even toast and tea. Please don't urge me," she begged, and I left her. At ten when I went to bed her room was dark.

At half-past eleven I got up, stole across the hall, and stood listening outside her closed door. At long intervals I could hear her move. She was not sleeping. I waited an hour and stole across the hall again. She was still awake. Poor Ruth— sleepless, tearless (there was no sound of sobbing) hour after hour, there she was lying all night long, staring into the darkness, waiting for the dawn. At three I opened the door gently and went in, carrying something hot to drink on a tray.

"What is the matter?" she asked calmly.

"Nothing, Ruth. Only you must sleep, and here is some hot milk with just a little pinch of salt. It's so flat without. Nobody can sleep on an empty stomach."

"I guess that's the trouble," she said, and sat up and took the milk humbly, like a child. Her fingertips were like ice. I went into the bath-room, filled a hot-water bag, and got out an extra down-comforter. I was tucking it in when she asked, "What time is it?" And I told her. "Only three? Oh, dear—don't go— just yet." So I wrapped myself up in a warm flannel wrapper and sat down on the foot of her bed with my feet drawn up under me.

"I won't," I said, "I'll sit here."

"You're awfully good to me," Ruth remarked. "I *was* cold and hungry, I guess. Oh, Lucy," she exclaimed, "I wish one person could understand, just *one*."

"I do, Ruth. I do understand," I said eagerly.

"It isn't suffrage. It isn't the parade. It isn't any *one* thing. It's just *everything*, Lucy. I'm made up on a wrong pattern for Bob. I hurt him all the time. Isn't it awful—even though he cares for me, and I for him, we hurt each other?"

I kept quite still. I knew that Ruth wanted to talk to some one, and I sat there hugging my knees, thankful that I happened to be the one. Always I had longed for this mysterious sister's confidence, and always I had seemed to her too simple, too obvious, to share and understand.

"You know, Lucy," she went on wistfully, "I was awfully happy at first—so happy—you don't know. Why, I would do anything for Bob. I was glad to give up riches for him. My worldly ambitions shriveled into nothing. Comforts, luxuries —what were they as compared to Bob's love? But, oh, Lucy, it is giving up little things, little independencies of thought, little daily habits, which I can't do. I tried to give up these, too. You know I did. I said that the book was just paper and print and the cards just pasteboard. But all the time they were symbols. I could destroy the symbols easily enough, but I couldn't destroy what they stood for. You see, Bob and I have different ideals. That's at the bottom of all the trouble. We tried for weeks not to admit it, but it had to be faced finally."

"Your ideals aren't very different way down at their roots— both clean, true, sincere, and all that," I said, with a little yawn, so she might not guess how tremblingly concerned I really was.

"You don't know all the differences, Lucy," she said sadly. "There's something the trouble with me—something left out —something that I cannot blame Bob for feeling sorry about. I believe I'll tell you. You see, Bob met me under a misapprehension, and I've been trying to live up to his misapprehension ever since. The first time he ever saw me I was tucked away in a little room by myself looking at the picture of a sick child. I was crying a little. He thought that I was feeling badly out of sympathy for the mother of the child—the mother in me, you see, speaking to the mother in her. I wasn't really. I was crying because the house that the picture happened to hang in was so dull and grimy beside Grassmere. I was crying for the luxuries I had lost. I never told Bob the truth about that picture until last week, and all this time he's been looking upon me as an ideal woman—a kind of madonna, mother of little children, you understand, and all that—and I'm not. Something must be wrong with me. I don't even long to be—yet. Oh, you see how unfitted I am for a man to weave idealistic pictures about—like that. It seemed to hurt Bob when I told him the truth about myself, hurt him terribly, as if I'd tumbled over and broken his image of me—at the cradle, you know. Oh, Lucy, what an unnatural girl I am! I don't admire myself for it. I wish I could be what Bob thinks, but I can't. I can't."

"You aren't unnatural. You're just as human as you can be, Ruth. I felt just the way you do before I was married, and most every girl does as young as you, too. Bob ought to give you chance to grow up."

"Grow up! Oh, Lucy, I feel so old! I feel used up and put by already. I've lived my life and haven't I made a botch of it?" She laughed shortly. "And what shall I do with the botch now? I can't stay here. It would break my heart to stay here where I had hoped to be so happy—everything reminding me, you know. No, I can't stay here."

"Of course you can't, Ruth. We'll think of a way."

"And I simply can't go back to Edith," she went on, "after knowing Bob. I don't want to go out to Michigan with Tom and Elise. I hate Michigan. Dear me! I don't know what I shall do. I'm discouraged. Once I was eager and confident, filled with enthusiasm and self-pride. Like that old hymn, you know. How does it go? 'I loved to choose my path and see, but now lead Thou me on. I loved the garish day, and spite of fears, Pride ruled my will. Remember not past years.' That is what I repeat over and over to myself. 'Lead, kindly light, amidst th' encircling gloom.' The encircling gloom! Oh, dear!" She suddenly broke off, "I wish morning would come." It did finally, and with it, when the approaching sun began to pinken the eastern sky, sleep for my tormented sister.

CHAPTER XVI

A FAMILY CONFERENCE

We all were seated about the table at one of Edith's sumptuous Sunday dinners at the Homestead when Ruth broke her news to the family. Tom had come East on a business trip, and was spending Sunday with Alec in Hilton; so Edith telephoned to all of us within motoring distance and invited us up for "Sunday dinner." This was two or three days after Ruth had told me that she and Bob were not to be married.

"Oh, yes, I'll go," she nodded, when I had clapped my hand over the receiver and turned to her questioningly, and afterward she said to me, "Concealing my feelings is one of the accomplishments my education *has* included. I'll go. I shan't tell them about Bob yet. I can't seem to just now."

I was therefore rather surprised when she suddenly abandoned her play-acting. She hadn't figured on the difficult requirements, I suppose, poor child. Bluff and genial Tom, grown rather gray and stout and bald now, had met her with a hearty, "Hello, bride-elect!" Oliver had shouted, "Greetings, Mrs. Prof!" And Madge, his wife, had tucked a tissue-paper-wrapped package under Ruth's arm: "My engagement present," she explained. "Just a half-a-dozen little guest-towels with your initials."

Later at the table Tom had cleared his throat and then remarked, "I like all I hear of this Robert Jennings. He's good stuff, Ruth. You've worried us a good deal, but you've landed on your feet squarely at last. He's a bully chap."

"And he's got a bully girl, too, now that she's got down to brass tacks," said Alec in big-brother style.

"Decided on the date?" cheerfully inquired Tom. "Elise said to be sure and find out. We're coming on in full force, you know."

"Yes, the date's decided," flashed Edith from the head of the table. "June 28th. It'll be hot as mustard, but Hilton will be lovely then, and all the summerites here. You must give me an hour on the lists after dinner, Kidlet. Bob's list, people, is three hundred, and Ruth's four, so I guess there'll be a few little remembrances. The envelopes are half directed already. I want you people to know this wedding is only seven weeks off, so hurry up and order your new gowns and morning coats. Simplicity isn't going to be the keynote of this affair."

"Hello!" exclaimed Tom abruptly, "I haven't inspected the ring yet. Let's see it. Pass it over, Toots."

Ruth glanced down at her hand. It was still there—Bob's unpretentious diamond set in platinum—shining wistfully on Ruth's third finger.

She started to take it off, then stopped and glanced over at me. "I think I'll tell them, Lucy," she said. "I've got something to tell you all," she announced. "I'm wearing the ring still, but— we've broken our engagement. I'm not going to marry Robert Jennings after all."

It sounded harsh, crude. Everybody stared; everybody stopped eating; I saw Tom lay down his fork with a juicy piece of duck on it. It had been within two inches of his mouth.

"Will you repeat that?" he said emphatically.

"Yes," complied Ruth, "I will. I know it seems sudden to you. I meant to write it, but after all I might as well tell you. My engagement to Robert Jennings is broken."

"Is this a joke?" ejaculated Edith.

"No," replied Ruth, still in that calm, composed way of hers. "No, Edith, it isn't a joke."

"Will you explain?" demanded Tom, shoving the piece of duck off his fork and abandoning it for good and all.

Ruth had become pale. "Why, there isn't much to explain, except I found out I wouldn't be happy with Bob. That's all."

"Oh," said Tom, "you found out you wouldn't be happy with Bob! Will you kindly tell us whom you mean to try your happiness on next?"

Ruth's gray eyes darkened. A little pink stole into her cheeks. "There's no good of your using that tone with me, Tom," she said.

"Did you know this?" asked Will of me from across the table.

I nodded.

"Do you mean to say it's *true*?" demanded Edith.

I nodded again.

"You're crazy, Ruth," she burst out, "you're simply stark mad. It would be a public disgrace. You've got to marry him now. You've simply got to. It's worse than a divorce. Why—the invitations are all ordered, even the refreshments. The whole world knows about it. You've *got* to marry him."

"My own disgrace is my own affair, I guess," said Ruth, dangerously low.

"It's *not* your own affair. It's ours; it's the whole family's; it's mine. And I won't stand it—not a second time. Here I have told *everybody*, got my Boston list all made up, too, and all my plans made. Didn't I have new lights put into the ball-room especially, and a lot of repairs made on the house—a new bathroom, and everything? And all my house-party guests invited? Why—we'll be the laughing-stock of this entire town, if you play this game a second time. Good heavens, you'll be getting the habit. No, sir! You *can't* go back on your word in this fashion. You've *got* to marry Robert Jennings *now*."

"I wouldn't marry Breck Sewall to please you, Edith, and I won't marry Robert Jennings to please you either," said Ruth. "She wanted me to elope with Breck!" she announced calmly.

"That isn't true," replied Edith sharply.

"Why don't you call me a liar and have done with it?" demanded Ruth.

"I wanted to save you from disgrace, and you know it. I wanted—" A maid came in.

"Let us wait and continue this conversation later," remarked Tom.

"We don't want *you*," flared Edith at the maid. "I didn't ring. Go out till you're summoned. You're the most ungrateful girl I ever knew, Ruth. You're—"

"Come," interrupted Alec. "This isn't getting anywhere. Let us finish dinner first."

"I'm sure I don't want any more dinner," said Edith.

"Nor I," commented Ruth, with a shrug.

There were a salad fork and a dessert spoon still untouched beside our plates. It would have been thoughtful if Ruth had waited and lit her fuse when the finger-bowls came on. It seemed a shame to me to waste two perfectly good courses, and unnecessarily sensational to interrupt the ceremony of a Sunday dinner. But it was impossible to sit there through two protracted changes of plates.

"I guess we've all had enough," remarked Tom, disgustedly shoving away that innocent piece of duck. We rose stragglingly.

"I don't care to talk about this thing any more," said Ruth, as we passed through the hall. "You can thrash it out by yourselves. Lucy, you can represent me!" And she turned away to go upstairs.

Tom called back, "No, Ruth. This is an occasion that requires your presence, whether you like it or not," he said. "Come back, please. There are a few questions that need to be settled."

Ruth acquiesced condescendingly. "Oh, very well," she replied, and strolled down the stairs and into the library. She walked over to the table and leaned, half sitting, against it, while the rest of us came in and sat down, and some one closed the doors.

"Fire away!" she said flippantly, turning to Tom. She picked up an ivory paper-cutter with a tassel on one end, twisted the cord tight, and then holding the cutter up by the tassel watched it whirl and untwist.

Pretty, graceful, nonchalant, armored in a half smile, Ruth stood before her inquisitors. Bob never would have recognized this composed and unmoved girl as the anxious Ruth who had tried so hard to please and satisfy.

"First," began Tom (he has always held the position of high judge in our family), "first, I should be interested to know if you have any plans for the future, and, if so, will you be kind enough to tell us what they may be."

"I have plans," said Ruth, and began twisting the cord of the paper-cutter again.

"Will you put that down, please," requested Tom.

"Certainly," Ruth smiled over-obligingly and laid the paper-cutter on the table. She folded her arms and began tapping the rug with her toe. She was almost insolent.

"Well, then—what are your plans?" fired Tom at her with an obvious effort to control himself.

"New York," she announced mysteriously.

"Oh, New York!" repeated Tom. It was a scornful voice. "New York! And what do you intend to do in New York?"

"Oh, I don't know. I haven't decided. Something," she said airily.

"Ruth," said Tom, "please listen to me carefully if you can for a minute. We've always given you a pretty loose rein. Haven't we?"

Ruth shrugged her shoulders.

"You've had every advantage; attended one of the most expensive schools in this country; had all the money you required, coming-out party and all that; pleasures, flattery, attention—everything to make a girl contented. You've visited any one you pleased from one end of the United States to the other; traveled in Europe, Florida—anywhere you wanted; come and gone at will. Nothing to handicap you. Nothing hard. Nothing difficult. You'll agree. And what have you done with your advantages? *What*—I want to know?"

Ruth shrugged her shoulders again.

"You can't blame any one but yourself. You haven't been

Olive Higgins Prouty

interfered with. I believed in letting you run your own affairs. Thought you were made of the right stuff to do it creditably. I was mistaken. You've had a fair trial at your own management and you've failed to show satisfactory results. Now *I'm* going to step in. *I'm* going to see if *I* can save you from this drifting about and getting nowhere. I don't ask you to go back and anchor with Robert Jennings again. I'm shocked to confess that I don't believe you're worthy of a man like Jennings. It is no small thing to be decided carelessly or frivolously—this matter of marriage. Engaged to two men inside of one year, and now both affairs broken off. It's disgraceful! You've got to learn somehow or other that although you are a woman, you're not especially privileged to go back on decisions."

"I don't want to be especially privileged," said Ruth, and then she added, "special privileges would not be expected by women, if they were given equal rights."

"Oh, Suffrage!!!" exclaimed Tom with three exclamation points. "So that's it! That's at the bottom of all this trouble."

"That's at the bottom of it," suddenly put in my husband, emphatically.

"Oh, I see. Well, first, Ruth, you're to drop all that nonsense. Suffrage indeed! What do *you* know about it? You ought to be married and taking care of your own babies, and you wouldn't be disturbed by all these crazy-headed fads, invented by dissatisfied and unoccupied females. Suffrage! And perhaps you think that this latest exhibition of your changeableness and vacillation is an argument in favor of it."

"You needn't throw women's vacillation in their faces, Tom," replied Ruth calmly. "Stable decisions are matters of training and education. Girls of my acquaintance lack the experience with the business world. They don't come in contact with big transactions. They're guarded from them. A lawyer does the thinking for a woman of property oftentimes, and so, of course, women do not learn the necessity of precise statements, accurate thought, and all that. From the time a girl is old enough to think she knows she is just a girl, who her family hope will grow up to be pretty and attractive and marry well. If her family believed she was to grow up into a responsible citizen who would later control by her vote all sorts of weighty questions that affect taxes and tariffs and things, they would have to devote more thought to making her intelligent, because it would have an effect upon their individual interests. I'm interested in suffrage, Tom, not for the good it is going to do politics, but for the good it's going to do women."

Tom made an exclamation of disgust. He was beside himself with scorn and disapproval.

"Nonsense! Utter rot! Women were made to marry and be mothers. Women were—"

"But we'd be better mothers," Ruth cut in. "Don't you see, if—"

"Oh, I don't want to discuss suffrage," interrupted Tom; "I want to discuss your life. Let's keep to the subject. I want to see you settled and happy some day, and as I'm so much older than you, you must put yourself into my hands, and cheerfully. First, drop suffrage. Drop it. Good Lord, Ruth, don't be a faddist. Then I want you to lay your decision about Jennings on the shelf. Let it rest for a while. Postpone the wedding if you wish—"

"But, Tom," tucked in Edith, "that's impossible. The invitations—"

"Never mind, never mind, Edith," interrupted Tom. Then to Ruth he went on. "Postpone the wedding—oh, say a month or two, and then see how you feel. That's all I ask. Reasonable, isn't it?" he appealed to us all. "I'll have a talk with Jennings in the meanwhile," he went on. "This suffrage tommy-rot is working all sorts of unnecessary havoc. I'm sick of it. I didn't suppose it had caught any one in our family though. You drop it, Ruth, for a while. You wait. I'm going back home next Wednesday. Now I want you to pack up your things and be ready to start with me Wednesday night from New York. We'll see what Elise and the youngsters will do for you."

"I'm sorry, Tom," replied Ruth pleasantly, "but my decision about Bob is final; and as for going out West with you and becoming a fifth wheel in your household—no, I've had enough of that. My mind is made up. I'm going to New York."

"But I shan't allow it," announced Tom.

"Then," replied Ruth, "I shall have to go without your allowing it."

"What do you mean?" demanded Tom.

"Why—just what I say. I'm of age. If I were a man, I wouldn't have to ask my older brother's permission."

"And how do you intend to live?"

"On my income," said Ruth. "I bless father now for that stock he left me. Eight hundred dollars a year has been small for me so far. I have had to have help, I know, but it will support my new life. I never was really grateful to father for that money till now. It makes me independent of you, Tom."

Edith, glaring inimically from her corner, exclaimed, "Grateful to her father! That's good!"

"My dear girl," said Tom, "we've never told you before, because we hoped to spare your feelings, but the time has come now. That stock father left you hasn't paid a dividend for a dozen years. It isn't worth its weight in paper. I have paid four hundred dollars, and Edith has been kind and generous enough to contribute four hundred dollars more, to keep you in carfares, young lady. It isn't much in order to talk of your independence around here."

The color mounted to Ruth's cheeks. She straightened. "What do you mean?" she asked.

"Exactly what I say. You haven't a penny of income. Edith and I are responsible for your living, and I want you to understand clearly that I shall not support a line of conduct which does not meet with my approval. Nor Edith either, I rather imagine."

"No, indeed, I won't," snapped out Edith. "I shan't pay a cent more. It's only rank ingratitude I get for it anyhow."

"Do you mean to say," said Ruth in a low voice—there was no flippancy to her now—"I've been living on Edith's charity, and yours, all these years? That I haven't anything of my own—not even my clothes—not even *this*," she touched a blue enameled watch and chain about her neck, "which I saved and saved so for? Haven't I any income? Haven't I a cent that's mine, Tom?"

"Not a red cent, Ruth—just some papers that we might as well put into the fireplace and burn up."

"Oh," she burst forth, "how unfair—how cruel and unfair!"

"There's gratitude for you," threw in Edith.

"To bring me up," went on Ruth, "under a delusion. To let me go on, year after year, thinking I was provided for, and then suddenly, when it pleases you, to tell me that I'm an absolute dependent, a creature of charity. Oh, how cruel that is! You tell me I ought to be grateful. Well, I'm not—I'm not grateful. You've been false with me. You've brought me up useless and helpless. I'm too old now to develop whatever talent I may have had. I can only drudge now. What is there I can do *now*? Nothing—nothing—except scrub floors or something like that."

"Oh, yes, there is, too," said Edith. "You can marry Robert Jennings and be sensible."

"Marry a man for support, whether I want to or not? I'll die first. You *all* want me to marry him," she burst out at us fiercely, "but I shan't—I shan't. I'm strong and healthy, and I'm just beginning to discover that I've got some brains, too. There's something I can do, surely, some way I can earn money. I shan't go West with you, Tom. Understand that. I can't quite see myself growing old in all your various households—old and useless and dependent like lots of unmarried women in large families. I can't see it without a fight anyhow. I don't care if I haven't any income. I can be a clerk in a store, I guess. Anyhow I shan't go West with you, Tom. I am of age. You can't make me. I know I'm just a woman, but I intend to live my own life just the same, and there's no one in this world who can bind and enslave me either!"

"You go upstairs, Ruth," ordered Tom. "I won't stand for such talk as that. You go upstairs and quiet down, and when you're reasonable, we'll talk again. We're not children."

"No, we're not," replied Ruth, "neither of us, and I shan't be sent upstairs as if I was a child either! You can pauperize me, and you can take away every rag I have on my back, too, if you want to, but I'll tell you one thing, you can't take away my independence. You think, Tom, you can frighten me, and conquer me, perhaps, by bullying. But you can't. Conditions are better for women than they used to be, anyhow, thank heaven, and for the courageous woman there's a chance to escape from just such masters of their fates as *you*—Tom Vars, even though you are my brother. And I shall escape somehow, *sometime*. See if I don't. Oh, I know what you all think of me," she broke off. "You all think I'm hard and heartless. Well—perhaps you're right. I guess I am. Such an experience as this would just about kill any softhearted person, I should think. But *I'm* not killed. Remember that, Tom. You've got money, support, sentiment on your side. I've got nothing but my own determination. But I'm not afraid to fight. And I will, if you force me. You'd better be pretty careful how you handle such an utterly depraved person as you seem to think I am. Why, I didn't know you had such a poor opinion of me."

She gave a short little laugh which ended in a sort of sob. I was afraid she was going to cry before us. But the armor was at hand. She put it on quickly, the cynical smile, the nonchalant air.

"There is no good talking any more, as I see," she was able to go on, thus protected. "This is bordering on a scene, and scenes are such bad taste! I'm going into the living-room."

She crossed the room to the door. "You all can go on maligning me to your hearts' content. I've had about enough, thank you. Only remember supper is at seven, and Edith's maids want to get out early Sundays. Consider the maids at least," she finished, and left us, colors flying.

CHAPTER XVII

RUTH GOES TO NEW YORK

The next morning when Will and I motored home we were alone. We approached the steeples of our town about noontime. I remember whistles were blowing and bells ringing as we passed through the Square. We saw Robert Jennings coming out of one of the University buildings on his way home from a late morning recitation. We slowed down beside him, and Will sang out to him to pile in behind; which he did, leaning forward and chatting volubly with Will and me for the next ten minutes about a new starter device for an automobile. When Will stopped in front of our walk, Robert hopped out of his back seat and opened the door for me.

It was when Will had motored out of hearing that Robert turned sharply to me and asked, "Did you leave her in Hilton?"

"No, Bob, Ruth isn't in Hilton. She's gone to New York," I told him gently.

"Whom is she staying with in New York? Your brother?" he asked.

"No, not Malcolm. No. But she's all right."

"What do you mean—'she's all right'?"

"Oh, I mean she has money enough—and all that."

"She isn't *alone* in New York!" he exclaimed. "You don't mean to say—"

"Now, Bob, don't *you* go and get excited about it. Ruth's all right. I'm just about worn out persuading my brother Tom that it is perfectly all right for Ruth to go to New York for a little while if she wants to. I can't begin arguing with you, the minute I get home. I'm all worn out on the subject."

"But what is she doing down there? Whom is she visiting? Who is looking out for her? Who went with her? Who met her?"

"Nobody, nobody. Nobody met her; nobody went with her; she isn't visiting anybody. Good heavens, Bob, you'd make a helpless, simpering little idiot out of Ruth if you had your way. She isn't a child. She isn't an inexperienced young girl. She's capable of keeping out of silly difficulties. She can be trusted. Let her use her judgment and good sense a little. It won't hurt her a bit. It will do her good. Don't you worry about Ruth. She's all right."

"But a girl—a pretty young girl like Ruth—you don't mean to say that Ruth—Ruth—"

"Yes, I do, too, Bob! And there are lots of girls just as pretty as Ruth in New York, and just as young, tapping away at typewriters, and balancing accounts in offices, and running shops of their own, too, in perfect safety. You're behind the times, Bob. I don't want to be horrid, but really I'm tired, and if you stay here and talk to me, I warn you I'm going to be cross."

We were in the house now. Bob had followed me in. I was taking off my things. He stared at me as I proceeded.

"I didn't see any sense at all in your breaking off your

engagement," I went on. "You both cared for each other. I should have thought—"

"It was inevitable," cut in Bob gravely. "It was inevitable, Lucy."

"Well, then, if it was, Bob, all right. I won't say another word about it. But now that Ruth is nothing to you—"

"Nothing to me!" he exclaimed.

"Yes, that is what I said—nothing to you," I repeated mercilessly, "I beg of you don't come here and show approval or disapproval about what she's up to. Leave her to me now. I'm backing her. I tell you, just as I told Tom and the others, she's all right. Ruth's *all right.*"

But later in my room I wondered—I wondered if Ruth really was all right. Sitting in my little rocking-chair by the window, sheltered and protected by kind, familiar walls, I asked myself what Ruth was doing now. It was nearing the dinner hour. Where would Ruth be eating dinner? It was growing dark slowly. It would be growing dark in New York. Stars would be coming out up above the towering skyscrapers, as they were now above the apple trees in the garden. I thought of Ruth's empty bed across the hall. Where would she sleep tonight? Oh, Ruth—Ruth—poor, little sister Ruth!

I remember when you were a little baby wrapped up in soft, pink, knitted things. The nurse put you in my arms, and I walked very carefully into my mother's room with you and stood staring down at you asleep. I was only a little girl, I was afraid I would drop you, and I didn't realize as I stood there by our mother's bed that she was bidding her two little daughters good-by. She couldn't take one of my hands because they were both busy holding you; but she reached out and touched my shoulder; and she told me always to love you and take care of you and be generous and kind, because you were little and younger. And I said I would, and carried you out very proud and happy.

That was a long while ago. I have never told you about it—we haven't found it easy to talk seriously together—but I have always remembered. I used to love to dress you when you were a baby, and feed you, and take you out in the brown willow baby carriage like the real mothers. But, of course, you had to outgrow the carriage; you had to outgrow the ugly little dresses father and I used to select for you at the department stores in Hilton; you had to outgrow the two little braids I used to plait for you each morning when you were big enough to go to school; you had to outgrow me, too. I am so plain and commonplace.

Yesterday when you put your arms about me there in the smoky train-shed in Hilton, and cried a little as I held you close, with the great noisy train that was to take you away snorting beside us, you became again to me the little helpless sister that mother told me to take care of. All the years between were blotted out. I remembered our mother's room, the black walnut furniture. I saw the white pillows and mother's long, dark braids lying over each of her shoulders. Again I heard her words; again I felt the pride that swelled in my heart as I bore you away.

"I hope you are safe tonight. You can always call on me. I will always come. Don't be afraid. And when you are unhappy, write to me. I shall understand. You are not hard, you are not heartless. You are tender and sensitive. Only your armor is made of flint. You are not changeable and vacillating. They didn't know. You are brave and conscientious." With some such words as these last did I write to Ruth before I slept that night. I believed in her as I never had before. I cherished her with my soul.

This is what had happened in Hilton. After Ruth had left the room the afternoon of her inquisition, the rest of us had sat closeted in serious consultation for two hours or more. It was after five when we emerged.

To Edith's inquiry as to Ruth's whereabouts, a maid explained that Miss Ruth had left word that she was going to walk out to the Country Club, and would return in time for supper at seven. I went upstairs to my room. A feeling of despair possessed me. I sat down and gazed out of the window. A maid knocked lightly as I sat staring and came in with a letter.

"Miss Ruth told me to wait until you were alone and then to give you this," she explained.

I thanked her and she departed. I locked the door, then tore open Ruth's note to me and read it.

> "Dear Lucy," it said. "I cannot help but overhear some of the conversation. Obviously, Tom is shouting so I may get the benefit of his remarks without effort. I must get out of this horrible place. How can I endure to meet the disapproval and bitterness and hatred— yes, *hatred*—when they come filing out upon me from that room across the hall. How can I sit down to supper with them all, ask for bread—for water? How can I keep up this farce of polite speech? I can't.

> "You are in favor of my going away somewhere. I can hear you urging them. Well, then, if you are, let me go *now*—tonight. I can't go back with you tomorrow. Even though I am hard and heartless, don't ask me to run the risk of seeing Bob by mistake just now. I can't see him now. I can't. I *won't* stay here at Edith's. I won't go with Tom. This isn't the Middle Ages. Then if ultimately I am to go away, alone somewhere, let me go immediately. After I've gone the responsibility of giving me permission will be lifted from Tom's shoulders. Don't you see? You can argue with him to better advantage if the step has been taken.

> "I shan't be blindly running away. I've been considering a change in my plans for so long that I've been enquiring. I know of a position I can get in New

York, and right off. I wrote about it last week. I heard of it through the Suffrage League. It's a position in the office there in New York. I would have explained all this to Tom if he had been decent, but he wasn't. He is narrow and prejudiced. Oh, Lucy, help me to escape. I've got fifteen dollars, of Tom's and Edith's, and I shall keep it, too! They owe *me* a debt instead of *I*, them. That's the way I feel. But fifteen dollars is not enough to start to New York with. There's a train at 6.20 and another at 8.15. I am going down to the station now, this *minute*, and wait for you to come down there with more money and help me off. If you get out of that room before six, I could take the earlier train. If not, then the 8.15. I will wait for you in the ladies' waiting-room where the couches are. If you think my going suddenly this way is out of the question, then I'll simply turn around and come back with you to the house here, and grin and bear the situation somehow. I'll have to. So meet me anyhow. Don't tell any one where I am. Just stroll out and we'll pretend we've been to the Country Club.

"I know that I've been horrid to you all my life, critical and pharisaic. You can pay me back for it now. You can refuse to help me if you want to. I shan't blame you. But, oh, dear, let me go away alone, just for a little while anyway. Let nature try and heal.

"I have my bag and toilet articles. Money is all I want—money and perhaps just one person in my family to wish me well.

"RUTH."

I glanced at the clock It was just quarter of six. There was no opportunity of laying this question on the table and waiting for the clearing light of morning to help me make a wise decision. This was an occasion when a woman's intuition must be relied upon. As I stood there with Ruth's letter in my hand, swift and sure was the conviction that came to me. I must help Ruth get away. She would surely escape sometime from the kind of bondage Tom was planning to place her under. If not tonight, or next week, then a month hence. Was it not better for her to go, even though suddenly and shockingly, with the God-speed and the trust of some one in her own family?

Is it ever wise to cut the last thread that holds a girl to those who have loved and cherished her? I thought not. Perhaps the slender thread that now existed between Ruth and me might be the means of drawing a stouter cord, which in its turn might haul a cable, strong and reliable. I did not think then of the possible dangers in New York—the difficulties, the risks; there was no time to discuss, no time for doubts and misgivings; there was simply time for me to fill out two blank checks for twenty-five dollars each, put on my hat and coat, and speed with all possible haste to the station.

I found Ruth eagerly awaiting me in the train-shed. There were crowds of people hastening here and there with bags and suit-cases. There were trucks and train-men. There was the roar of an incoming train. Through the confusion Ruth's anxious eyes looked straight into mine.

"Well?"

"Is this your train?" I asked with a nod toward the sweating monster that had just come to a standstill on the first track.

"It's the New York train," said Ruth.

"Well, I've brought some money," I went on quickly. "Fifty dollars. It will last for a while. They don't know about it yet, back there at the house. I shall have to tell them when I go back. I can't predict. Tom may wire Malcolm to meet you and drag you back home. I don't know. But I'll use all the influence I can against it. I'll do my very best, Ruth."

Ruth's hand found mine in a sudden grasp and held it tightly.

Another train roared into the train-shed.

"Where shall you stay tonight?" I shrieked at her.

She gave the name of a well-known hotel reserved especially for women. "I shall be all right," she called. "I'll drop you a line tomorrow. You needn't worry about me. I'll let you know if I need anything."

A deep megaphoned voice announced the New York train.

"Your ticket?" I reminded.

"I have it. I was going anyway," she replied.

"Well, then," I said, and opened my bag and produced the two checks. She took them. "Promise me, Ruth, promise *always* to let me know—always if you need anything, or are unhappy."

Her eyes suddenly brimmed with tears. Her under lip quavered. She broke down at last. I held her in my arms.

"Oh, Lucy, Lucy," she cried. "You're so good to me. I miss him so. I left the ring in the corner of your top drawer. You give it to Bob. I can't. You're all I have. I've been so horrid to you all my life. I miss Bob so. I hate Tom. I almost hate Tom. Oh, Lucy, what's to become of me? Whatever is to become of me?"

The train gave a little jerk.

"All aboard, Miss," called a porter.

"Your train, Ruth dear," I said gently and actually pushed her a little toward New York, which even now was beginning to appall me. She kissed me good-by. I looked up and saw her floating away in a cloud of fitful steam.

CHAPTER XVIII

A YEAR LATER

That was nearly a year ago. Until one day last week I have not seen Ruth since, not because of the busy life of a young mother—for such I have become since Ruth went away—no, though busy I have been, and proud and happy and selfish, too, like every other mother of a first son in the world, I suppose—but because Ruth hasn't wished to be seen. That is why I have heard from her only through letters, why I direct my answers in care of a certain woman's club with a request to forward them, and why I have neither sent down Will, nor appointed Malcolm to look her up and find out how she was getting along.

Ruth has requested that I make no endeavor to drag her forth into the light of criticism and comment. She has written every week punctually; she has reported good health; and has invariably assured me that she is congenially employed. I have allowed her her seclusion. In olden days broken-hearted women and distracted men withdrew to the protection of religion, and hid their scars inside the walls of nunneries and monasteries. Why not let Ruth conceal her wounds, too, for a while, without fear of disturbance from commenting friends and an inquisitive family?

However, a fortnight ago, I had a letter from Ruth that set me to planning. It casually referred to the fact that she was going to march in the New York suffrage parade. I knew that she is still deeply interested in suffrage. Any one of her letters bore witness to that. I decided to see that parade. My son was six months old; I hadn't left him for a night since he was born; he was a healthy little animal, gaining ounces every week; and for all I knew the first little baby I had been appointed to take care of was losing ounces. I made up my mind to go down to New York and have a look at Ruth anyway. I told Will about it; he fell in with my scheme; and I began to make arrangements.

When I announced to Robert Jennings that we were going to New York, I tried to be casual about it.

"I haven't been down there for two years," I said one night when he dropped in upon us, as was his occasional custom. "I require a polishing in New York about every six months. Besides I want to begin disciplining myself in leaving that little rascal of mine upstairs, just to prove that he won't swallow a safety-pin or develop pneumonia the moment my back's turned. Don't you think I'm wise?"

"New York?" took up Bob. "Shall you—do you plan to see anybody I know?" he inquired.

He was a different man that falteringly asked me this question from the Robert Jennings of a year ago—the same eyes, the same voice, the same persistent smile, and yet something gone out from them all.

"No, Bob," I replied, "I'm not going to look up Ruth." We seldom spoke of her. When we did it was briefly, and usually when Will happened to be absent.

"There's a suffrage parade in New York, Wednesday," Robert informed me. "While you're there, you know. Had you an idea that she might be in it?"

"Why, I shouldn't be a bit surprised," I allowed.

"Well, then, of course you'll see her," he brought out.

"Well, I might. It's possible. I shall see the parade, I hope. They say they're rather impressive."

"She's well?" asked Bob.

"She writes so," I told him briefly.

"And happy?"

"She seems so."

"What should you think of the idea of my seeing that parade, too?" he asked a little later.

"I shouldn't think very well of it, Bob."

"Should I be in the way?" he smiled, "interrupt yours and Will's *tete-a-tete*?"

"Oh, no, of course not. But—O Bob," I broke off, "why keep on thinking about Ruth? I wish you wouldn't. Life has such a lot else in it." He colored a little at my frankness. "Oh, I know you don't want me to talk about it, but I can't help it. You knew her such a little while, scarcely six months in all, and besides she wasn't suited to you. I see it now myself. She's stark mad about all these suffrage things. You wouldn't have been happy. She's full of theories now. I wish you'd drop all thought of her and go about the next thing. I'm sure Ruth is going about the next thing. *You* ought to."

"Nevertheless," he said, "should I be in the way?"

Of course he went. I could see his mind was made up in spite of what I might say. The three of us—Robert Jennings and Will and I—stood for two hours on the edge of a curbing in New York City waiting for Ruth to walk up Fifth Avenue.

We were a merry little party. A spark of Robert's old fun seemed to have stolen into his eyes, a little of the old crispness into his voice.

"They're going to walk several abreast," he explained. "It will be hard work finding her in such a crowd. She might get by. So this is my plan. I'll take as my responsibility the rows farthest over, you take the middle, Will, and Lucy, you look out for those nearest the curb. See? Now between the three of us we'll see her. Hello! I believe they're coming!"

I looked down Fifth Avenue, lined with a black ribbon of people on each side. It was free from traffic. Clear and uninterrupted lay the way for this peculiar demonstration. I saw in the distance a flag approaching. I heard the stirring strains of a band.

Ruth was very near the front of the parade. One band had passed us and disappeared into dimness and Ruth preceded the second one.

It was a lovely sunny day, with a stiff sharp breeze that made militant every flag that moved. Ruth wore no slogan of any sort. She carried one symbol only—the American flag. She was not walking. Ruth rode, regally, magnificently. We were hunting for her in the rank and file, and then some little urchin called out, "Gee! Look at the peach!"

And there she was—Ruth! Our Ruth, on a black horse, a splendid creature flecked with foam.

"Some girl!" said a man beside me.

"Who's she?" exclaimed somebody else.

Then abruptly the band that she immediately preceded broke into thundering music, and drowned everything but the sight of her.

But oh, such a sight! She was in her black habit and wore the little tri-cornered hat that so became her. She has always

Olive Higgins Prouty

ridden horseback. Confidently, easily she sat in her saddle, with one white-gloved hand holding the reins, and the other one the pole of the flag, which waved above her head. In Ruth's eyes there was an expression that was ardent. Neither to left nor right did she look. She seemed oblivious of her surroundings. Straight ahead she gazed; straight ahead she rode; unafraid, eager, hopeful; the flag her only staff. She epitomized for me the hundreds and hundreds of girls that were following after. Where would they all come out? Where, *where* would Ruth come out? She had sought liberty. Well, she had it. Where was it taking her? With a choking throat I watched my sister's stars and stripes vanish up Fifth Avenue. I thought it would satisfy me to see Ruth well and happy—for she looked well, she looked happy—but it didn't satisfy me. I was hungry for more of her.

None of us, Will, Robert or I, had spoken as she rode by. It had been too impressive. I had not looked at Robert. I had observed only his hand as it grasped his coat sleeve as he stood with folded arms. One hand, I thought, had tightened its grasp a little. We all stood perfectly speechless for at least three minutes after Ruth went by. Finally it was Robert who spoke.

"Have you had enough?" he asked of me, leaning down.

"Have you?" I inquired.

"Yes, I have. Let's go. Come on, Will, let's get out," he said. There was a note of impatience in his voice. We wormed our way back to the entrance of a shop.

"What's the rush?" said Will.

Robert replied. I could see his emotion now. "It's this. I'll tell you. I'm going to clear right out of this crowd and look that girl up. You've got that address in Madison Avenue, Lucy. I'm going to look her up—"

"But, Bob," I remonstrated. "She doesn't live there, and she doesn't want to be looked up. She has asked me not to—and besides—"

"I can't help that—I shall be doing the looking up. I'll take the blame," he rather snapped at me.

"Now, look here, Bob, old man," said Will, and he put a hand on one of Robert's shoulders. "What's the good in it *now*? Don't you see she'll be hotter than ever on this thing just now? Wait till she cools off a bit. That's the idea!"

"Oh, it isn't to dissuade her. I don't care about that. It's simply to find out if she's all right. She may need help of some kind or other. She's a proud girl. Good heavens, she isn't going to send for any one. I don't know what we've been thinking of—a whole year down in this place, and no knowledge of what kind of a life she's had to live. That isn't right—no. Lucy, if you'll be kind enough to give me that address, I'll be off."

"I don't believe you can trace her through that."

"I'll see to that end of it." He was really almost sharp with me.

"What do you think, Will?" I inquired.

"Oh, give it to him, give it to him, my dear."

And so I did at last.

Will and I went to the theater that night, and supper afterward. It was after midnight when we strolled into the hotel. Robert Jennings was sitting in one of the big chairs in the corridor with a paper up before his face. Will had gone to the desk to get our key, and I went up and spoke to Bob.

"Well, hello!" I blurted out cheerfully. "What success? Did you see her?"

He stood up, and I saw his face then.

"Yes, I saw her," he replied, then with difficulty added, "Don't ask me about it," and abruptly he turned away, tossed aside the paper, and walked straight out of the hotel. He might have been in a play on the stage.

We had arranged to leave for home the following morning. Will called up Robert's room about nine to find out if he was still planning to return with us. There was no answer. I felt anxious about Bob. Will felt simply irritated.

"Ought to have known more than to have gone pressing his suit on a person in Ruth's frame of mind," he grumbled.

Robert Jennings didn't show up until three minutes before the train pulled out. His reservation hadn't been canceled, but I had little hope of his appearance. My heart gave a bound of relief when I saw him coming into the car at the farther end.

"Oh, here you are!" I said. "I'm so glad you've come. We've been looking for you."

"Hello there," put in Will.

"Have you? That's good of you," said Bob. He had himself well in hand now. I was glad of that. "I went out for breakfast," he explained. "I was sure to show up, however. I have a five o'clock appointment this afternoon," and he took off his overcoat, swung his chair about, and sat down.

For two hours he sat opposite me there without a single reference to the night before. You might have thought I never had seen him cast that newspaper aside and unceremoniously burst out of the hotel. We talked about all sorts of indifferent subjects. Finally I leaned over and asked Will if he didn't want to go into the smoking-car.

"Understand?" I inquired.

"Surely," he replied, "surely, I do, Miss Canny," and left us.

A half-an-hour outside New London Bob began to talk. "Do you want to hear about last night?" he asked me.

"If you want to tell me," I replied.

"Well, I found her. I found Ruth."

"Yes, I know you did, Bob."

"Do you know *where* I found her?"

"Why, no. Of course I don't."

"Well, I'll tell you. After I left you I went first to the Madison Avenue address. It wasn't until I gave the lady at the desk of that club the impression that I came bearing news of some serious nature connected with Ruth's family, that she gave me the address where Ruth's mail is forwarded. She told me it was Ruth's place of business. It was an address up near the region of the Park, no name, just the bare street and number. I called 'information,' and finally the house on the 'phone. I was informed Miss Vars would not be in until after dinner. So I waited, and about half-past eight went up there. I found the house—a big, impressive affair, grilled iron fence close to it in front, very fine, very luxurious; all the windows curtained darkly, with a glow of brightness through the cracks here and there. I hesitated to present myself. I walked up and down twice in front of the house, wondering if it would be wiser to call Ruth by telephone and make an appointment. Then suddenly some one inside opened an upper window—it was a warm night. I saw a man draw aside the laces, raise the shade, and throw up the sash. I saw beyond into the room. I saw Ruth. She was sitting beneath a bright light, on a sofa. She was sewing. She seemed quite at home. I saw the man turn away from the window and go back and sit down on the sofa beside her. I saw him stretch out, put one hand in his pocket, lean back luxuriously, and proceed to smoke. It was all very intimate. A policeman passed me as I stood there staring.

"'Who lives there?' I asked him—and he told me. 'Oh, that's the Sewall place,' he said, 'Young Breckenridge Sewall, you know.' I looked up at the window again. The man was closing it now. Is he dark, quite dark, stoops a little, with a receding forehead?" asked Robert of me.

I nodded. I couldn't speak.

"It was he, it was Sewall without a doubt. What is Ruth doing in that house?" demanded Bob. "What is she doing, sitting there alone with that man at nine o'clock at night—sewing? What does it mean? I didn't go in. I walked back to the hotel and sat there, and then I went out and walked again. What does it mean? For heaven's sake, Lucy—tell me what she's doing there?"

"O Bob," I said tremblingly, "don't think anything awful about Ruth. Whatever she's doing there, it's all right."

"You don't know," he groaned.

"I know Ruth, and that's enough. Of course she's all right. Don't let's get absurd. I can't understand it, of course, but after all—"

"Oh, please," almost shuddered Bob, "don't let's talk about it. I don't want to think about it. She has been such a beautiful memory, and now—please don't talk about it."

"All right," I said and leaned back and gazed out of the window, stunned by his news, frightened more than I dared to show.

We rumbled on in silence for half an hour. I was dimly aware that Bob bought a magazine. Will joined us later, sat down, and fell off to sleep. Bob got up and announced that he was going into the smoking-car. His composure of the early afternoon had left him. He appeared nervous and disturbed. He looked distressed. Just outside Providence he returned to the car with a porter and began gathering up his belongings.

"What is it?" I asked.

"Nothing much," he replied shortly, "only I'm going back to New York. I'm going back now—tonight, that's all."

CHAPTER XIX

RUTH RESUMES HER OWN STORY

I had no idea what I was undertaking when I went to New York. I had had no experience with the difficulties that exist between announcing you intend to live your own life, and living it. The world is a bewildering place for one unused to it. All the savoir-faire and sophistication acquired in reception-rooms didn't stand me in very good stead when it came to earning my own living in New York City. I was timid, full of fears—imaginary and real. I had been to New York many times before, but the realization that I was in the big city alone, unanchored, afloat, filled me with panic. I was like a young bird, featherless, naked, trembling, knocked out of its nest before it could fly. Every sound, every unknown shape was a monster cat waiting to devour me. I was acutely aware of dangers lurking for young girls in big cities. For two or three days I had all I could do to control myself and keep my nerve steady.

I arrived on a cold, gray, cloudy morning; unaccustomed to reaching destinies unmet; my heart torn and bleeding; nobody to turn to for help and advice; no plan formed in my confused mind; afraid even to trust myself to the care of a taxicab driver. For such a timid pilgrim in quest of freedom, to start out in search of an address she treasures because of the golden apple of immediate employment that it promises, and to learn on arrival that the position already has been filled, is terribly disheartening. To wake up the second morning in a two-dollar hotel room, which she has locked and barred the night before with all the foolish precautions of a young and amateurish traveler, to pay a dollar for a usual breakfast served in her room and a dollar-and-a-half for a luncheon of nothing but a simple soup and chicken-a-la-King, and then to figure out on a piece of paper that at such a rate her fifty dollars will last just about two weeks, is enough to make any young fool of a girl wish she had been taught something else besides setting off expensive gowns. I didn't know what I ought to do. I didn't know how to begin. I was so self-conscious, at first, so fearful that my being at that hotel, alone, unchaperoned, might be questioned and cause unpleasant comment, that I stayed in my room as much as possible. When I look back and see myself those first few days I have to smile out of self-pity. If it hadn't been for my lacerated pride, for the memory of Tom's arrogance and Edith's taunts, I might have persuaded myself to give up my dangerous enterprise, but every time I rehearsed that scene at the Homestead (and, imprisoned as I was, I rehearsed it frequently), something flamed up in me higher and higher each time. I could not go back with self-respect. It was impossible. I concluded that I might as well get singed in New York, as bound in slavery by Tom and Edith.

As soon as I became fully convinced that my lot was cast, I ventured out to look for cheaper accommodations.

Ever since I have been allowed alone on a railroad train, the Y. W. C. A. has been preached to me as a perfectly safe place to ask advice in case of being stranded in a strange city. So I trudged down there one late afternoon and procured a list of several lodging-houses, where my mother's young parlor-maid could stay for a week with safety while we were moving from our summer house. I didn't know whether I could bring myself really to undress and get into the little cot in the room which I finally engaged, but at least the room had a window. I could sit by that. I had been assured that the place was reputable. I moved down there in a taxicab one rainy Saturday afternoon. Lucy had sent me my trunk, and I had to convey it somehow. I didn't sleep at all the first night. There was a fire-escape immediately outside my open window, and there was not a sign of a lock on the door. On Monday I bought a screw-eye and hook for fifteen cents, and put nails in the sash for burglar stops.

At first I used to crawl back to that smelly little hall bedroom at the earliest sign of dusk; at first, if a man on the street spoke to me, I would tremble for five minutes afterward; at first the odor of the continual boiling of mutton bones and onions that met me every time I opened the door of Mrs. Plummet's lodging-house used to make me feel sick to my stomach. I became hardened as time went on, but at first it was rather awful. I don't like to recall those early experiences of mine.

I learned a great deal during my first fortnight at Mrs. Plummet's. I never knew, for instance, that one meal a day, eaten at about four o'clock in the afternoon, takes the place of three, very comfortably, if aided and abetted in the morning by crackers spread with peanut butter, and a glass of milk, a whole bottle of which one could buy for a few cents at the corner grocery store. The girl who roomed next door to me gave me lots of such tips. I had no idea that there were shops on shabby avenues, where one could get an infinitesimal portion of what one paid for a last season's dinner-gown; that furs are a wiser investment than satin and lace; and that my single emerald could be more easily turned into dollars and cents than all the enameled jewelry I owned put together. The feeling of reenforcement that the contents of my trunk gave me did a lot in restoring confidence. The girl next door and I reckoned that their value in secondhand shops would see me through the summer, at least. Surely, I could become established somewhere by fall.

I didn't know how to approach my problem. I didn't know what advertisements in the newspapers were the false ones. I felt shy about applying for work at stores and shops. For whom should I ask? To what department present myself? What should I say first? One day I told a benevolent-looking woman, one of the officers at the Y. W. C. A., the truth about myself, that I, and not my mother's parlor-maid, was occupying the room in the lodging-house. Not until that woman put her hand kindly on my shoulder and advised me to go home—did I realize how determined I had become. New York had not devoured me, the lodging-house had not harmed me. I had found I could sleep, and very well, too, on the lumpy, slumped-in cot with the soiled spread. No one climbed the fire-escape, no one tried my locked door at night. I had pawned my last winter's furs, but my character seemed quite clean and unsmirched. Go home! Of course I wasn't going home. Not yet. The lady gave me a list of reputable employment agencies at last. If Mrs. Plummet's hadn't daunted me, employment offices couldn't either, I said. I was told to provide suitable references.

Now references were just what I couldn't very well provide. I had left home under disagreeable circumstances. I tried to make it clear without too much detail that, except for my sister, my connections with my people were severed, and I couldn't apply to Lucy. I hadn't even given her my actual address. She would be sure to come looking me up, or send some one in her place. Very likely she would ask my brother Malcolm to drop in on me sometime. I was in deadly fear I would run across him on the street, and if Malcolm had ever smelled the inside of the house where I roomed, I fear his nose never would have come down. If Lucy had ever seen the dirt on the stairs she would have pronounced the house disreputable, and dragged me home. Secrecy was my only chance for success, at least for a while. I would have to discover what could be done without references.

It was due to a little new trick I learned of looking on at myself that it was not impossible for me to seek a position through an employment agency. I had become, you see, one of those characters I had read about in short stories dozens of times before—an unemployed girl in New York, even to the hall-bedroom, the handkerchiefs stuck on my window-pane in process of ironing, the water-bugs around the pipes in the bath-room. It was this consciousness of myself that made many of the hardships bearable—this and the grim determination not to give up.

I told the lady in charge of the intelligence office where I first applied that I was willing to try anything, but thought I was best suited as a mother's-helper, or a sort of governess. She shrugged when I told her I had no reference, but occasionally she gave me an opportunity for an interview.

There was something about me that, lacking a reference, impressed my would-be employers unfavorably; possibly it was the modish cut of the hundred-dollar spring suit I wore, or the shape of my hat. Anyhow, they all decided against me. If I had persisted long enough, I might have found some sort of place, but on the fourth or fifth day of my ordeal in intelligence offices, something happened.

I was sitting with the rest of my unemployed sisters in the little inner room provided for us off the main office, when I glanced through the door to see Henrietta Morgan and her mother. I looked hastily away. Here I had been avoiding Fifth Avenue and the region of shops, for fear some of my old friends about New York (and I have many) might run across me, and stupidly I had walked into the very place infested by them. I accomplished my escape easily enough. Naturally Mrs. Morgan wasn't looking for me in such a place, but I didn't take the chance again.

I was lonely and discouraged many times during that first bitter summer of mine in New York. I felt no charity for Edith, no forgiveness for Tom. I hadn't wanted to leave home—not really—I hadn't sought an experience like this. They had forced me to it. If only Tom hadn't treated me like a naughty child! If only Bob—oh if *only* Bob—(no, there were some things I could not dwell upon. It was wiser not to). Some pains are dull and steady. One can endure them and smile. Others recur at intervals, occasioned by some unimportant detail like a man on the street selling roasted chestnuts, which reminds one of saffron woods in late October. Such pain is like the stab of a sharp stiletto.

Mine is the same old story of hope and despair, of periods of courage occasioned by opportunities that flickered for a while and went out. I was not utterly without employment. The first three dollars I earned at directing envelopes in a department store made me happy for a fortnight. It was a distinct triumph. I felt as if I had been initiated into a great society. I had been paid money for the labor of my hands! The girl who roomed next to me had helped me to get the position. I was not without associates. There were twenty-five girls besides myself who carried away in their clothes each morning the odor of Mrs. Plummet's soup-stock. Mrs. Plummet let rooms to girls only, and only rooms. We didn't board with Mrs. Plummet. I wondered how she and old Mr. Plummet ever consumed, alone, so much lamb broth.

For a fortnight I was a model for trying on suits in a downtown wholesale house; several times the Y. W. C. A. found opportunities for me to play accompaniments; in October when the suffrage activities began I was able to pick up a few crumbs of work in the printing office of one of their papers. But such a thing as permanent employment became a veritable will-o'-the-wisp. I was strong and willing, and yet I could not—absolutely *could not*—support myself. I tried writing fiction. I had always yearned to be literary, but the magazines sent all my stuff back. I tried sewing in a dressmaker's shop, but after three days the Madam announced that her shop would be closed during August, the dull season. She had hired me simply to rush a mourning order. From one thing to another I went, becoming more and more disheartened as fall approached, and my stock of clothes and jewelry, on the proceeds of which I was living, became lower and lower. My almost empty trunk stared at me forlornly from its corner; it foretold failure. What should I do when the last little frumpery of my old life had been turned into money to support my new one? To whom turn? I could not ask for help from those who had admonished and criticized. I had written Lucy weekly that I was prospering. I could not acknowledge failure even to her. I bent every nerve to the effort.

One day in a magazine that some one had discarded in a subway train I ran across an advertisement for "a young lady of education and good family, familiar with social obligations, to act as a private secretary to a lady in a private home." I answered that advertisement. I had answered dozens similar before. This, like the others no doubt, would end in failure. But I couldn't sit and fold my hands. I must keep on trying. I answered it—and six others at the same time. Of the seven I had a reply only from the one mentioned above.

It was a unique reply. It was typewritten. "If still interested in the position referred to in attached clipping reply by complying to requirements enclosed—and mail answer by the evening of the day that this communication is received.

"1st.   Write a formal acceptance to a formal dinner.

2nd.   Write a few words on suffrage appropriate to an older woman who is mildly opposed.

3rd.   Write a polite note of refusal to the treasurer of a charitable institution in reply to a request to donate sum of money.

4th.   Write a note of condolence to an acquaintance upon the death of a relative.

5th.   Write a note of congratulation to a debutante announcing her engagement.

6th.   Write an informal invitation to a house-party in the country.

7th.   Acknowledge a gift of flowers sent to you during an illness."

I sat down with zest to this task. It was an original way to weed out applicants. I spent the whole afternoon over it. It was late in the evening before I had all my questions answered, neatly copied, sealed, and dropped inside a green letter-box.

A day or two later I received in the same non-committal typewritten form a brief summons to appear the following morning between twelve and one o'clock at a certain uptown hotel, and to inquire at the desk for Miss A. S. Armstrong.

It was a clear starry night. I pinned a towel over my suit, put it on a coat-hanger, and hung it securely to the blind-catch outside my window. I didn't know who Miss A. S. Armstrong was, but at any rate I would offer up to the stars what I possessed of Mrs. Plummet's soup-stock.

CHAPTER XX

THE FIFTH WHEEL GAINS WINGS

Miss A. S. Armstrong proved to be a thin angular creature with no eyelashes. She saw me come in through the revolving doors of the hotel at sharp twelve o'clock. When I enquired for her at the desk, she was at my elbow. She was not the lady I had come to be interviewed by; she was merely her present private secretary; the lady herself, she explained, was upstairs awaiting me.

"You're younger than we thought," she said, eyeing me critically. She was a very precise person. Her accent was English. My hopes dimmed as I looked upon her. If she had been selected as desirable, then there was little chance for me. My short experience in employment offices had proved to me the undesirability of possessing qualities that impress a would-be employer as too attractive.

"Do you have young men callers?" "Do you like 'to go'?" "Do you want to be out late?" Such inquiries were invariably made when I was trying to obtain a position as a mother's-helper or child's-companion; and though I was able to reply in the negative, my inquisitors would look at me suspiciously, and remain unconvinced. Now, again, I felt sure as we ascended to the apartment above that my appearance (Miss Armstrong had called it my youth) would stand in my way.

I was ushered into a room high up in the air, flooded with

New York sunshine. It dazzled me at first. Coming in from the dimness of the corridor, I could not discern the features of the lady sitting in an easy chair.

"I beg your pardon," ejaculated Miss Armstrong at sight of her, "I thought you were in the other room. Shall we come in?"

"Certainly, certainly." There was a note of impatience.

Miss Armstrong turned to me. I was behind her, half hidden. "Come in," she said. "I wish to introduce you to Mrs. Sewall—Mrs. F. Rockridge Sewall. The applicant to your advertisement, Mrs. Sewall."

Miss Armstrong stood aside. I stepped forward (what else could I do?) and stood staring into the eyes of my old enemy. It was she who recovered first from the shock of our meeting. I had seen a slight flush—an angry flush I thought—spread faintly over Mrs. Sewall's features as she first recognized me. But it faded. When she spoke there wasn't a trace of surprise in her voice.

"My applicant, did I understand you to say, Miss Armstrong?"

"Yes," I replied in almost as calm a manner as hers, "I answered your advertisement for a private secretary, and followed it by responding to the test which you sent me, and received word to appear here this morning."

"I see, I see," said Mrs. Sewall, observing me suspiciously.

"But," I went on, "I did not know to whom I was applying. I answered six other advertisements at the same time. I have, of course, heard of Mrs. F. Rockridge Sewall. I doubt if I would be experienced enough for you. Miss Armstrong spoke of my youth downstairs." Mrs. Sewall still continued to observe me. "To save you the trouble of interviewing me," I went on, "I think I had better go. I am not fitted for the position, I am quite sure. I am sorry to have taken any of your time. I would never have answered your advertisement had you given your name." I moved toward the door.

"Wait a minute," said Mrs. Sewall. "Kindly wait a minute, and be seated. Miss Armstrong, your note-book please. Are you ready?"

Miss Armstrong, seated now at a small desk, produced a leather-bound book and fountain-pen. "Quite ready," she replied.

Mrs. Sewall turned to me. "I always finish undertakings. I have undertaken an interview with you. Let us proceed with it, then. Let us see, Miss Armstrong, what did the young lady sign herself?"

"Y—Q—A."

"Yes. 'Y—Q—A.' First then—your name," said Mrs. Sewall.

It was my impulse to escape the grilling that this merciless woman was evidently going to put me to; my first primitive instinct to strike my adversary with some bitterly worded accusation and then turn and fly. But I stood my ground. Without a quiver of obvious embarrassment, or more than a second's hesitation, I replied, looking at Mrs. Sewall squarely.

"My name is Ruth Chenery Vars."

Miss Armstrong scratched it in her book.

"Oh, yes, Ruth Chenery Vars. Your age, please, Miss Vars?" Mrs. Sewall coldly inquired.

I told her briefly.

"Your birthplace?"

And I told her that.

"Your education?" she pursued.

"High-school," I replied, "one year of boarding-school, one year coming out into society, several years stagnating in society, some travel, some hotel life, one summer learning how to live on seven dollars a week."

"Oh, indeed!" I thought I discerned a spark of amusement in Mrs. Sewall's ejaculation. "Indeed! And will you tell me, Miss Vars," she went on, a little more humanely, "why you are seeking a position as private secretary?"

"Why, to earn my living," I replied.

"And why do you wish to earn your living?"

"The instinct to exist, I suppose."

"Come," said Mrs. Sewall, "why are you here in New York, Miss Vars? You appear to be a young lady of good birth and culture, accustomed to the comforts, and I should say, the luxuries of life, if I am a judge. Why are you here in New York seeking employment?"

"To avoid becoming a parasite, Mrs. Sewall," I replied.

"'To avoid becoming a parasite'!" (Yes, there was humor in those eyes. I could see them sparkle.) "Out of the mouths of babes!" she exclaimed, "verily, out of the mouths of babes! You are young to fear parasitism, Miss Vars."

"I suppose so," I acknowledged pleasantly, and looked out of the window.

Beneath Mrs. Sewall's curious gaze I sat, quiet and unperturbed, contemplating miles of roofs and puffing chimneys. I was not embarrassed. I had once feared the shame and mortification that would be mine if I should ever again encounter this woman, but in some miraculous fashion I had opened my own prison doors. It flashed across me that never again could the bogies and false gods of society rule me. I was free! I was independent! I was unafraid! I turned confident eyes back to Mrs. Sewall. She was considering me sharply, interrogatively, tapping an arm of her chair as she sat thinking.

"Well," I said smiling, and stood up as if to go. "If you are through with me—"

"Wait a minute," she interrupted. "Wait a minute. I am not through. Be seated again, please. I sent out about thirty copies of the papers such as you received," she went on. "Some fifteen replies were sent back. Yours proved to be the only possible one among them. That is why I have summoned you here today. The position of my private secretary is a peculiar one, and difficult to fill. Miss Armstrong has been with me some years. She leaves to be married." (Married! This sallow creature.) "She leaves to marry an officer in England. She is obliged to sail tomorrow. Some one to take her place had been engaged, but a death—a sudden death—makes it impossible for the other young lady to keep her contract with me. Now the season is well advanced. I am returning to town late this year. My town house is being prepared for immediate occupancy. The servants are there now. I return to it tomorrow. On Thursday I have a large dinner. My social calendar for the month is very full. You are young—frightfully young—to fill a position of such responsibility as Miss Armstrong's. My private secretary takes care of practically all my correspondence. But many of the letters I asked you to write in the test I sent are letters which actually must be written within the next few days. Your answers pleased me, Miss Vars—yes, pleased me very much, I might say." She got up (I rising too) and procured a fresh handkerchief from a silver box on a table. She touched it, folded, to her nose.

"The salary to begin with is to be a hundred and twenty-five dollars a month," she remarked. She shook out the handkerchief, then she added, coughing slightly first behind the sheer square of linen, "I should like you to start in upon your duties, Miss Vars, as soon as possible—tomorrow morning if it can be arranged."

I was taken unawares. I had not expected this.

"Why—but do you think—I'm sorry," I stumbled, "but on further consideration I feel that I—"

"Wait a minute, please. Before you give me an answer it is fair to explain your position more in detail. It is an official position. Your hours are from ten to four. You are in no sense maid or companion. You live where you think best, are entirely independent, quite free, the mistress of your own affairs. I am a busy woman. The demands upon my time are such that I require a secretary who can do more than add columns of figures, though that she must do too. She must in many cases be my brains, my tact, convey in my correspondence fine shades of feeling. It is a position requiring peculiar talent, Miss Vars, and one, I should say, which would be attractive to you. During the protracted absence of an only son of mine, who is occupying my London house, I shall be alone in my home this winter. You may have until this evening to think over your answer. Don't give it to me now. It is better form, as well as better judgment, never to be hasty. I liked your letters," she smiled graciously upon me now. "After this interview I like them still. I like *you*. I think we would get on."

A hundred and twenty-five dollars a month! The still unmarried Breck safe in England! My almost empty trunk! Why not? Why not accept the position? Was I not free from fear of what people would say? Had I not already broken the confining chains of "what's done," and "what isn't done?" I needed the work; it was respectable; Breck was in England; a hundred and twenty-five dollars a month; my trunk almost empty.

"Well," I said, "I need a position as badly as you seem to need a secretary, Mrs. Sewall. We might try each other anyway. I'll think it over. I won't decide now. I will let you know by five o'clock this afternoon."

I accepted the position. Mrs. Plummet shed real tears when I told her my good news at six o'clock that night; and more tears a fortnight later when I moved out of my little hall bedroom, and my feather-weight trunk, lightsomely balanced on the shoulders of one man, was conveyed to the express-wagon and thence to new lodgings in Irving Place.

It was in the new lodgings that my new life really began. Its birth had been difficult, the pains I had endured for its existence sharp and recurring, but here it was at last—a lovely, interesting thing. I could observe it almost as if it was something I could hold in my two hands. Here it was—mine, to watch grow and develop; mine to tend and nurture and persuade; my life at last, to do with as I pleased.

At the suffrage headquarters I had run across a drab-appearing girl by the name of Esther Claff, and it was with her that I shared the room in Irving Place.

She was writing a book, and used to sit up half the night. She was a college-educated girl, who had been trained to think logically. Social and political questions were keen delights to Esther Claff. She took me to political rallies; we listened to speeches from anarchists and socialists; we attended I. W. W. meetings; we heard discussions on ethical subjects, on religion, on the white-slave traffic, equal suffrage, trusts. Life at all its various points interested Esther Claff. She was a plain, uninteresting girl to look at, but she possessed a rare mind, as beautifully constructed as the inside of a watch, and about as human, sometimes I used to think.

She was very reticent about herself, told me almost nothing of her early life and seemed to feel as little curiosity about mine. I lived with Esther Claff a whole winter with never once an expression from her of regard or affection. I wondered sometimes if she felt any. Esther was an example, it seemed to me, of a woman who had risen above the details of human life, petty annoyances of friendships, eking demands of a community. I had heard her voice tremble with feeling about some reforms she believed in, but evidently she had shaken off all desire for the human touch. I wished sometimes that Esther wasn't quite so emancipated.

My associates were Esther's associates—college friends of hers for the most part, a circle of girls who inspired me with their enthusiasms and star-high aspirations. They were living economically in various places in New York, all keenly interested in what they were doing. There was Flora Bennett, sleeping in a tiny room with a skylight instead of uptown with her family, because her father wouldn't countenance his daughter's becoming a stenographer, making her beg spending money from him every month like a child. There was Anne DeBois who had left a tyrannical parent who didn't believe in educating girls, and worked her way through college. There was a settlement worker or two; there was poor, struggling Rosa who tried to paint; Sidney, an eager little sculptor; Elsie and Lorraine, two would-be journalists, who lived together, and who were so inseparable we called them Alsace and Lorraine; there was able Maria Brown, an investigator who used to spend a fortnight as an employee in various factories and stores and write up the experience afterwards.

There were few or no men in our life. Esther and I frequented our friends' queer little top-story studios in dark alleys for recreation, and got into deep discussions on life and reforms. Sometimes we celebrated to the extent of a sixty-cent table d'hote dinner in tucked-away restaurants. We occupied fifty-cent seats at the theater occasionally, and often from dizzying heights at the opera would gaze down into the minaret boxes below, while I recalled with a little feeling of triumph that far-distant time when I had sat thus emblazoned and imprisoned.

I had cut loose at last. I was proud of myself. In the secret of my soul I strutted. I was like a boy in his first long trousers. I might not yet show myself off to the family. They would question the propriety of my occupation with Mrs. Sewall, but nevertheless I had not failed. Sometimes lying in my bed at night with all the vague, mysterious roar of New York outside, my beating heart within me seemed actually to swell with pride. I was alone in New York; I was independent; I was self-supporting; I was on the way to success. I used to drop off to sleep on some of those nights with the sweet promise of victory pervading my whole being.

One day I ran across an advertisement in the back of a magazine representing a single wheel with a pair of wings attached to its hub. It was traveling along without the least difficulty in the world. So was I. The fifth wheel had acquired wings!

CHAPTER XXI

IN THE SEWALL MANSION

In spite of Mrs. Sewall's crowded engagement calendar, she was a woman with very few close friends. She was very clever; she could converse ably; she could entertain brilliantly; and yet she had been unable to weave herself into any little circle of loyal companions. She was terribly lonely sometimes.

For the first half-dozen weeks our relations were strictly official. And then one day just as I was leaving to walk back to my rooms as usual, Mrs. Sewall, who was just getting into her automobile, asked me if I would care to ride with her. The lights were all aglow on Fifth Avenue. We joined the parade in luxurious state. This was what I once had dreamed of—to be seated beside Mrs. F. Rockridge Sewall in her automobile, creeping slowly along Fifth Avenue at dusk. Life works out its patterns for people cunningly, I think. I made some such remark as I sat there beside Mrs. Sewall.

"How? Tell me," she said, "how has it worked out its pattern cunningly for you?"

We had never mentioned our former relations. I didn't intend to now.

"Oh," I said, side-stepping what was really in my mind, "cunningly, because here I am, in a last winter's hat and a sweater for warmth underneath my old summer's suit, and yet

Olive Higgins Prouty

I'm happy. If life has woven me into such a design as that—I think it's very clever of it."

"*Are* you happy?" questioned Mrs. Sewall.

"Yes, I believe I am," I replied honestly. "That, of course, isn't saying I am not just a little lonely sometimes. But I'm interested. I'm terribly interested, Mrs. Sewall."

"Well, but weren't you interested when you were a debutante? You referred to having been a debutante, you remember, once. Weren't you, as you say, terribly interested *then*?"

"Yes, in a way, I suppose I was. But I believe *then* I was interested in myself, and what was good for my social success, and now—it sounds painfully self-righteous—but now I'm interested in things outside. I'm interested in what's good for the success of the world." I blushed in the dusk. It sounded so affected. "I mean," I said, "I'm interested in reforms and unions, and suffrage, and things like that. I used to be so awfully individualistic."

"Individualistic! Where do you run across these ideas? A girl like you. Parasitism, and suffrage! Is my secretary a suffragette?" she asked me smilingly.

"Well," I replied, "I believe that woman's awakening is one of the greatest forces at work today for human emancipation."

"Well, well," ejaculated Mrs. Sewall. "So my secretary thinks if women vote, all the wrinkles in this old world will be ironed out."

I knew I was being made fun of a little, but I was willing nevertheless.

"The influence suffrage will have on politics will not be so important as the influence it will have on ethics and conventions," I replied, "and I believe it will have such a beneficial influence that it will be worth Uncle Sam's trouble to engage a few more clerks to count the increased number of ballots."

"Well—well. Is that so?" smiled Mrs. Sewall, amused. "Do you think women competent to sit on juries, become just judges, and make unbiased and fair decisions? What have you to say to that, Miss Enthusiast?"

"Women are untrained now, of course, but in time they will learn the manners of positions of trust, as men have, through being ridiculed in print, through bitter experiences of various kinds. If they are given a few years at it, they'll learn that they can't afford to be hasty and pettish in public positions, as they could in their own little narrow spheres at home. A child who first goes to school is awfully new at it. He sulks, cries, wants his own way; he hasn't learned how to work with others. Neither have women yet, but suffrage will help us toward it."

"I had no idea you were such a little enthusiast. Come, don't you want to have tea with me and my friend Mrs. Scot-Williams? I'm to meet her at the Carl. She enjoys a girl with ideas."

"In this?" I indicated my suit. We were drawing up to the lighted restaurant, where costly lace veiled from the street candle-lighted tables.

"In that?" Mrs. Sewall looked at me and smiled. "Talk as you have to me, my dear, and she will not see what your soul goes clothed in."

My enemy—Mrs. Sewall! My almost friend now! She could sting, but she could make honey too. Bittersweet. I went with her to drink some tea.

That was the beginning of our intimate relations. Mrs. Sewall invited me the very next day to lunch with her in the formal dining-room, with the Sewall portraits hanging all around. We talked more suffrage. It seemed to amuse her. She was not particularly interested in the woman's movement. It simply served as an excuse.

One stormy evening not long after the luncheon invitation Mrs. Sewall invited me to stay all night. She was to be alone and had no engagement. She asked me frequently after that. We slipped into relations almost affectionate. I discovered that Mrs. Sewall enjoyed my reading aloud to her. I found out one day, when her maid, who was an hourly irritation to her, was especially slow about arranging her veil, that my fingers pleased and satisfied. Often, annoyed beyond control, she would exclaim, "Come, come, Marie, how clumsy you are! All thumbs! Miss Vars, do you mind? Would you be so kind?" Often I found myself buttoning gloves, untangling knots in platinum chains, and fastening hooks.

As late fall wore into early winter, frequently I presided at the tea-table in Mrs. Sewall's library—the inner holy of holies, upstairs over the drawing-room. "Perkins is so slow" (Perkins was the butler) "and his shoes squeak today. Would you mind, Miss Vars? You're so swift and quiet with cups."

Once she said, in explanation of her friendliness: "I've never had anything but a machine for a private secretary before. Miss Armstrong was hardly a companionable person. No sense of humor. But an excellent machine. Oh, yes—excellent. Better at figures than you, my dear Miss Vars, but oh, her complexion! Really I couldn't drink tea with Miss Armstrong. I never tried it, but I'm sure it would not have been pleasant. You have such pretty coloring, my dear. Shan't I call you Ruth some day?"

Spontaneously it burst out. I had never had the affection of an older woman. I grasped it.

"Do, yes, do call me Ruth," I exclaimed.

I had once believed I could please this difficult woman. I had not been mistaken. It was proved. I did please her. She called me Ruth!

I wrote her letters for her, I kept her expenses, I cut her coupons, I all but signed her generous checks to charitable institutions. Most willingly I advised her in regard to them. She sent five hundred dollars to Esther Claff's settlement house in the Jewish quarter on my suggestion, and bought one of Rosa's paintings, which she gave to me. She wanted me to go with her to her dressmaker's and her milliner's. She consulted me in regard to a room she wanted to redecorate, a bronze that she was considering. She finally confided in me her rheumatism and her diabetes. I was with her every day. Always after her late breakfast served in her room, she sent for me. After all it wasn't surprising. I should have to be very dull and drab indeed not to have become her friend. I was the only one in her whole establishment whom she wasn't obliged to treat as servant and menial.

Of everything we talked, even of Breckenridge—of Breckenridge as a baby, a boy, a college-man. She explained his inheritance, his weaknesses, his virtues. She spoke of Gale Oliphant and the interrupted marriage. Once—once only—she referred to me.

"Oh, dear, oh, dear," she began one day with a sigh, "the best-laid plans of mice and men"—Oh, dear, oh, dear! Sometimes I think I have made a great many mistakes in my life. For instance, my son—this Breckenridge I talk so much about—he, well, he became very fond of some one I opposed. A nice girl—a girl of high principles. Oh, yes. But not the girl whom his mother had happened to select for him. No. His mother wished him to marry his second cousin—this Gale you've heard me speak of—Gale Oliphant. Breckenridge was fond of her—always had been. She was worth millions, *millions!*

"You see, a short time before Breckenridge formed the attachment for the young lady with the high principles, his mother's lawyer had persuaded her into a most precarious investment. For two years, a large part of her fortune trembled uncertainly on the edge of a precipice. She believed that her son required less a girl with high principles of living, than a girl with principles represented by quarterly dividends. Breckenridge would not make a success as a man without means. But as I said—'the best-laid plans of mice and men!'

"Oh, well, perhaps you read the story. Most unfortunate. It was in the papers. It nearly broke me. A law-suit on the eve of my son's marriage to Miss Gale Oliphant. After I had successfully brought the affair to the desired climax too! Oh, most unfortunate!

"The suit was brought by a creature who had no claims. Put up to it by unscrupulous lawyers of no repute. We paid the money that she asked to hush up the notoriety of the affair, but not before the mischief of breaking off the relations with Miss Oliphant had been nicely accomplished. That was over a year ago. My investments have proved successful. Gale is married to a man twice her age. Breckenridge is still in England."

"And what's become of the girl you didn't approve of?" I asked lightly, threading my needle. I was sewing that day.

"The girl with the high principles?" Mrs. Sewall queried. "I don't know," she said distinctly, slowly. "I don't know, I wish I did. If you should ever run across her, tell her to come and make herself known to me, please. I've something to say."

"I will," I said, carefully drawing the thread through my needle and making a knot. "If I ever run across her. I doubt if I do. I've learned that *that* girl has gone on a long journey to a new and engrossing country."

"Oh? I must send a message to her somehow then. Come here, my dear. Come here. I've got my glasses caught."

I laid down my work and crossed over to Mrs. Sewall. It was

true. The chain was in a knot. I untangled it.

"How deft you are!" she exclaimed softly. "Thank you, dear. Thank you." Then she put her cold white fingers on my arm, and patted it a little. She smiled very sweetly upon me.

"My private secretary pleases me better every day!" she said.

CHAPTER XXII

THE PARADE

I didn't tell Lucy that I was with Mrs. Sewall. I had my mail directed to Esther's college club. I rather hated to picture the terrible curses that Edith would call down upon my head when she heard that I was occupying a position which she would certainly term menial. I dreaded to learn what Tom would say of me. Already I had seen Malcolm one day on Fifth Avenue, and bowed to him from the Sewall automobile. Surely, he would report me; but either he didn't recognize me, or else he didn't recognize Mrs. Sewall, for Lucy's letters proved she was still ignorant of my occupation. I accepted kind fate's protection of me; I lived in precious and uninterrupted seclusion.

Of course, I marched in the suffrage parade when it took place in May. I rode on Mrs. Scot-Williams' beautiful, black, blue-ribbon winner. Mrs. Scot-Williams, Mrs. Sewall, and a group of other New York society women tossed me flowers from a prominent balcony as I rode up Fifth Avenue. I carried only the American flag. It was my wish. I wanted no slogan. "Let her have her way," nodded Mrs. Scot-Williams to the other ladies. "The dear child's eyes will tell the rest of the story."

The parade was a tremendous experience to me. Even the long tedious hours of waiting before it started were packed with significance. There we all were, rich and poor; society women and working girls; teachers, stenographers, shirtwaist makers;

actresses, mothers, sales-women; Catholic and Protestant; Jew and Gentile; black and white; German, French, Pole and Italian—all there, gathered together by one great common interest. The old sun that shone down upon us that day had never witnessed on this planet such a leveler of fortune, station, country and religion. The petty jealousies and envies had fallen away, for a period, from all us women gathered there that day, and the touch of our joined hands inspired and thrilled. Not far in front of me in the line of march there was a poor, old, half-witted woman, who became the target of gibes and jeers; I felt fierce protection of her. Behind me were dozens of others who were smiled or laughed at by ridiculing spectators; I felt protection of them all.

For hours before the parade started I sat on the curbing of the side-walk with a prominent society woman on one side, and a plain little farmer's wife from up state on the other. We talked, and laughed, and ate sandwiches together that I bought in a grimy lunch-room.

When finally the parade started, and I, mounted on Mrs. Scot-Williams' beautiful Lady F, felt myself moving slowly up Fifth Avenue to the martial music of drums, brass horns, and tambourines; sun shining, banners waving, above me my flag making a sky of stars and stripes, and behind me block upon block of my co-workers; I felt uplifted and at the same time humbled.

"Here we come," I felt like saying. "Here we come a thousand strong—all alike, no one higher than another. Here we come in quest. We come in quest of a broader vision and a bigger life. We come, shoe-strings dragging, skirts impeding, wind disheveling, holding on to inappropriate head-gear, feathers awry, victims of old-time convictions, unadapted to modern conditions, amateur marchers, poorly uniformed—but here we come—just count us—here we come! You'll forget the shoe-strings after you've watched a mile of us. You'll forget the conspicuous fanatics among us (every movement has its lunatic fringe, somebody has said), you'll forget the funny remarks, the jokes of newsboys, and the humorous man you stood beside, after your legs begin to feel stiff and weary, and still we keep on coming, squad upon squad, band upon band, banner upon banner."

As I rode that day with all my sisters I felt for the first time in my life the inspiration of cooeeperation. It flashed across me that the picture of the wheel with the wings was as untrue as it was impossible. I had made a mistake. I was not that sort of wheel. I wasn't superfluous. I was a tiny little wheel with cogs. I was set in a big and tremendous machine—Life, and beside me were other wheels, which in their turn fitted into other cogs of more and larger wheels. And to make life run smoothly we all must work together, each quietly turning his own big or small circumference as he had been fashioned. Alone nothing could be accomplished. Wings indeed! Fairy-tales. Cog-wheels must mesh. Human beings must cooeperate.

That night I had promised to spend with Mrs. Sewall. I didn't want to. I wanted to see Esther Claff. I wanted to hear the tremor of her voice, and watch her faint blue eyes grow bright and black. Tonight she would put on her little ugly brown toque and gray suit, and join the other girls, in somebody's studio or double bedroom. There would be great talk tonight! We had all marched in one company or another. I wanted to hear how the others felt. My feelings were tumultuous, confused. I longed for Esther's fervor and calm eloquence. But I had promised Mrs. Sewall; she had been particularly anxious; I couldn't go back on my word now; she dreaded lonely evenings; and I was glad that I hadn't telephoned and disappointed her when I finally did arrive a little before dinner.

She took my hand in both of hers; she looked straight into my eyes, and if I couldn't hear Esther's voice tremble, then instead I could hear Mrs. Sewall's.

"My dear," she said, "I am very proud of you. You were very beautiful, this afternoon. You will always do me credit."

I leaned and kissed her hand half playfully. "I shall try anyhow," I said lightly.

Mrs. Sewall took out her handkerchief and touched it to her eyes, then slipped one of her arms through mine, and rested her jeweled hand on my wrist, patting it a little.

"What a dear child you are!" she murmured. "I have grown fond of you. I want you to know—tonight, when your eyes are telling me the fervor that is glowing in that arduous soul of yours, how completely you satisfy me. It may be one more little triumph to add to your day's joy. I want you to know that if ever it was in my power to place my wealth and my position on you, dear child, it would be the greatest happiness of my life. I have given myself the liberty of confiding much in you, of taking you into the inner courts, my dear. You are as familiar with my expenditures as with your own; you are acquainted with my notions upon distribution, charitable requests, wise and foolish investments; you appreciate my ideas in regard to handling great fortunes; you agree with me that masters of considerable amounts of money are but temporary keepers of the world's wealth, and must leave their trust for the next steward in clean, healthy, and growing condition; you have been apprenticed to all my dearest hopes and ambitions. Ah, yes, yes, very creditably would you wear my crown. With what grace, intelligence, and appreciation of values would you move among the other monitors of great fortunes, admired by them, praised, and loved, I think. What a factor for good you could become! Your expansive sympathies—what resources they would assume. Ah, well, well, you see I like to paint air-castles. I like to put you into them. This afternoon when I saw you mounted like some inspired goddess on that superb creature of Mrs. Scot-Williams', and caught the murmur that passed over the little company on the balcony as you approached, I thought to myself, 'She's made for something splendid.' And you are, my dear—you are. Something splendid. Who knows, my air-castles may come true."

"O Mrs. Sewall," I said softly, "I'm not worthy of such kind words as those."

"There, there," she interrupted. She had heard the catch in my voice. "There. Think nothing more about it. We won't talk seriously another moment. Dinner will be announced directly. Let us have Perkins light a fire."

CHAPTER XXIII

AN ENCOUNTER WITH BRECK

Mrs. Sewall didn't remain long with me in the library after dinner. She excused herself to retire early. I was to read aloud to her later, when Marie called me. I was dawdling over a bit of sewing as I waited. My thoughts were busy, my cheeks hot. The experience of the day, climaxing in Mrs. Sewall's warm words, had excited me, I suppose. I wondered if first nights before footlights on Broadway could be more thrilling than this success of mine. Was it my new feeling of sisterhood that so elated me—or was it, more, Mrs. Sewall's capitulation? Was I still susceptible to flattery?

"Well, hello!" suddenly somebody interrupted.

I recognized the voice. My heart skipped a beat, I think, but my practiced needle managed to finish its stitch.

"Hello, there," the voice repeated, and I looked up and saw Breckenridge Sewall smiling broadly at me from between heavy portieres.

"Hello, Breck," I said, and holding my head very high I inquired, "What are you doing *here*?"

"Oh, I'm stopping here," he grinned. "What are *you* doing?"

"You know very well what I'm doing," I replied. "I'm your

mother's private secretary. What are you doing around here, Breck?"

He laughed. "You beat 'em all. I swear you do! What am I doing around here! You'd think I didn't have a right in my own house. You'd think it was your house, and I'd broken in. Well, seeing you ask, I'll tell you what I'm doing. I'm observing a darned pretty girl, sitting in the corner of one of my sofas, in my library, and I don't object to it at all—not at all. Make yourself quite at home, my girl. Look here, aren't you glad to see a fellow back again?" He came over to me. "Put your hand there in mine and tell me so then. I've just come from the steamer. Nobody's extended greetings to me yet. I'm hurt."

"Haven't you seen your mother?" I inquired coolly.

"Not yet. The old lady'll keep. You come first on the program, little private secretary. Good Lord—private secretary! What do you know about that? Say, you're clever. Gee!" he broke off, "but it's good to get back. You're the first one I've seen except Perkins. Surprised?" He rested both hands on the table beside me, and leaned toward me. I kept on sewing. "Come, come," he said, "put it down. Don't you recollect I never was much on patience? Come, little private secretary, I'm just about at the end of my rope."

"I think you ought to go upstairs and see your mother," I replied calmly. "Did she expect you?"

"Sure. Sure, my dear. I 'phoned the mater to vanish. Savvy?" He was still leaning toward me. "Come, we're alone. I dropped everything on the spot to come to *you*. Now don't you suppose you can manage to drop that fancy-work stuff to say you're glad to see me?"

"Please, Breck," I said, moving away from him a little. He was very near me. "Don't be in such a hurry. Please. You always had to give me time, you know. Would you mind opening a window? It's so warm in here. And then explain this surprising situation? I'd thank you if you would."

"It is hot in here," he said, leaning still nearer, "hot as hell, or else it's the sight of you that makes my blood boil," he murmured.

I moved away again, reeled off some more thread and threaded my needle.

"You don't fall off!" Breck went on. "You don't lose your looks. By gad, you don't!"

"If you touch the bell by the curtain there," I said, "Perkins will come and open the window for us."

"Good Lord," Breck exclaimed, "you're the coolest proposition I ever ran across. All right. Have your own way, my lady. You always have been able to twist me around your little finger. Here goes." And he strode across to the front window, pulled the hangings back and threw open a sash. I felt the cool air on the back of my neck. Breck came back and stood looking down at me quizzically. I kept on taking stitches. "Keep right at it, industrious little one," he smiled. "Sew as long as you want to. *I* don't mind. I don't have to go out again to get home tonight. I'm satisfied. Stitch away, dear little Busy Bee." He took out a cigarette and lit it; then suddenly sat down on the sofa beside me, leaned back luxuriously, and in silence proceeded to send little rings of smoke ceilingward. "Lovely!" he murmured. "True felicity! I've dreamed of this! This is something like home now, my beauty. This is as it ought to be! I always wear holes in the heels too, my love. And no knots, kindly."

"Breck," I interrupted finally, "is your mother in this?"

"We're all in it, my dear child."

"Will you explain?"

"Sure, delighted. Sit up on my hind legs and beg if you want me to. Anything you say. It was this way. I was in London when mater happened to mention the name of her jewel of a secretary. I was about to start off on a long trip in the yacht— Spain, Southern France, Algiers. Stocked all up. Supplies, crew, captain—everything all ready. 'I don't care what becomes of 'em,' I said, when I got news where you were. 'I don't care. Throw 'em overboard. Guests too. I don't give a hang. Throw them over—Lady Dunbarton, and the Grand Duke too. Drown 'em! There's somebody back in New York who has hung out her little Come-hither sign for me, and I'm off for the little home-burg in the morning.'"

"Come-hither sign! O Breck, you're mistaken. I—"

"Hold on, my innocent little child, I wasn't born day before yesterday. But let that go. I won't insist. I've come anyhow." He leaned forward. "I'm as crazy about you as ever," he said earnestly. "I never cared a turn of my hand for any one but you. Queer too, but it's so. I'm not much on talking love—the real kind, you know—but I guess it must be what I feel for you. It must be what is keeping me from snatching away that silly stuff there in your hand, and having you in my arms now—whether you'd like it or not. Say," he went on, "I've come home to make this house really yours, and to give you the right of asking what I'm doing around here. You've won all your points—pomp, ceremony, big wedding, all the fuss, mater's blessing. The mater is just daffy about you—ought to see her letters. You're a winner, you're a great little diplomat, and I'm proud of you too. I shall take you everywhere— France, England, India. You'll be a queen in every society you enter—you will. By Jove—you will. Here in New York, too, you'll shine, you little jewel; and up there at Hilton, won't we show them a few things? You bet! Say—I've come to ask you to marry me. Do you get that? That's what I've come for—to make you Mrs. Breckenridge Sewall."

I sat very quietly sewing through this long speech of Breck's. The calm, regular sticking in and pulling out of my needle concealed the tumult of my feelings. I thought I had forever banished my taste for pomp and glory, but I suppose it must be a little like a man who has forsworn alcohol. The old longing returns when he gets a smell of wine, and sees it sparkling within arm's reach.

As I sat contemplating for a moment the bright and brilliant picture of myself as Breck's wife, favored by Mrs. Sewall, envied, admired by my family, homaged by the world, the real mistress of this magnificent house, I asked myself if perhaps fate, now that I had left it to its own resources in regard to Breck, did not come offering this prize as just reward. And then suddenly, borne upon the perfumed breeze that blew through the open window, I felt the sharp keen, stab of a memory of a Spring ago—fields, New England—fields and woods; brooks; hills; a little apartment of seven rooms, bare, unfurnished; and somebody's honest gray eyes looking into mine. It seemed as if the very embodiment of that memory had passed near me. It must have been that some flowering tree outside in the park, bearing its persuasive sweetness through the open window, touched to life in my consciousness a memory imprinted there by the perfume of some sister bloom in New England. I almost felt the presence of him with whom I watched the trees bud and flower a Spring ago. Even though some subtle instinct prompted Breck at this stage to rise and put down the window, the message of the trees had reached me. It made my reply to Breck gentle. When he came back to me I stood up and put aside my needle-work.

"Well?" he questioned,

"I'm so sorry. I can't marry you, Breck. I can't."

"Why not? Why can't you? What's your game? What do you want of me? Don't beat around. I'm serious. What do you mean 'you can't?'"

"I'm sorry, but I don't care enough for you, Breck. I wish I did, but I just don't."

"Oh, you don't! That's it. Well, look here, don't let that worry you. I'll make you care for me. I'll attend to that. Do you understand?" And suddenly he put his arms about me. "I'll marry you and make you care," he murmured. I felt my hot cheek pressed against his rough coat, and smelled again the old familiar smell of tobacco, mixed with the queer eastern perfume which Breck's valet always put a little of on his master's handkerchief. "You've got to marry me. You're helpless to do anything else—as helpless as you are now to get away from me when I want to hold you. I'm crazy about you, and I shall have you some day too. If it's ceremony you want, it's yours. Oh, you're mine—*mine*, little private secretary. Do you hear me? You're mine. Sooner or later you're mine."

He let me go at last.

I went over to a mirror and fixed my hair.

"I wish you hadn't done that," I said, and rang for Perkins. He came creaking in, in his squeaky boots.

"Perkins," I said, "will you call a taxi for me? I'm not staying with Mrs. Sewall now that she has her son here. Please tell her that I am going to Esther's."

"I shall see that you get there safely," warned Breck. "I've rights while you're under this roof."

"It isn't necessary, Breck. I often walk. I'm used to going about alone. But do as you please. However, if you do come, I'm going to ask you not to treat me as if—as if—as you just did. I've given all that to somebody else."

"Somebody else," he echoed.

"Yes," I nodded. "Yes, Breck; yes—somebody else."

"Oh!" he said. "Oh!" and stared at me. I could see it hit him.

"I'll go and put my things on," I explained, and went away.

When I came back he was standing just where I had left him. Something moved me to go up and speak to him. I had never seen Breckenridge Sewall look like this.

"Good-night, Breck," I said. "I'm sorry."

"You! Sorry!" he laughed horribly. Then he added, "This isn't the last chapter—not by a long shot. You can go alone tonight—but remember—this isn't the last chapter."

I rode away feeling a little uneasy. I longed to talk to some one. What did he mean? What did he threaten? If only Esther—but no, we had never been personal. She knew as little about the circumstances of my life as I about hers. She could not help me. Anyway it proved upon my arrival at the rooms in Irving Place that Esther was not there.

I sat down and tried to imagine what Breck could imply by the "last chapter." At any rate I decided that the next one was to resign my position as Mrs. Sewall's secretary. That was clear. I wrote to her in my most careful style. I told her that until she was able to replace me, I would do my best to carry on her correspondence in my rooms in Irving Place. She could send her orders to me by the chauffeur; I was sorry; I hoped she would appreciate my position; she had been very good to me; Breckenridge would explain everything, and I was hers faithfully, Ruth Chenery Vars.

Esther didn't come back all night—nor even the next day. I could have sallied forth and found some of our old associates, I suppose; but I knew that they would all still be discussing the parade, and somehow I wanted no theorizing, no large thinking. I wanted no discussion of the pros and cons of big questions and reforms. I wanted a little practical advice—I wanted somebody's sympathetic hand.

About seven o'clock the next evening, the telephone which

Esther and I had indulged in interrupted my lonely contemplations with two abrupt little rings. I got up and answered it weakly. I feared it would be Mrs. Sewall—or Breck, but it wasn't.

"Is that you, Ruth?"

Bob! It was Bob calling me! Bob's dear voice!

"Yes," I managed to reply. "Yes, Bob. Yes, it's I."

"May I see you?"

"Yes, you may see me."

"When? May I see you now?"

"Why, yes. You may see me *now*."

"All right. I'm at the Grand Central. Just in. I called your other number and they gave me this. I don't know where it is. Will you tell me?"

I could feel the foot that my weight wasn't on trembling. "Yes, I'll tell you," I said, "but I'd rather meet *you*—some nicer place. Couldn't I meet you?"

"Yes—if you'd rather. Can you come *now*?"

"Yes, now, Bob, this very minute."

"All right, then." He named a hotel. "The tea-room in half an hour. Good-by."

"Good-by," I managed to finish; and I was glad when I hung up the receiver that Esther wasn't there.

CHAPTER XXIV

THE OPEN DOOR

No one would have guessed who saw a girl in a dark-blue, tailored suit enter the tea-room that evening about seven o'clock, and greet a man, with a brief and ordinary hand-shake, that there was a tremor of knees and hammering of heart underneath her quiet colors; and that the touch of the man's bare hand, even through her glove, sent something zigzagging down through her whole being, like a streak of lightning through a cloud. All she said was: "Hello, Bob. I've come, you see." And he quietly, "Yes, I see. You've come."

He dropped her hand. They looked straight into each other's eyes an instant.

"Anything the matter with anybody at home?" she questioned.

"Oh, no, nothing," he assured her. "Everybody's all right. Are you all right, Ruth?"

"Yes," she smiled. (How good it was to see him. His kind, kind eyes! He looked tired—a little. She remembered that suit. It was new last Spring. What dear, intimate knowledge she still possessed of him.) "Yes," she smiled, "I'm all right."

"Had dinner?" he questioned.

"No, not a bite." She shook her head. (How glowing and fresh he was, even in spite of the tired look. She knew very well what he had done with the half-hour before he met her; he had made himself beautiful for her eyes. How well acquainted she was with all the precious, homely signs, how completely he had been hers once. There was the fountain-pen, with its peculiar patent clasp, in its usual place in his waistcoat pocket. In that same pocket was a pencil, nicely sharpened, and a small note-book with red leather covers. She knew! She had rummaged in that waistcoat pocket often.)

They went into the dining-room together. They sat down at a small table with an electric candle on it, beside a mirror. A waiter stood before them with paper and raised pencil. They ordered, or I suppose they did, for I believe food was brought. The girl didn't eat a great deal. Another thing I noticed—she didn't trust herself to look long at a time into the man's eyes. She contented herself with gazing at his cuffed wrist resting on the table's edge, and at his hands. His familiar hands! The familiar platinum and gold watch chain too! Did it occur to him, when at night he wound his watch, that a little while ago it had been a service she was wont to perform for him? How thrillingly alive the gold case used to seem to her—warmed by its nearness to his body. Oh, dear, oh, dear—what made her so weak and yearning tonight? What made her so in need of this man? What would Esther Claff think? What would Mrs. Scot-Williams say?

"Well, Ruth," the man struck out at last, after the waiter had brought bread and water and butter, and the menu had been put aside, "Well—when you're ready, I am. I am anxious to hear all that's happened—if you're happy—and all that."

The girl dragged her gaze away from him. "Of course, Bob," she said, "of course you want to know, and I am going to tell you from beginning to end. There's a sort of an end tonight, and it happens I need somebody to tell it to, quite badly. I needed an old friend to assure me that I've nothing to be afraid of. I think you're the very one I needed most tonight, Bob." And quite simply, quite frankly, the girl told him her story—there was nothing for her to hide from him—it was a relief to talk freely.

The effect of her story upon the man seemed to act like stimulant. It elated him; she didn't know why. "What a brick you are, Ruth," he broke out. "How glad I am I came down here—what a little brick you are! I guess you're made of the stuff, been dried and baked in a kiln that insures you against danger of crumbling. It's only an unthinking fool who would ever be afraid for you. You need to fear nothing but a splendid last chapter to your life, whoever may threaten. Oh, it's good to see you, Ruth—how good you cannot quite guess. I saw you yesterday in the parade—Lucy and Will too—and I got as near home as Providence, when suddenly I thought I'd turn around and come back here. I was a little disturbed, anxious—I'll acknowledge it—worried a bit—but now, *now*—the relief!"

"You thought I was wasting away in a shirtwaist factory!" she laughed.

He laughed too. "Not quite that. But, never mind, we don't need to go into what I thought, but rather into what I think— what I *think*, Ruth—what I shall always think." Compelling voice! Persuasive gaze! She looked into his eyes. "Ruth!" The man leaned forward. "We've made a mistake. What are you down here for all alone, anyhow? And what am I doing, way up there, longing for you day after day, and missing you every hour? My ambitions have become meaningless since you have dropped out of my future. What is it all for? For what foolish notion, what absurd fear have we sacrificed the most precious thing in the world? Yesterday when I saw you—Oh, my dear, my dear, I need you. Come as you are. I shan't try to make you over. There's only one thing that counts after all, and that is ours."

With some such words as these did Bob frighten me away from the sweet liberties my thoughts had been taking with him. I had been like some hungry little mouse that almost boldly enters human haunts if he thinks he is unobserved, but at the least noise of invitation scampers away into his hole. I scampered now—fast. My problems were not yet solved. I had things I must prove to Lucy, to Edith, to Tom—things I must test and prove to myself. I could not go to him now. Besides, all the reasons that stood in the way of our happiness existed still, in spite of the fact that our joy of meeting blinded us to them for the moment. I tried to make it clear to Bob.

"You can't have changed in a winter, Bob, and I haven't. We decided so carefully, weighed the consequences of our decision. We were wise and courageous. Let's not go back on it. I don't know what conclusions about life I may reach finally, but I want to be able to grow freely. I'm like a bulb that hasn't been put in the earth till just lately. I don't know what sort of flower or vegetable I am, and you don't either. It's been good to see you, Bob, and I needed some one to tell me that I was all right, but now you must go away and let me grow."

"You wouldn't want to come and grow in my green-house then?" he smiled sadly.

I shook my head. "That's just it, Bob. I don't want to grow in any green-house yet. I want to be blown and tossed by all the winds of the world that blow."

"I'll let you grow as you wish," he persisted.

"Please, Bob," I pleaded. "Please—"

He turned away. I didn't want to hurt him.

"Bob," I said gently, "please understand. It isn't only that I think the reasons for our decision of a year ago still exist, but I've just *got* to stay here now, Bob, even though I don't want to. I've got it firmly fixed in my mind *now* that I'm going to see my undertaking through to a successful end. I'm bound to show Tom and the family what sort of stuff I'm made of. I'm going to prove that women aren't weak and vacillating. Why, I haven't been even a year here yet. I couldn't run to cover the first time I found myself out of a position. Besides the first position wasn't one I could exhibit to the family. I *must* stay. I'm just as anxious to prove myself a success as a young man whose family doesn't think he's got it in him. Please understand, and help me, Bob."

"Shall we see each other sometimes?" he queried.

"It's no use. It doesn't help," I said. "I do care for you, somehow, and seeing you seems to make foggy what was so clear and crystal, as if I were looking at it through a mist. I mean sitting here with you makes me feel—makes me forget what I marched for day before yesterday. I was so full of it—of all it meant and stood for—and now—No, Bob. No. You must let me work these things out alone. I shall never be satisfied now until I do."

He left me at my door. There was a light in the windows upstairs, and I knew that Esther had come home. Bob left me with just an ordinary hand-shake. It hurt somehow—that formal little ceremony from him. It hurt, too, afterward to stand in the doorway and watch him walking away. It hurt to hear the sound of his steady step growing fainter and fainter. O Bob, you might have turned around and waved!

I went upstairs. "Hello," said Esther. "Where have you been?" and I told her to dinner with a man from home. A little later I announced to her that I had resigned my position as private secretary to Mrs. Sewall. She asked no questions but she made her own slow deductions.

I must have impressed her as restless and not very happy that night. I caught her looking at me suspiciously, once or twice, over her gold-bowed reading-glasses. Once she inquired if I was ill, or felt feverish. My cheeks did burn.

"Oh, no," I said, "but I guess I'll go to bed. It's almost midnight."

Esther took off her glasses and rubbed her eyes.

"One gets tired, sometimes, climbing," she observed. I waited. "The trail up the mountain of Self-discovery is not an easy one. One's unaccustomed feet get sore, and one's courage wavers when the trail sometimes creeps along precipices or shoots steeply up over rocks. But I think the greatest test comes when the little hamlets appear—quiet, peaceful little spots, with smoke curling out of the chimneys of nestling houses. They offer such peace and comfort for weary feet. It's then one is tempted to throw away the mountain-staff and accept the invitation of the open door and welcoming hearth."

"Oh, Esther," I exclaimed, "were you afraid I was going to throw away my mountain-staff?"

"Oh, no, no. I was simply speaking figuratively." She would not be personal.

"I'm not such a poor climber as all that," I went on. "I am a bit discouraged tonight. You've guessed it, but I am not for giving up."

"If one ever gets near the top of the mountain of Self-discovery," Esther pursued dreamily, "he becomes master not only of his own little peak, but commands a panorama of hundreds of other peaks. He not only conquers his own difficult trail, but wins, as reward for himself, vision, far-reaching."

I loved Esther when she talked like this.

"Well," I assured her, "I am going to get to the top of my peak, if it takes a life-time. No hamlets by the wayside for me," I laughed.

"Oh, no," she corrected. "Never to the top, Ruth—not *here*. The top of the mountain of Self-discovery is hidden in the clouds of eternity. We can simply approach it. So then," she broke off, "you aren't deserting me?"

"Of course I'm not, Esther," I assured her.

"What do you mean to do next, then—if you're leaving Mrs. Sewall?"

"I don't know. Don't ask. I'm new at mountain-climbing, and when my trail crawls along precipices, I refuse to look over the edge and get dizzy. Something will turn up."

The next morning's mail brought a letter from Mrs. Sewall. My services would not be needed any longer. Enclosed was a check which paid me up to the day of my departure. In view of the circumstances, it would be wiser to sever our connections immediately. Owing to the unexpected return of her son, they were both starting within a few days for the Pacific coast. Therefore, she would suggest that I return immediately by express all papers and other property of hers which chanced to be in my possession. It was a regret that her confidence had been so misplaced.

I read Mrs. Sewall's displeasure in every sentence of that curt little note. If I had been nursing the hope for understanding from my old employer, it was dead within me now. The letter cut me like a whip.

My feeling for Mrs. Sewall had developed into real affection. Her years, her reserve, her remoteness had simply added romance to the peculiar friendship. I had thrilled beneath the touch of her cold fingertips. There had been moments lately when at the kindness in her eyes as they dwelt upon me, I had longed to put my arms around her and tell her how happy and proud I was to have entered even a little way into the warm region near her heart. I loved to please her. I would do anything for her except marry Breck, and she could write to me like this! She could misunderstand! She could all but call me traitor!

Very well. With bitterness, and with grim determination never to plead or to explain, I sent back by the next express the check-books and papers I was working on evenings in my room, and also by registered mail returned the bar of pearls she had once playfully removed from her own dress and pinned at my throat. "Wear it for me," she had said. "If I had had a daughter I would have spoiled her with pretty things, I fear. Allow an old lady occasionally to indulge her whims on you, my dear."

I lay awake a long time that night, preparing myself for the struggle that awaited me. I had as little chance now to obtain steady employment as when I made my first attempt. I was still untrained, and, stripped of Mrs. Sewall's favor, still unable to provide the necessary letters of reference. I hadn't succeeded in making any tracks into which, on being pushed to the bottom again, I could stick my toes, and mount the way a second time more easily. Lying awake there, flat on my back, I was reminded of a little insect I once watched climbing the slippery surface of a window-pane. It was a stormy day, and he was on the outside of the window, buffeted by winds. I saw that little creature successfully cover more than half his journey four successive times, only to fall wriggling on his back at the bottom again. When he fell the fourth time, righted himself, and, dauntless and determined, began his journey again, I picked him up bodily and placed him at the top. Possibly— how could such a small atom of the universe as I know— possibly my poor attempts were being watched too!

However, I didn't wait to find out. At least I didn't wait to be picked up. The very next day I set forth for employment agencies.

CHAPTER XXV

MOUNTAIN CLIMBING

There followed a long hot summer. There followed days of hopelessness. There followed a wild desire for crisp muslin curtains, birds to wake me in the morning, a porcelain tub, pretty gowns, tea on somebody's broad veranda. There were days in mid-July when if I had met Bob Jennings, and he had invited me to green fields, or cool woods, I wouldn't have stopped even to pack. There were days in August when a letter from Breck, post-marked Bar Harbor, and returned like three preceding letters unopened, I didn't dare read for fear of the temptation of blue sea, and a yacht with wicker chairs and a servant in white to bring me things.

If it hadn't been for Esther's quiet determination I might have crawled back to Edith any one of those hot stifling nights and begged for admittance to the cool chamber with the spinet desk. My head ached half the time; my feet pained me; food was unattractive. The dead air of the New York subway made me feel ill. In three minutes it could sap me of the little hope I carried down from the surface. I used to dream nights of the bird-like speed of Breckenridge Sewall's powerful automobiles. I used to wake mornings longing for the strong impact of wind against my face.

The big city, the crowds of working people that once inspired, the great mass of congregated humanity had lost its romance. Even my own particular struggle seemed to have no more

Olive Higgins Prouty

"punch" in it. The novelty of my undertaking, the adventure had worn away. They had been right at the Y. W. C. A. when they advised me a year ago to go home and give up my enterprise. I had been dauntless then, but now, although toughened and weathered, discouragement and despair possessed me. I allowed myself to sit for days in the room in Irving Place, without even trying for a position.

It was Esther who obtained a steady job for me at last, in a book-binding factory down near the City Hall. From eight in the morning until five at night I folded paper, over and over and over again, with a bone folder; the same process—no change—no variation. The muscles that I used ached like a painful tooth at first. Some nights we worked until nine o'clock. Accuracy and speed were all that was required to be an efficient folder—no brains, no thought—and yet I never became expert. The sameness of my work got on my nerves so at last—the everlasting repetition of sound and motion—that occasionally I lost all sense of time and place. It was like repeating some common word over and over again until it loses all significance except that of a peculiar sound.

It broke me at last. I became ill. What hundreds of other girls were able to do every day the year round, had finished me in three weeks. I was as soft as a baby. It was my nerves that gave way. I got to crying one night over some trivial little thing, and I couldn't stop. They took me to a hospital, I don't remember how or when. I became aware of trained nurses. I drifted back to the consciousness of a queer grating sound near the head of my bed, which they told me was an elevator; I smelled anesthetics. I realized a succession of nights and days. There were flowers. There was a frequent ringing of bells. Heaven couldn't have been more restful. I loved to lie there and watch a breeze blow the sash-curtains at the windows, in and out with a gentle, ship-like motion. Esther visited me often. Sometimes she sat by the window alone, correcting proof (she had secured a position in a publishing house the first of the summer), and sometimes one of the other girls of our little circle was with her. I never talked with them; I never questioned; they came and went; I felt no curiosity. They tell me I lay there like that for nearly three weeks, and then suddenly with no warning and with no sense of shock or surprise the veil lifted.

Esther and the struggling artist we called Rosa were by the window. They had both come from the same little town in Pennsylvania. I'd been watching them for half an hour or more. They had been talking. I had liked the murmur of their low voices. In the most normal fashion in the world I began to listen to their conversation.

"I wouldn't have had the courage," I heard Rosa say.

"Why not?" replied Esther. "Her family could do no more than is being done. If they took her home now, she'd never come back again. Her spirit would be broken. That wouldn't be good for her. Besides *they* don't need her, while I—why, she's the only human being in the world that's ever meant anything in my life, and I am thirty-three. It has been almost like having had a child dependent on me—having had *her*, giving her a new point of view, taking care of her *now*."

"Well, but how long can you stand the expense of this private room, and the doctors?"

"You needn't worry about that," Esther shrugged.

"But it seems a shame, Esther," burst out Rosa, "just when your father's estate begins to pay you enough income to live on, and you could devote the best of yourself to your book—it seems a shame not to be able to take advantage of it. You've always said," she went on, "that a woman can't successfully begin to create after she's thirty-five. This will certainly put you behind a while. And the room rent too! Does she know yet that you didn't tell her the truth about the price of the room in Irving Place?"

"No, Ruth doesn't know," replied Esther. "She's very proud

about such matters. When she first came she had only an empty trunk, a new job, and a few dollars. Later, when I was going to explain, she lost her position with Mrs. Sewall. I was thankful I hadn't told her then."

"Well, I must say!" exclaimed Rosa warmly, "I must say!"

"Rosa," said Esther. "You don't understand. If Ruth did pay her full share of the room, she would be obliged to leave me sooner. Don't you see? My motives are selfish. You're the one person who knew me back there at home. You have seen all along how stark and empty my life has been—just my independence, my thoughts, my ambitions. That's all. No one to care, no one to make sacrifices for, no man, no child— Good heavens, if some human being has fallen across my way, don't be surprised if I prize my good fortune."

I lay very still listening to Esther's voice. I closed my eyes for fear she might glance up and meet the tears in them, and sudden understanding. I had never known her till now. I could feel the tears, in spite of me, creeping down my cheeks.

I left the hospital a week later. They sent me back to the room in Irving Place with orders for long walks in the fresh air, two-hour rest periods morning and afternoon, and a diet of eggs, chicken, cream and fresh green vegetables. Ridiculous orders for a working girl in New York! They disturbed Esther. She was very quiet, more uncommunicative than ever. I used to catch her looking at me in a sort of anxious way. It seemed as if I couldn't wait to help her with her too-heavy burden. Although I had brought back from the hospital fifteen pounds less flesh on my bones, there was something in my heart instead that was sure to make me strong and well. My new incentive was the secret knowledge of Esther's devotion. To prove to her that her sacrifices had not been in vain became my ambition. For a few days I idled in the room, as the doctor ordered; strolled about Gramercy Park near-by, feeding my eyes on green grass and trees; indulged in bus rides to the Park occasionally; and walked for the exercise.

It's strange how easily some opportunities turn up, and others can't be dug with spade and shovel. One day, aimlessly strolling along a side street, up among the fifties, a card in a milliner's shop chanced to meet my eye. "Girl Wanted," it said, in large black letters.

It was late in the afternoon. If I had set out in quest of that opportunity, the position would have been filled before I arrived. But this one was still open. They wanted a girl to deliver, and perhaps to help a little in the work-room—sewing in linings, and things like that. The hours were short; the bundles not heavy; I needed exercise; it had been ordered by the hospital.

The work agreed with me perfectly. It was very easy. I liked the varied rides, and the interesting search for streets and numbers. It was just diverting enough for my mending nerves. The pay was not much. I didn't object. I was still convalescing.

Crossing Fifth Avenue one day, rather overloaded with two large bandboxes which, though not heavy, were cumbersome, I saw Mrs. Sewall! A kindly policeman had caught sight of me on the curbing and signaled for the traffic to stop. As I started across, I glanced up at the automobile before which I had to pass. Something familiar about the chauffeur caught my attention. I looked into the open back of the car. Mrs. Sewall's eyes met mine. She didn't smile. There was no sign of recognition. We just stared for a moment, and then I hurried along.

I didn't think she knew me. My illness had disguised me as if I wore a mask.

I was, therefore, surprised the next morning to receive a brief note from Mrs. Sewall asking me to be at my room, if possible, that evening at half-past eight.

CHAPTER XXVI

THE POT OF GOLD

Esther was out canvassing for suffrage. She canvassed every other evening now. She had not touched the manuscript of her book for weeks.

Esther could earn a dollar an evening at canvassing. One evening's canvassing made a dozen egg-nogs for me. Esther poured them down my throat in place of chicken and fresh vegetables. I couldn't stop her. I wasn't allowed even to say "Thank you."

"I'd do the same for any such bundle of skin and bones as you," she belittled. "Don't be sentimental. You'd do it for me. We'd both do it for a starved cat. It's one of the unwritten laws of humanity—women and children first, and food for the starving."

She was out "egg-nogging," as I used to call it, when Mrs. Sewall called. I had the room to myself. Mrs. Sewall had never visited my quarters before. I lit the lamp on our large table, drew up the Morris-chair near it, straightened our couch-covers, and arranged the screen around the chiffoniers. Mrs. Sewall was not late. I heard her motor draw up to the curbing, scarcely a minute after our alarm clock pointed to the half-hour.

Marie accompanied her mistress up the one flight of stairs to our room. I heard them outside in the dim corridor, searching for my name among the various calling cards tacked upon the half-dozen doors. It was discovered at last. There was a knock. I opened the door.

"That will do," said Mrs. Sewall, addressing herself to Marie, who turned and disappeared, and then briefly to me, "Good evening."

"Good evening, Mrs. Sewall. Come in," I replied. We did not shake hands. I offered her the Morris-chair.

"No," she said, "no, thank you. This will do." And she selected a straight-backed, bedroom chair, as far away as possible from the friendly circle of the lamp-light. "I'm here only for a moment," she went on, "on a matter of business."

I procured a similar straight-backed chair and drew it near enough to converse without too much effort. It was awkward. It was like trying to play an act on a stage with nothing but two straight chairs in the middle—no scenery, nothing to elude or soften. Mrs. Sewall, sitting there before me in her perfect black, a band of white neatly edging her neck and wrists, veil snugly drawn, gloves tightly clasped, was like some hermetically sealed package. Her manner was forbidding, her gaze penetrating.

"So this is where you live!" she remarked.

"Yes, this is where I live," I replied. "It's very quiet, and a most desirable location."

"Oh! Quiet! Desirable! I see." Then after a pause in which my old employer looked so sharply at me that I wanted to exclaim, "I know I'm a little gaunt, but I'm not the least disheartened," she inquired frowning, "Did you remain in this quiet, desirable place all summer, may I ask?"

"Well—not all summer. I was away for three weeks—but my

room-mate, Miss Claff, was here. It isn't uncomfortable."

"Where were you then, if not here?"

"Why, resting. I took a vacation," I replied.

"You have been ill," Mrs. Sewall stated with finality, and there was no kindness in her voice; it expressed instead vexation. "That is evident. You have been ill. What was the trouble?"

"Oh, nothing much. Nerves, I suppose."

"Nerves! And why should a girl like you have nerves?"

"I don't know, I'm sure," I smiled. "I went into book-binding. It's quite the fad, you know. Some society women take it up for diversion, but I didn't like it."

"Were you in a hospital? Did your people know? Were you properly cared for?" Each question that she asked came with a little sharper note of irritation.

"Yes. Oh, yes. I was properly cared for. I was in a private room. I have loyal friends here."

"Loyal friends!" scoffed Mrs. Sewall. "Loyal friends indeed! And may I ask what loyal friend allows you to go about in your present distressing condition? You are hardly fit to be seen, Miss Vars."

I flushed. "I'm sorry," I said.

"Disregard of one's health is not admirable."

"I'm being very careful," I assured Mrs. Sewall. "If you could but know the eggs I consume!"

"Miss Vars," inquired Mrs. Sewall, with obvious annoyance in her voice , "was it you that I saw yesterday crossing

Fifth Avenue?"

"With the boxes? It was I," I laughed.

She frowned. "I was shocked. Such occupation is unbecoming to you."

"It is a perfectly self-respecting occupation," I maintained.

The frown deepened. "Possibly. Yes, *self-respecting*, but, if I may say so, scarcely respecting your friends, scarcely respecting those who have cared deeply for you—I refer to your family— scarcely respecting your birth, bringing-up, and opportunities. It was distinctly out of place. The spectacle was not only shocking to me, it was painful. Not that what I think carries any weight with you. I have been made keenly aware of how little my opinions count. But—"

"Oh, please—please, Mrs. Sewall," I interrupted. "Your opinions *do* count. I've wanted to tell you so before. I was sorry to leave you as I did. I've wanted to explain how truly I desired to please you. I would have done anything within my power except—I couldn't do that one special thing, *anything* but that."

Mrs. Sewall raised her hand to silence me. There was displeasure in her eyes. "We will not refer to it, please," she replied. "It is over. I prefer not to discuss it. It is not a matter to be disposed of with a few light words. I have not come here to discuss with you what is beyond your comprehension. Pain caused by a heedless girl, or a steel knife, is not less keen because of the heartlessness of either instrument. I have come purely on business. We will not wander further."

There was a pause. Mrs. Sewall was tapping her bag with a rapid, nervous little motion. I was keeping my hands folded tightly in my lap. We were both making an effort to control our feelings. We sat opposite each other without saying anything for a moment. It was I who spoke at last.

"Very well," I resumed. "What is the business, Mrs. Sewall? Perhaps," I suggested coldly, "I have failed to return something that belongs to you."

"No," replied Mrs. Sewall. "On the contrary, I have something here that belongs to *you*." She held up a package. "Your work-bag. It was found by the butler on the mantel in the library."

"Oh, how careless! I'm sorry. It was of no consequence." My cheeks flamed. It hurt me keenly that Mrs. Sewall should insult the dignity of our relations by a matter so trivial. My work-bag indeed! Behind her, in the desk, were a few sheets of her stationery!

I rose and took the bag. "Thank you," I said briefly.

"Not at all," she replied.

I waited a moment. Then, as she did not move, I inquired, "Shall I call your maid, or will you allow me to take you to your car?"

Mrs. Sewall did not reply. I became aware of something unnatural in her attitude. I noticed her tightly clasped hands.

"Oh, Mrs. Sewall!" I exclaimed. She was ill. I was sure of it now. She was deathly pale. I kneeled down on the floor and took her hands. "You are not well. Let me help—please. You are in pain."

She spoke at last. "Call Marie," she ordered, and drew her hands away.

I sped down to the waiting car. Marie seemed to comprehend before I spoke.

"Oh! Another attack! Mon Dieu! The tablets! I have them. They are here. Make haste. It is the heart. They are coming more often—the attacks. Emotion—and then afterwards the pain. She had one yesterday, late in the afternoon. And now tonight again. Mon Dieu—Mon Dieu! The pain is terrible." All this from Marie as we hastened up the stairs.

Mrs. Sewall sat just where I had left her in the straight-backed chair. She made no outcry, not the slightest moan, but there were tiny beads of perspiration on her usually cool brow, and when she took the glass of water that I offered, her hand shook visibly. She would not lie down. She would have nothing unfastened. She would not allow me to touch her.

"No, no. Marie understands. No. Kindly allow Marie. Come, Marie. Hurry. Stop flying about so. I'm not going to die. Hurry with the tablets. Don't be a fool. Make haste. There! Now I shall be better. Go away—both of you. Leave me. I'll call when I'm ready."

We stepped over to the window and stood looking out, while behind us the heroic sufferer, silently and alone, fought a fresh onslaught of pain. I longed to help her, and she would not let me. I might not even assist her to her automobile. Ten minutes later on her own feet and with head held erect she left my room. The only trace of the struggle was a rip across the back of one of the tight black gloves, caused by desperate clenching of hands. I had heard the cry of the soft kid as I stood by the window with Marie.

I opened my work-bag later. The square of fillet lace was there, the thread and the thimble, the needle threaded just as I had left it when Breck stepped in and interrupted. There was something else in the bag, too—something that had not been there before, a white box, long and thin. It contained the bar of diamonds and pearls, with a note wrapped around it.

> "This pin," the note said, "was not a loan as your returning it assumes. My other employees received extra checks at Easter-time when you received this. If you prefer the money, you can, at any time, receive the pin's value at —'s, my jewelers, from my special agent,

Mr. Billings. It is my hope that you will make such use of this portion of your earnings with me that I may be spared the possibility of the spectacle you afforded me this afternoon on the Avenue.

"FRANCES ROCKRIDGE SEWALL."

The next night when Esther came in from canvassing, there lay upon her desk the neglected manuscript of her book, found in a bottom drawer. Before it stood a chair; beside it a drop-light. A quill pen, brand new, bright green and very gay, perched atop a fresh bottle of ink. Near-by appeared a small flat book showing an account between Esther Claff and Ruth Vars and an uptown bank. Inside, between roseate leaves of thin blotting paper, appeared a deposit to their credit of five hundred dollars.

The tide of my fortune had changed. One good thing followed another. It is always darkest before the storm breaks that clears the sky. My horizon so lately dim and obscure began to clear. As if five hundred dollars, safely deposited in a marble-front bank, wasn't enough for one week to convince me that life had something for me besides misfortune, three days after Mrs. Sewall called I received a summons from Mrs. Scot-Williams, whose horse I rode in the suffrage parade. Out of a sky already cleared of its darkest clouds there shot a shaft of light. I could see nothing at first but the brightness of Mrs. Scot-Williams' proposition. It blinded me to all else. I felt as if some enormous searchlight from heaven had selected poor, battered Ruth Chenery Vars for special illumination.

Mrs. Scot-Williams had observed that my place at Mrs. Sewall's was now filled by another. Therefore it had occurred to her that I might be free to consider another proposition. If so, she wanted to offer me a position in a decorator's shop which she was interested in. I might have heard of it—Van de Vere's, just off Fifth Avenue.

Van de Vere's—good heavens—it was all I could do to keep

the tears out of my eyes! Five hundred dollars in the bank—
and now kind fate offering me a seat in heaven that I hadn't
even stood in line for! What did it mean?

Mrs. Scot-Williams, across a two by four expanse of tablecloth
(we were lunching at her club), slowly unfolded her
proposition to me, held it up for me to see, turned it about, as
it were, so that I could catch the light shining on it from all
sides, offered it to me at last to have and to hold. I accepted
the precious thing.

"Rainbows really do have pots of gold, then!" I remember I
exclaimed.

CHAPTER XXVII

VAN DE VERE'S

Van de Vere's was a unique shop. It had grown from a single ill-lighted sort of studio into a very smart and beautifully equipped establishment, conveniently located in the shopping district. It looked like a private house, had been, originally. There were no show windows. The door-plate bore simply the sign V. de V's. A maid in black and white met you at the door (you had to ring), and while she went to summon Miss Van de Vere or her assistant, you were asked to be seated in a reception-room, done in black and white stripes.

Virginia Van de Vere was as unique as her shop. She wore long, loose clinging gowns, with heavy, silver chains clanking about her neck or waist. She wore an enormous ring on her forefinger. Her hair, done very low and parted, covered both her ears. It was black, so were her eyes. She hadn't any color. She led a smart and fashionable life outside business hours, going out to dinner a good deal (I had seen her once at Mrs. Sewall's) and making an impression with free and daring speech. She lived in a gorgeous apartment of her own, and for diversion had adopted a little curly-headed Greek boy, for whom she engaged the services of a French nurse. She was very temperamental.

Mrs. Scot-Williams had found Virginia Van de Vere some half dozen years before, languishing in the ill-lighted studio, on the verge of shutting up shop and going home for want of patronage. It was just that kind of talented girl that Mrs. Scot-Williams liked to help and encourage. She established Virginia Van de Vere.

Mrs. Scot-Williams is a philanthropic woman, and enormously wealthy. Her pet charity is what she calls "the little-business woman." New York is filled with small industries run by women, in this loft, or that shop—clever women, too, talented, many of them, and it is to that class that Mrs. Scot-Williams devotes herself. She takes keen delight in studying the tricks and secrets of business success. When some young woman to whom she has lent capital to start a cake and candy shop complains of dull trade, or a little French corsetier finds her customers falling off, Mrs. Scot-Williams likes to investigate the difficulties and suggest remedies—more advertising, a better location, a new superintendent in the workshop, one thing or another—perhaps even a little more capital, which, if she lends and loses it, she simply puts down under the head of charity in her distribution of expenses.

I had occurred to Mrs. Scot-Williams as a possible means for improving conditions at Van de Vere's. Miss Van de Vere possessed so highly a developed artistic temperament that her manner sometimes antagonized. Her assistant's duty, therefore, would be that of a cleverly constructed fly, concealing beneath tact and pretty manners ("and pretty gowns, my dear," added Mrs. Scot-Williams) a hook to catch reluctant customers.

I was fitted for such a position. I had been used as bait before, for other kind of fish. I purchased my fine feathers. Within a fortnight after my interview with Mrs. Scot-Williams, I was cast upon the waters.

There was no jealousy between Virginia Van de Vere and me. Beauty to her was something pulsing and alive. If any one suggested marring it, it tortured her. I was not so sensitive. The result was, I took charge of the customers who mentioned leatherette dens and Moorish libraries , and Virginia's genius was spared injury. She loved me for it. We worked beautifully together.

Van de Vere's was my great chance. It was indeed my pot of gold. I had always loved beautiful things, and here I was in the midst of their creating! Heaven had been kind. The joy of waking in the morning to a day of congenial work, setting forth to labor that was constructing for me a trade of my own, was like a daily tonic. I was very happy, full of ambition. I used to lie awake nights planning how I could make myself able and efficient. I discovered a course I could take evenings in Design and Interior Architecture, and I took advantage of it. I read volumes at the library on period furniture and decorating. I haunted antique shops. I perused articles on good salesmanship. Mornings I was up with the birds (the pigeons, that is) and half-way to my place of business by eight o'clock. It agreed with me. I grew fat on it. I regained the pounds of flesh that I had lost at the hospital with prodigious speed. Color came back to my cheeks, song to my lips.

Esther's book actually towered. It wasn't necessary for her to keep her position in the publishing house any longer. It wasn't necessary for her to conceal from me the price of our room. My salary was generous, and with Esther's little income we were rich indeed. We could drink all the egg-nogs we wanted to. We could even fare on chicken and green vegetables occasionally. We could buy one of Rosa's paintings for twenty-five dollars, and lend fifteen, now and then, if one of the girls was in a tight place. We could afford to canvass for suffrage for nothing. We could engage a bungalow for two or three weeks at the sea next year.

As soon as I felt that my success at Van de Vere's was assured, I wrote to my family and asked them to drop in and see me. The first of the family to arrive was Edith, one day in February. Isabel, the maid, announced Mrs. Alexander Vars to me. I sent down for her to come up.

The second floor of Van de Vere's looks almost like a private house—a dining-room with a fine old sideboard, bedroom hung with English chintz, a living-room with books and low lamps—sample rooms, of course, all of them, but with very little of the atmosphere of shop or warehouse.

I met Edith in the living-room.

"Hello, Edith," I said. She looked just the same, very modish, in some brand-new New York clothes, I suppose.

"Toots!" she exclaimed, and put both arms about me and kissed me. Then to cover up a little sign of mistiness in her eyes that would show, she exclaimed, "You're just as good-looking as ever. I declare you are!"

"So are you, too, Edith!" I said, misty-eyed, too, for some reason. I had fought, bled and died with Edith once.

"Oh, no, I'm not. I've got a streak of gray right up the front."

"Really? Well, it doesn't show one bit," I quavered, and then, "It's terribly good to see some one from home."

Edith got out her handkerchief.

"I, for one, just hate squabbles," she announced.

And "So do I," I agreed.

Later we sat down together on the sofa. She looked around curiously.

"What sort of a place is this, anyhow?" she asked in old, characteristic frankness. "I didn't know what I was getting into. It seems sort of—I don't know—not quite—not quite—I feel as if I might be shut up in here and not let out."

I laughed. Later I took her up to our showrooms on the top floor.

"Good heavens, do you sell people things, Ruth?" she demanded.

"Of course I do," I assured her.

"Just the same as over a counter almost?"

"Yes—not much difference."

"But don't you feel—oh, dear—that seems so queer—what *is* your social position?"

"Oh, I don't know. I've cut loose from all that."

"I know, but still you've got to think about the future. For instance, how would we feel if Malcolm wrote he was going to marry a clerk—or somebody like that—or a manicurist?"

"If she had education to match his—I should think it was very nice."

"Oh, no, you wouldn't. That's talk. Most people wouldn't anyhow. You are awfully queer, Ruth. You aren't a bit like anybody I know. Don't you sometimes feel hungry for relations with people of your own class? Friendly relations, I mean? Something different from the relations of a clerk to a customer? I would. You are just queer." Then suddenly she exclaimed, "Who's that?"

Virginia had passed through the room.

"Oh, that's Virginia. That's Miss Van de Vere."

"My dear," said Edith, impressed, "she was a guest at Mrs. Sewall's once, when you were out West. She's so striking! I saw her at the station when she arrived—Van de Vere—yes, that was the name. It was in the paper. They spoke of her as a talented artist. Everybody was just crazy about her in Hilton. She was at Mrs. Sewall's two weeks. She was reported engaged to a duke Mrs. Sewall had hanging around. I remember distinctly. What is she doing around here?"

"Why, she and I run this establishment," I announced.

"Good heavens! Does she sell people things?"

"Why, of course, Edith, why not?"

"Well—of all things! I don't know what we're coming to. I should think England *would* call us barbarians. Why, in England, even a man who is in trade has a hard time getting into society. But do introduce me to her if there's a chance before I go."

Later Edith exclaimed, "By the way, my dear, you'll be interested to know I've turned suffrage."

"How did that happen?"

"Of course I wouldn't march or anything like that, and I think militancy is simply awful, but you'd be surprised how popular suffrage is getting at home. I gave a bridge in interest of it. Lots of prominent people are taking it up. Look here," she broke off abruptly, "when can you come up for a Sunday? I'm just crazy to get hold of you and have a good old talk."

"Oh, almost any time. I'm anxious to see nice old Hilton again."

"Well, we must plan it. How would you like to bring that Miss Van de Vere? In the spring when the summer people get here. She has quite a number of admirers among them. I'd just love to give you a little tea or something."

Same old Edith! A wave of tenderness swept over me for her—faults and all. "Of course we'll come," I laughed. "I'll arrange it."

I knew in a flash that I should never quarrel with my sister-in-law again. She was no more to blame than a child with a taste for sweets. Why feel bitterness and rancor? She was only a victim of her environment after all. My tenderness—was a revelation. I hadn't realized that tolerance had been part of my soul's growth—tolerance even toward the principles from which I had once fled in righteous indignation.

Tom dropped in at Van de Vere's some time in the spring.

"Looks like a woman's business," he almost sneered, critically surveying the striped walls of the reception-room; and later, "Impractical and affected, I call it," he said. "If I was building a house I'd steer clear of any such place as this."

"Wait a minute," I replied pleasantly. "Come with me," and I took Tom into the well-lighted rooms at the rear, where our workers were engaged, at the time, on a rush order. "Does that look affected, Tom?" I asked. "Every one of those girls is living a decent and self-respecting life, many of them are helping in their family finances; and besides, the few stockholders of Van de Vere's are going to get a ten per cent dividend on their holdings next year. Does that strike you as impractical and affected, too?"

Tom looked at me, shut his mouth very tight, and shook his head. "I suppose all this takes the place of babies in your life. It wouldn't satisfy some women ten minutes. Elise wouldn't give up one of her babies for a business paying thirty per cent."

"But Tom," I replied calmly. "We all can't marry. Some of us—"

"*You* could have. This is not natural. 'Tisn't according to nature. No, sir. Abnormal. Down here in New York living like a man. What do you want to copy men for? Why don't you devote yourself to becoming an ideal woman, Ruth? That's what I want to know. I don't approve of this sort of thing at all."

I felt no anger. I felt no impulse to strike back. I had reached such an elevation on my mountain of Self-discovery, as Esther would have put it, that I commanded vision at last. Tom and his ideas did not obstruct my progress, like the huge blow-down that he had once been in my way, against which I had blindly beaten my fists raw. I had found my way around Tom. I could look down now and see him in correct proportion to other objects in the world about me. I saw from my height that such obstructions as Tom could be circumvented—a path worn around him, as more and more girls pursued the way I had chosen. I looked down and perceived, already, girls trooping after me. There was no use hacking away at Tom any more. Nature herself removes blow-downs on mountain-trails in time, by a process of slow rot and disintegration. When time accomplishes the same with the Toms of the world then we shan't need even to walk around. We can walk over!

So, "I know you don't approve, Tom," I replied almost gently, "and there's truth in what you say—that women are made to run homes and families, instead of businesses, most of them. Of course Elise wouldn't give up one of her babies! She's one of the 'most-of-them.' How are the babies anyway?"

CHAPTER XXVIII

A CALL FROM BOB JENNINGS

One day, however, I realized that I hadn't walked around Tom. I really hadn't circumvented, by persistence and determination, the obstacles that lay in the way to triumph. Some one, like a fairy godmother from Grimm's, had waved a wand and wished the obstacles away. Virginia told me about it. I learned that except for Mrs. Sewall I might still be delivering bandboxes. The searchlight following me about wherever I went for the last six months, making my way bright and easy, came not from heaven. It came instead from a lady in black who chose to conceal her good offices beneath an unforgiving manner, as she hid the five hundred dollars inside a trivial bag.

Mrs. Sewall called one day at the shop. She asked for Miss Van de Vere. She was contemplating redecorating a bed-chamber, it seemed. Virginia came to me in the workshop, and told me about it.

"Your old lady is out there," she said. "You'd better take her order."

"My old lady?"

"Yes, Mrs. Sewall, who landed you in our midst, my dear."

I stared at Virginia.

"Certainly, and pays a portion of your ridiculous salary, baby-mine." She went on pinching my cheek playfully. She delights in patronizing me. "You're an expensive asset, my dear—not but what I am glad. I always urged somebody of your sort to relieve me. Mrs. Scot-Williams never saw it that way, however, until the old lady Sewall came along and crammed you down our throats. I wasn't to tell you, but I see no harm in it. Go on in, and whatever the tiff's about make it up with the old veteran. She's not a bad sort."

I went upstairs. My heart was bursting with gratitude. I had vexed, displeased, cruelly hurt my benefactress—she had likened me to a steel knife—and yet she had bestowed upon me my greatest desire. Much in the same way as I had rescued the little bug, buffeted by winds, Mrs. Sewall had picked me up and placed me at the zenith of my hopes. But for her, no Mrs. Scot-Williams, no Van de Vere's, no trade of my own, no precious business to work for, and make succeed!

"Mrs. Sewall," I began eagerly (I found her alone in the living-room), "Mrs. Sewall—" and then I stopped. There was no encouragement in her expression.

"Ah, Miss Vars," she remarked frostily.

"Mrs. Sewall—please," I begged, "please let me—"

"My time is limited this morning," she cut in. "Doubtless Miss Van de Vere has sent you to me to attend to my order. If so, let us hasten with it. I am hunting for a cretonne with a peacock design for a bed-chamber. I should like to see what you have."

"But Mrs. Sewall—"

"My time is limited," she repeated.

"I know, but I simply *must* speak."

She raised her hand. "I hope," she said, "that you are not going to make me ill again, Miss Vars."

I surrendered at that. "No, no," I assured her. "No, I'm not. I'm thoughtless. I think only of myself. I'll go and call Miss Van de Vere."

"That will not be necessary," said Mrs. Sewall. "You may show me the cretonne, now that you are here."

For half an hour we hunted for peacocks. I had the samples brought down to the living-room, piled on a chair near-by, and then dismissed the attendant. Mrs. Sewall appeared only slightly interested. In fact, I think we both were observing each other more closely than the cretonnes. They acted simply as a screen, through the cracks of which we might surreptitiously gaze.

I noted all the familiar points—the superb string of pearls about Mrs. Sewall's neck; the wealth of diamonds on her slender fingers when she drew off her glove; the band of black on the lower edge of the veil, setting off her small features in a heavy frame. I noted, too, the increased pallor beneath the veil. There was a sort of emaciated appearance just behind the ears, which neither carefully-set earring nor cleverly arranged coiffure could conceal. The veins on Mrs. Sewall's hands, moreover, were prominent and blue.

But for a tangle in the chain of Mrs. Sewall's glasses she would have left me with no sign of friendliness. It was when I passed her a small sample in a book, and she attempted to put on her glasses, that I observed the fine platinum cord was in a knot. I offered my services. I didn't suppose she would accept them. I was surprised at her cool, "Yes, if you will."

Mrs. Sewall was sitting down. I had to kneel to my task. The chain proved to be in a complicated snarl. My fingers trembled. I was very clumsy. I was afraid Mrs. Sewall would become exasperated. "Just a moment," I said, and looked up.

Our eyes met. I was so close I could see the tiny network of wrinkles in the face above me. I could see the sudden tenderness in the eyes.

"It seems to be a particularly difficult snarl," I quavered, then bent my head and worked in silence for a moment. We were so near, we could hear each other breathe.

Suddenly in a low voice, almost a whisper, Mrs. Sewall asked, "Are you happy here?"

"Oh, so happy," I replied.

"Are you better? Are you well?" she pursued.

I dropped my hands in her lap, looked up, and nodded. I could not trust myself to speak. I knelt there in silence for a moment.

Finally I said, "Are *you* happy? Are *you* better? Are *you* well, dear Mrs. Sewall?"

"What does it matter? I am an old woman," she replied, in that disparaging little way of hers.

Our old intimacy shone clear and bright in that stolen moment. We were like two lovers forbidden to each other, whispering there together, when the lights suddenly go out, and they are enfolded in the protecting dark. "You are not too old to have created great happiness!" I exclaimed softly.

She shrugged and smiled.

It was a rare moment. I did not mean to spoil it. I ought to have been content. My eagerness was at fault.

"Oh!" I burst out crudely, "if you knew how sorry I am to have done anything to *you*, of all people, that displeased. If—" She recoiled; she drew back. I had ventured where angels feared to tread. The chain was not yet untangled, but she would not let me kneel there any longer. She rose; I too.

"My time is limited, as I said," she reminded me; "I am here on business. Let us endeavor to complete it, Miss Vars."

"Yes," I said, blushing scarlet, "let us, by all means. I'm sorry, excuse me, I'll go upstairs and see what else we have."

* * * * *

When Bob finally called at Van de Vere's I hadn't seen him for over a year. While I had been working so hard to establish myself in my new venture, Bob had been starting a brand-new law firm of his own, in a little town I had never heard of in the Middle West. He had severed all connections with the University when his mother had died. I knew as well as if he had told me that when he broke loose from any sort of steady salary he had abandoned all hope of persuading me to come and grow in his green-house, as he had once put it. It had been our original plan that Bob would work gradually into a law firm in Boston, at the same time retaining some small salaried position at the University enabling us to be married before he became established as a lawyer. Bob had been able to lay little by. His mother had required specialists and trained nurses. When I first realized that Bob had gone West and set about planning his life without reference to me I felt peculiarly free and unhampered. When he as much as told me that it was easier for him not to hear from me at all, than in the impersonal way I insisted upon, I was glad. I cared for Bob too much not to feel a little pang in my breast every time I saw my name and address written by his hand. And I wanted nothing to swerve me away from the goal I had my eyes set on—the goal of an acknowledged success as an independent, self-supporting human being.

When Bob first dropped in at Van de Vere's I hardly recognized him as the romantic figure who had wandered over brown hillsides with me, a volume of poetry stuffed into his overcoat pocket. No one would have guessed from this man's enthusiastic interest in the progressive spirit of the West that he had been born on Beacon Hill behind violet-shaded panes of glass. No one would have guessed, when he talked about cleaning out a disreputable school-board by means of the women's vote, that he had once opposed parades for equal suffrage in Massachusetts. When Bob shook hands with me, firmly, shortly, as if scarcely seeing me at all, I wondered if it might have slipped his mind that I was the girl he had once been engaged to marry.

He explained that he was in town on business, leaving the same evening. He could give me only an hour. There was a man he had to meet at his hotel at five. Bob was all nerves and energy that day. He talked about himself a good deal. They wanted to get him into politics out there in that wonderful little city of his. He'd been there only fourteen months, but it was a great place, full of promise—politics in a rather rotten condition—needed cleaning and fumigating. He'd a good mind to get into the job himself—in fact, he might as well confess he was in it to some extent. He was meeting the governor in Chicago the next night, or else he'd stay over and ask me to go to the theater with him.

I don't suppose Bob would have referred to the old days if I hadn't. It was I, who, when at last a lull occurred, said something about that time when he had found me struggling in a mire that threatened to drown, and I had grasped his good, strong arm.

"Wasn't it better, Bob," I asked, "that I should learn to swim myself, and keep my head above water by my own efforts?"

"It certainly seems to be what women are determined to do," he dodged.

"Well, isn't it better?" I insisted.

"I'll say this, Ruth," he generously conceded. "I think there would be less men dragged down if all women learned a few strokes in self-support."

"Oh, Bob!" I exclaimed. "Do you really think that? So do I. Why, *so do I!* We agree! Women would not lose their heads so quickly in times of catastrophe, would they? You see it, too! Women would help carry some of the burden. All they'd need would be one hand on a man's shoulder, while they swam with the other and made progress."

He laughed a little sadly. "Ruth," he said, for the first time becoming the Bob I had known, "I fear you would not need even one hand on a shoulder. It looks to me," he added, as he gazed about the luxuriously furnished living-room of Van de Vere's, "that you can reach the shore quite well alone."

CHAPTER XXIX

LONGINGS

The days at Van de Vere's grew gradually into a year, into two years, into nearly three. From assistant to Virginia Van de Vere I became consultant, from consultant, partner finally. Van de Vere's grew, expanded, spread to the house next door. To the two V's upon the door-plate was added at last a third. Van de Vere's became Van de Vere and Vars.

My life, like that of a child's, assumed habits, personality, settled down to characteristics of its own. I remained with Esther in Irving Place, in spite of Virginia's urgent invitation to share her apartment, adding to the room an old Italian chest, a few large pieces of copper and brass, and a strip or two of antique embroidery. I preferred Irving Place. It was simple, quiet, and detached.

I came and went as I pleased; ate where I wanted to and when; wandered here and there at will. Evenings I sometimes went with Esther, when she could leave the book, or with Rosa, or with Alsace and Lorraine, to various favorite haunts; sometimes with Virginia to the luxurious studios of artists who had arrived; sometimes with Mrs. Scot-Williams to suffrage meetings, where occasionally I spoke; sometimes to dinner and opera with stereotyped Malcolm; sometimes simply to bed with a generous book. A beautiful, unhampered sort of existence it was—perfect, I would have called it once.

My relations with the family simmered down to a friendly basis. They accepted my independence as a matter of course. It had been undesired by them, true enough, its birth painful, but like many an unwanted child, once born, once safely here, they became accustomed to it, fond, even proud, as it matured. I spent every Christmas with Edith in Hilton, going up with Malcolm on the same train, and returning with him in time for a following business day. I often ran up for a week-end with Lucy and Will. Once I spent a fortnight with Tom and Elise in Wisconsin. The family seldom came to New York without telephoning to me, and often we dined together and went to the theater. I ought to have been very happy. I had won all I had left home for. I worked; I produced. At Van de Vere's my creative genius had found a soil in which to grow. I, as well as Virginia, conceived dream rooms, sketched them in water-colors, created them in wood, and paint, and drapery. I had escaped the stultifying effects of parasitism, rescued body and brain from sluggishness and inactivity, successfully shaken off the shackles of society. Freedom of act and speech was mine; independence, self-expression—yes, all that, but where —where was the promised joy?

When I look back and observe my life, I see the sharp, difficult ascent that led to my career at Van de Vere's with clearness. As if it was a picture taken on a sunny day I observe the details of the first joyous days of realized ambition. Just when my happiness began to blur I do not know. Less distinct are the events that led to my discontent. Gradual was the tarnishing of the metal I thought was gold within the pot. I closed my eyes to the process, at first refused to recognize it. I wouldn't admit the possibility of lacks and deficiencies in my life. When they became too obvious to ignore, I searched for excuses. I was tired; I had overworked; I needed a change. Never was it because I was a woman, and just plain hungry for a home. The slow disillusion that crept upon me expressed itself at odd and unexpected moments. In the middle of a fine discussion with the girls of the old circle, the "mountain-climbers," as Esther sometimes called us, the ineffectualness of our lives would sweep over me. To my chagrin, immediately after an inspired argument on suffrage a kind of reactionary longing to be petted, and loved, and indulged occasionally would possess me. Sometimes coming home to the room in Irving Place, after a long day at the shop, I would be more impressed by the loneliness of my life than the freedom.

I hid these indications of what I considered weakness, buried them deep in my heart, at first, and covered them over with a bright green patch of exaggerated zest and enthusiasm. One never realizes how many people are suffering with a certain disease until he himself is afflicted. I didn't know, until my little patch of green covered a longing, how many other longings were similarly concealed. As I became more intimately acquainted with the members of our little circle I discovered that there was frequently expressed a desire for human ties. I recalled Esther's confession at the hospital. Her words came back to me with startling significance. "A stark and empty life," she had said, "no man, no child, no one to make sacrifices for—just my thoughts, my hopes and my ambitions—that's all." Virginia, too—successful and brilliant Virginia Van de Vere! For what other reason had Virginia adopted the curly-headed Greek boy except to cover a lack in her life? For what reason than for a desire for some one to love and to be loved by were Alsace and Lorraine so devoted to each other? I read that a philanthropist of world renown, a woman whose splendid service had been praised the country over, was quoted as saying she would give up her public life a second time and choose the seclusion and the joy of a home of her own. At first I stoutly said to myself, "Well, anyhow, *I* shall not run to cover. I needed no one two years ago. Why should I now?" Why, indeed? A nest of gray hairs, discovered not long after, answered me. They set me to thinking in earnest. Gray hairs! Growing old! Creative years slipping by! Good heavens—was there danger that my life would become stark and empty too? I had chosen the mountain trail. Had I lost then the joy and the comfort of the nestling house and curling smoke? There were still interesting contracts of course, engrossing work. There was still the success of Van de Vere's to live for, but the ecstasy had all faded by the time I first realized that I was no longer a young girl.

Mrs. Sewall never came again to the shop after that single call. I was told she was in Europe. I never heard from her. Her son—poor Breck—had died at sea when a huge and luxurious ocean liner had tragically plunged into fathoms of water. I learned that an English girl had become Mrs. Sewall's companion. They were occupying the house in England. No doubt they were very happy together. Sometimes it would sweep over me with distressing reality that nobody really needed me—Breck, or Mrs. Sewall, or self-sufficient Bob in his beloved West. Bob was fast becoming nothing but a memory to me. If I thought of him at all it was as if my mind gazed at him through the wrong end of a pair of opera glasses. He seemed miles away. He must have come to New York occasionally but he didn't look me up. I heard of his activities indirectly through Lucy and Will. With the help of the women voters he had succeeded in cleaning out a board of aldermen, and now the women wanted him to run for mayor. This all interested me, but it didn't make me long for Bob. I wasn't conscious of wanting anything specific. My discontent was simply a vague, empty feeling, a good deal like being hungry, when no food you can call to mind seems to be what you want.

Mrs. Scot-Williams of her own accord suggested a vacation of two months for me. I know she must have observed that my spirits had fallen below normal. Mrs. Scot-Williams said she was afraid I had been working too steadily, and needed a change. I was looking a little tired. She invited me to go to Japan with her, starting in mid-July. We'd pick up some antiques for the shop in the East. It would do me a world of good. Perhaps Mrs. Scot-Williams was right. Such a complete change might help me to regain my old poise. I told her I would go with pleasure.

However, before I ever got started my loneliness culminated one dismal night, two days before the Fourth of July. I had been away for two weeks with Mrs. Scot-Williams on a suffrage campaign, combining a little business en route. Mrs. Scot-Williams had had to return in time to celebrate the holiday with her college-boy son and some friends of his at her summer place on Long Island.

I arrived at the Grand Central alone, hot and tired. It was an exceedingly warm night. I felt forlorn, returning to New York for an uncelebrated holiday. I took the subway down town. The air was stifling. It always manages to rob me of good-cheer. When I reached the room in Irving Place I found Esther writing as usual. Esther had grown pale and anemic of late. Her book had met with success, and it seemed to make her a little more impersonal and remote than ever. I had been away two weeks, but Esther didn't even get up as I came in. That was all right. We're never demonstrative.

"Hello," she said, "you back?" She dipped her pen into the ink-well.

"I'm back," I replied, and went over and raised the shade. A girl all in white and a young man carrying her coat went by, laughing intimately. Oh, well! What of it? I shrugged. I had my career, my affairs, Van de Vere's. "Want to come out somewhere interesting for dinner?" I suggested to Esther.

"Sorry," she said. "Can't possibly. Got to work."

I stared at Esther's back a moment in silence. Her restricted affection was inadequate tonight. I glanced around the room. It was unbeautiful in July. Where was the lure of it? Where had disappeared the charm of my life anyhow? Why should I be standing here, fighting a desire to cry? I could go out and find some one to dine with me. Of course—of course I could. I went to the telephone. Should it be Virginia, Rosa, Alsace and Lorraine, Flora Bennett? None—none of them! My heart cried out for somebody of my own tonight, upon whom I had a claim of some kind or other. I called Malcolm, my own older brother. We had grown a little formal of late. That was true. Never mind. I'd break through the reserve somehow. I'd draw near him. There was the bond of our parents. I wanted bonds tonight.

I got Malcolm's number at last. I was informed by a house-mate of his that my brother had gone to a reunion with his people for over the Fourth of July. His people! What a sound it had for my hungry soul. His people! *My* people, too, bound in loyalty by identical traditions. I, too, would go to them for a day or two. There would probably be a letter for me.

I went to my desk and glanced through my waiting mail. There was nothing, absolutely nothing. I looked through the pile twice. A family reunion and they had not notified me! I had become as detached as all that! I glanced at Esther again. She was scratching away like mad. I heard the drone of a hurdy-gurdy outside. I would not stay here. The thought of a holiday in Irving Place became suddenly unendurable. I must escape it somehow. There was a train north an hour later. My suitcase was still packed.

"Esther," I said quietly, "I believe I'll go up to Hilton for the holiday. I don't seem to be especially needed here."

"Mind not interrupting?" said Esther, scratching away hard. "I'm right in the midst of an idea."

I picked up my suitcase, and stole out.

CHAPTER XXX

AGAIN LUCY NARRATES

No one was more surprised than I on the morning of the Fourth of July, when Ruth unexpectedly arrived from New York.

We Vars were all at Edith's in Hilton, even to Tom and Elise, who had taken a cottage on the Cape for the summer and were able to run up and join us all for the holiday. Will and I had motored up from our university town, and even Malcolm had put in an appearance. I had advised Edith not to bother to write Ruth about the impromptu reunion. I had understood that she was traveling around somewhere with her prominent suffrage leader, Mrs. Scot-Williams. Ruth is a woman of affairs now, and I try not to disturb her with family trivialities. The reunion was not to be a joyful occasion anyhow. A cloud hovered over it. We're a loyal family, and if one of us is in trouble, the others all try to help out. Oliver was the one to be helped just at present. The Fourth of July holiday offered an excellent opportunity for us all to meet and talk over his problem.

Oliver has always been financially unfortunate. In fact, life has dealt out everything in the line of blessings stingily to Oliver, except, possibly, babies. To Oliver and Madge had been born four children. With the last one there had settled upon Madge a persistent little cough. We didn't consider it anything serious. She didn't herself, and when Oliver dropped in one

Olive Higgins Prouty

night at Will's and my house, just a week before the Fourth of July, and said something about spots on her lungs, and Colorado immediately, it was a shock. The doctor wanted Madge to start within a week. He was going out to Colorado with another patient and could take her along with him at the same time. He would allow only Marjorie, the oldest little girl, to accompany her mother. The others must positively be left behind. He couldn't predict anything. The lungs were in a serious condition. However, if the climate proved beneficial, Madge would have to stay in Colorado at least six months.

Now Oliver and Madge live very economically. They can't afford governesses and trained nurses. Madge, poor girl, had to go away not knowing what arrangement was to be made for the care of the two little girls and infant son, the first Vars heir, by the way, whom she left behind. Oliver went as far as Hilton with her and got off there with his motherless brood, joining us at Edith's, while Madge and Marjorie were whisked away out West with the doctor and the other patient.

I felt sorry for Oliver. He was anxious and worried, seemed helpless and inadequate. The children hung on him and asked endless questions. He was tired, poor boy, and disheartened. The arrangement we suggested for the children did not please him. Edith had generously offered to assume the care of the little Vars heir. I had said that I would take. Emily, and to Elise was allotted Becky, aged three. We were all in Edith's living-room talking about it, when Ruth suddenly appeared on the scene.

Now Ruth is an interior decorator. Her shop is one of the most successful and exclusive in New York City. We're all very proud of Ruth. When she appeared that day so unexpectedly at the Homestead, I spied her first coming up the walk to Edith's door.

"Well—look what's coming!" I exclaimed, for Ruth was not alone. She was carrying Oliver's littlest girl, Becky.

"Good gracious!" exclaimed Edith.

"Is it Ruth?" asked Malcolm, staring hard through his thick, near-sighted glasses.

"Has she got Becky?" inquired Oliver.

"Explain yourself," laughed Alec, going to the screen door and letting Ruth in.

We all gathered round her.

"Hello, everybody," she smiled at us over Becky's shoulder. She was warm with walking. "Nothing to explain. Just decided to run up here, that's all, and found this poor little thing crying down by the gate. It's Becky, isn't it, Oliver? I haven't seen her for a year."

"It's just a shame you didn't let us meet you," said Edith. "Walking in this weather! I declare it is. Come, give that child to me, and you go on upstairs and get washed up. She's ruining your skirt. Come, Becky."

Becky is an extremely timid little creature. She hadn't let any one but Oliver touch her since Madge had gone the day before. She had been crying most of the time. Her lip quivered at the sight of Edith's outstretched hands. I saw her plump arm tighten around Ruth's neck.

"Here, come, Becky," said Oliver sternly, and offered to take her himself. She turned away even from him. "She takes fancies," explained Oliver. "You're in for it, I'm afraid, Ruth."

"Am I?" Ruth said, flushing unaccountably. "Well, you see," she went on apologetically, "I came upon her down there by the gate just as she had fallen down and hurt her knee. I was the only one to pick her up, so she had to let me. I put powder on the bruised knee. It interested her. It made her laugh. We had quite a game, and when I came away she insisted upon coming, too."

"You see, Madge has started for Colorado," I explained, "and Becky—"

"Colorado!" exclaimed Ruth. Of course she didn't know.

We told her about it.

"Poor little lonely kiddie," Ruth said softly afterward, giving Becky a strange little caress with the tip of her finger on the end of the child's infinitesimal nose. "Most as forlorn as some one they don't invite to family reunions any more."

"Why, Ruth," I remonstrated. "We thought—you see—"

"Never mind," she interrupted lightly. "I wasn't serious. I'll run upstairs now, and freshen up a bit."

"Come, Becky," ordered Oliver, "get down."

I saw Becky's arm tighten around Ruth's neck again. She's an unaccountable child.

Ruth said quietly, "Let her come upstairs with me, if she wants. I haven't had a welcome like this since the days of poor little Dandy."

An hour later Edith and I found Ruth sitting in a rocking-chair in the room that used to be hers years ago when she was a young girl. She was holding Becky.

"What in the world are you doing?" asked Edith.

"I never held a sleeping child before, and I'm discovering," replied Ruth, softly so as not to disturb Becky. "Aren't the little things limp?"

"Well, put her down now, do," said practical Edith. "We want you downstairs. Luncheon is nearly ready."

"I can't yet," said Ruth. "Every time I start to leave her she cries, and won't let me. Isn't it odd of the little creature? You two go on down. I'll be with you as soon as I can."

Later that afternoon we continued the discussion that Ruth had interrupted. Oliver didn't seem to be any more reconciled to the arrangement than before.

"I hate to break the home all up," he objected. "I want to keep the children together. Madge does, too. I should think there ought to be some one who likes children, and who wants a home, who could come and help me out for six months, who wouldn't cost too much."

"Hired help! No, no. Never works," Tom said, shaking his head.

"You have to be away so much on business, you know, Oliver," I reminded.

Suddenly Ruth spoke, picking up a magazine and opening it. "How would I do, instead of the hired help, Oliver?" she asked, casually glancing at an advertisement. "Becky didn't seem to mind me."

"You!" echoed Malcolm.

"Why, Ruth!" I exclaimed.

"What in the world do you mean?" demanded Edith.

"Oh, thanks," smiled Oliver kindly upon her. "Thanks, Ruth. It is bully of you to offer, but, of course, I wouldn't think of such a thing."

"Why not?" she inquired calmly. "I could give you the entire summer. I'm taking a two months' vacation this year."

"Oh, no, no. No, thanks, Ruth. Our apartment is, no vacation spot. I assure you of that. Hot, noisy, one general housework girl. It certainly is fine of you, but no, thanks, Ruth. Such a sacrifice is not necessary."

"It wouldn't be a sacrifice," remarked Ruth, turning a page of the magazine.

"Oh, come, come, Ruth!" broke in Tom irritably. "Let us not discuss such an impossibility. We're wasting time. You have your duties. This is not one of them. It's a fine impulse, generous. Oliver appreciates it. But it's quite out of the question."

"I don't see why," Ruth pursued. "For an unattached woman to come and take care of her brother's children during her vacation seems to me the most natural thing in the world."

"You know nothing about children," snorted Tom.

"I can learn," Ruth persisted.

Ruth's offer proved to be no passing whim, no sentimental impulse of the moment. Scarcely a week later, and she was actually installed in Oliver's small apartment. The family talked of little else at their various dinner-tables for weeks to come. Of all Ruth's vagaries this seemed the vaguest and most mystifying.

Oliver's apartment is really quite awful, disorderly, crowded, incongruous. It contains a specimen of every kind of furniture since the period of hair-cloth down to mission—cast-offs from the homes of Oliver's more fortunate brothers and sisters. When I first saw Ruth there in the midst of the confusion of unpacking, the room in Irving Place with its old chests and samovars, Esther Claff quietly writing in her corner, the telephone bell muffled to an undisturbing whirr, flashed before me.

The baby was crying. I smelled the odor of steaming clothes, in process of washing in the near-by kitchen. I heard the deep voice of the big Irish wash-woman I had engaged, conversing with the rough Norwegian. Becky was hanging on to Ruth's skirt and begging to be taken up. In the apartment below some one was playing a victrola. I hoped Ruth was not as conscious as I of Van de Vere's at this time in the morning—low bells, subdued voices, velvet-footed attendants, system, order.

"Well, Ruth," I broke out, "I hope you'll be able to stand this. If it's too much you must write and let me know."

She picked up Becky and held her a moment. "I think I shall manage to pull through," she replied.

CHAPTER XXXI

RUTH DRAWS CONCLUSIONS

Will and I were buried in a little place in Newfoundland all summer, and Ruth's letters to us, always three days old when they reached me, were few and infrequent. What brief notes she did write were non-committal. They told their facts without comment. I tried to read between the practical lines that announced she had changed the formula for the baby's milk, that she had had to let down Emily's dresses, that she had succeeded in persuading Oliver to spend his three weeks' vacation with Madge in Colorado, finally that Becky had been ill, but was better now. I was unable to draw any conclusions. I knew what sort of service Ruth's new enterprise required— duties performed over and over again, homely tasks, no pay, no praise. I knew the daily wear and tear on good intentions and exalted motives. I used to conjecture by the hour with Will upon what effect the summer would have on Ruth's theories. She has advanced ideas for women. She believes in their emancipation.

Edith and Alec had gone to Alaska. They could not report to me how Ruth was progressing. Elise had been unable to leave her cottage on the Cape for a single trip to Boston. Only Oliver's enthusiastic letters (Oliver who never sees anything but the obvious) assured me that, at least on the surface, Ruth had not regretted her undertaking.

Will and I returned the first of September. Ruth's two months would terminate on September tenth, and I had come back early in order to help close Oliver's apartment and prepare for the distribution of the children, which we had arranged in the early summer. Oliver was still in Colorado when I returned. He was expected within a week, however. I called Ruth up on the telephone as soon as I could, and told her I would be over to see her the next day, or the day after. I couldn't say just when, for Elise and Tom, who were returning to Wisconsin, were to spend the following night with me. Perhaps after dinner we would all get into the automobile and drop in upon her.

We all did. Oliver's apartment is on the other side of Boston from Will and me. We didn't reach there until after eight o'clock. The children, of course, were in bed. Ruth met us in the hall, half-way up the stairs. She was paler than usual. As I saw her it flashed over me how blind we had been to allow this girl—temperamental, exotic, sensitive to surroundings—to plunge herself into the responsibilities that most women acquire gradually. Her first real vacation in years too!

Elise and I kissed her.

"You look a little tired, Ruth," said Elise.

"A woman with children expects to look tired sometimes," Ruth replied, with the sophistication of a mother of three. "I had to be up a few nights with Becky."

I slipped my arm about Ruth as we mounted the stairs. "Has it been an awful summer?" I whispered.

She didn't answer me—simply drew away. I felt my inquiry displeased her. At the top of the landing she ran ahead and opened the door to the apartment, inviting us in. I was unprepared for the sight that awaited us.

"Why, Ruth!" I exclaimed, for I recognized all about me familiar bowl and candlestick from Irving Place, old carved chest, Russian samovar, embroidered strips of peasant's handicraft.

"How lovely!" said Elise, pushing by me into Oliver's living-room.

It really was. I gazed speechless. It made me think of the inside of a peasant's cottage as sometimes prettily portrayed upon the stage. It was very simple, almost bare, and yet there was a charm. At the windows hung yellowish, unbleached cotton. On the sills were red geraniums in bloom. A big clump of southern pine filled an old copper basin on a low tavern table. A queer sort of earthen lamp cast a soft light over all. In the dining-room I caught a glimpse of three sturdy little high chairs painted bright red, picked up in some antique shop, evidently. On the sideboard, a common table covered with a red cloth, I saw the glow of old pewter.

"You've done wonders to this place," commented Tom, gazing about.

"Oliver gave me full permission before he went away," Ruth explained. "I've stored a whole load-full of his things. It *is* rather nice, I think, myself."

"Nice? I should say it was! But did it pay for so short a time?" I inquired.

"Oliver can keep the things as long as he wants them," said Ruth.

"But it must make your room in Irving Place an empty spot to go back to," I replied.

Ruth went over to the lamp and did something to the shade. "Oh," she said carelessly, "haven't I told you? I'm not going back. I've resigned from Van de Vere's. Do all sit down."

Ruth might just as well have set off a cannon-cracker. We were startled to say the least. We stood and stared at her.

"Do sit down," she repeated.

"But, Ruth, why have you done this? Why have you resigned?" I gasped at last. She finished with the lamp-shade before she spoke.

"I insist upon your sitting down," she said. "There. That's better." Then she gave a queer, low laugh and said, "I think it was the sight of the baby's little flannel shirt stretched over the wooden frame hanging in the bath-room that was the last straw that broke me before I wrote to Mrs. Scot-Williams."

"But—"

"There was some one immediately available to take my place at Van de Vere's—another protegee of Mrs. Scot-Williams. I had to decide quickly. Madge is improving every week, Oliver writes, but she has got to stay in Colorado at least during the winter, the doctor says. Becky is still far from strong. She was very ill this summer. She doesn't take to strangers. I think I'm needed here. It seemed necessary for me to stay."

"Perfect nonsense," Tom growled. "There's no more call for you to give up your business than for Malcolm his. Perfectly absurd."

"But oh, how fine—how fine of you, Ruth!" exclaimed Elise.

"You shan't do it. You shan't," I ejaculated.

"Don't all make a mistake, please," said Ruth. "It is no sacrifice. There's no unselfishness about it, no fine altruism. I'm staying because I want to. I'm happier here. Can't any of you understand that?" she asked. There was a quality in her voice that made us all glance at her sharply. There was a look in her eyes which reminded me of her as she had appeared in the suffrage parade. This sister of mine had evidently seen another vision. If it had made her cheeks a little pale, it had more than made up for it in the exalted tone of her voice and expression of her eyes.

"You say you're happier here?" asked Elise. "Weren't you happy then, down there in New York, Ruth?"

"Yes, for a while. But you see my life was like a circle uncompleted. In keeping trimmed the lights of a home even though not my own, even only for a short period, I am tracing in, ever so faintly, the yawning gap."

"Gap! But Ruth, we thought—"

She flushed a little in spite of herself. We were all staring hard at her. "You see," she went on, "I've never been needed before as I have this summer. A home has never depended upon me for its life before. I've liked it. I don't see why you're so surprised. It's natural for a woman to want human ties. Contentment has stolen over me with every little common task I have had to do."

"But, Ruth," I stammered, "we never thought that this—housekeeping—such menial work as this, was meant for *you*."

"Nor love and devotion either, I suppose," she said a little bitterly, "nor the protection of a fireside," she shrugged. "Such rewards are not given without service, I've heard. And service paid by love does not seem menial to me."

Tom laid down his hat upon the table, and leaned forward. He had been observing Ruth keenly. I saw the flash of victory in his eye. Tom had never been in sympathy with Ruth's emancipation ideas, and I saw in her desire for a home and intimate associations the crumbling of her strongest defense against his disapproval. I wished I could come to her aid. Always my sympathies had instinctively gone out to her in the controversies that her theories gave rise to. Would Tom plant at last his flag upon her long-defended fortress?

"This is odd talk for you, Ruth," said Tom.

"Is it?" she inquired innocently. Did she not observe Tom calling together his forces for a last charge?

"Certainly," he replied. "You gave up home, love, devotion— all that, when you might have had it, years ago. You emancipated yourself from the sort of service that is paid by the protection of a fireside."

"Well?" she smiled, unalarmed.

"You see your mistake now," he hurried on. "You make your mad dash for freedom, and now come seeking shelter. That is what most of 'em do. You tried freedom and found it lacking."

"And what is your conclusion, Tom?" asked Ruth, baring herself, it seemed to me, to the onslaught of Tom's opposition.

"My conclusion! Do I need even to state it?" he inquired, as if flourishing the flag before sticking its staff into the pinnacle of Ruth's defense. "Is it not self-evident? If you had married five years ago, today you would have a permanent family of your own instead of a borrowed one for eight months. Your freedom has robbed you of what you imply you desire—a home, I mean. My conclusion is that your own history proves that freedom is a dangerous thing for women."

Ruth answered Tom quietly. I thrilled at her mild and gentle manner. We all listened intently.

"Tom," she said slowly and with conviction, "my own history proves just the opposite. The very fact that I do feel the deficiencies of freedom, is proof that it has not been a dangerous tool. If it had killed in me the home instinct, then I might concede that your fears were justified, but if, as you say, most women do not rove far but come home in answer to their heart's call, then men need not fear to cut the leash." With some such words Ruth pulled Tom's flag from out her fortress where he had planted it. As Tom made no reply she went on talking. "Once I had no excuse for existence unless I married. My efforts were narrowed to that one accomplishment. I sought marriage, desperately, to escape the stigma of becoming a superfluous and unoccupied female. Today if I marry it will be in answer to my great desire, and, whether married or not, a broader outlook and a deeper appreciation are mine. I believe that working hard for something worth while pays dividends to a woman always. If I never have a home of my own," Ruth went on, "and I may not—spinsters," she added playfully, "like the poor must always be with us—at least I have a trade by which I can be self-supporting. I'm better equipped whatever happens. Oh, I don't regret having gone forth. No, Tom, pioneers must expect to pay. I'm so convinced," she burst forth eagerly, "that wider activities and broader outlooks for women generally are a wise thing, that if I had a fortune left me I would spend it in establishing trade-schools in little towns all over the country, like the Carnegie libraries, so that all girls could have easy access to self-support. I'd make it the custom for girls to have a trade as well as an education and athletic and parlor accomplishments. I'd unhamper women in every way I knew how, give them a training to use modern tools, and then I'd give them the tools. They won't tear down homes with them. Don't be afraid of that. Instinct is too strong. They'll build better ones."

My brother shook his head. "I give you up, Ruth, I give you up," he said.

"Don't do that," she replied. "I'm like so many other girls in this age. Don't give us up. We want you. We need your conservatism to balance and steady. We need our new freedom guided and directed. We're the new generation, Tom. We're the new spirit. There are hundreds—thousands—of us. Don't give us up." I seemed to see Ruth's army suddenly swarming about her as she spoke, and Ruth, starry-eyed and victorious, standing on the summit in their midst.

CHAPTER XXXII

BOB DRAWS CONCLUSIONS TOO

It was Edith who told me the news about Mrs. Sewall. I ought to have been prepared for anything. Ever since Ruth had been employed as secretary to Mrs. Sewall there had been something mysterious about their relations. Ruth had never explained the details of her life in the Sewall household—I had never inquired too particularly—but whenever she referred to Mrs. Sewall there was a troubled and sort of wistful expression in her eyes which made me suspicious. She admired Mrs. Sewall, no doubt of that. She felt deep affection for her. Several times she had said to me during our intimate talks together, of which we had had a good many lately, "Oh, Lucy, I wish the ocean wasn't so wide. I'd run across for over a Sunday." I knew, without asking, that Ruth was thinking of Mrs. Sewall. She was living in London.

Edith called me on the telephone early one Monday morning. She frequently is in Boston, shopping. From the hour, evidently she had just arrived from Hilton.

"Well," she began excitedly, "what have you got to say?"

"Say? What about?"

"Haven't you seen the paper?" she demanded.

"Not yet," I had to confess. "I've been terribly rushed

this morning."

"You don't know what has happened, then?"

"No. What has? Out with it," I retorted a little alarmed. Edith's voice was high-pitched and strained.

"The old lady Sewall has died."

"Oh, I'm sorry," I replied, relieved, however.

"In London—a week ago," went on Edith.

"Really? What a shame! Does Ruth know?"

"She ought to. It rather affects her."

"How's that?"

"How's that!" repeated Edith. "Good heavens, if you'd read your paper you'd understand how. The old lady's will is published. It's terribly thrilling."

The color mounted to my face. "What do you mean, Edith?"

"Never you mind. You go along and read for yourself, and then meet me at one o'clock—no, make it twelve. I've got to talk to some one—quick. I never saw the article myself until I was on the train coming down. I'm just about bursting. Good gracious, Lucy, hustle up, and make it eleven o'clock, sharp."

We agreed on a meeting-place and I hung up the receiver, went upstairs to my room, sat down, and opened the paper. I found the article Edith referred to easily enough. It was on the inside of the front page printed underneath large letters. It was appalling! The third sentence of the headlines contained my sister's name. There must be some mistake. Wasn't such news as this borne by a lawyer with proper ceremony and form, or at least delivered by mail, inside an envelope sealed with red wax?

Ruth had known nothing of this three days ago when I called to see her. It could not be true. All the way into Boston on the electric car, I felt self-conscious and ill-at-ease. I was afraid some one I knew would meet me, and refer to the newspaper announcement. I would dislike to confess, "I know no more about it than you." I hate newspaper notoriety anyhow.

Edith greeted me as if we hadn't met for years, kissed me ecstatically and grasped both my hands tight in hers. Her sparkling eyes expressed what the publicity of the hotel corridor, where we met, prevented her from proclaiming aloud.

"Where can we go to be alone for half a minute?" she whispered.

"Let's try in here," I said, and we entered a deserted reception-room, and sat down in a bay-window.

"Did you telephone to Ruth?" was Edith's first remark.

I shook my head. "No. I didn't like to," I said.

"Nor I," confessed Edith. "She's always been touchy with me on the subject of Mrs. Sewall since the row. Isn't it too exciting?"

"Can it be legal, Edith?" I inquired.

"Of course, silly. Wills aren't published until they're looked into. Legal? Of course it is. I always said Ruth would do something splendid, one of these days, and she has, she has—the rascal."

"You've got so much money yourself, Edith, why does a little more in the family please you so?" I asked. Edith was extremely excited.

"A little. It isn't a little. It's a *lot*. But it isn't just the money.

It's more. It's what the money does. There has always been a kind of pitying attitude toward us in Hilton since that Sewall affair of Ruth's, for all my efforts. This clears it up absolutely. Haven't you read the way the thing's worded? Wait a minute." She opened her folded paper. "Here, I have it." Her eyes knew exactly where to look. Ruth's name appeared in the will at the very end of a long list of bequests to various charitable institutions.

"Listen. 'All the rest, residue, and remainder of my property, wheresoever and whatsoever, including my house in New York City, my house in Hilton, Massachusetts, known as Grassmere; my furniture, books, pictures and jewels, I give, devise, and bequeath to the former fiancee of my son, now deceased, in affectionate memory of our relations. This portion of my estate to be used and to be directed, according to the dictates of her own high discretion, during the term of her natural life and at her death to pass to her lawful issue.' Did you ever hear anything to equal it?" demanded Edith. "Don't you see the old lady recognizes Ruth before the world? Don't you see, however humiliated I was at that distressing affair three or four summers ago, it's all wiped off the slate now, by this? She makes Ruth her heir, Lucy. Don't you see that? And she does it affectionately, too. I can't get over it! I don't know what made the old veteran do such a thing. I don't care much either. All I know is, that we're fixed all right in Hilton society *now*. Grassmere Ruth's! Good heavens—think of it! Think of the power in my hands, if only Ruth behaves, to pay back a few old scores. I only wish Breck was alive. She'd marry him now, I guess, with all this recognition. I wonder whatever she'll do with Grassmere anyhow."

"Turn it into some sort of institution for making women independent human beings, I'll wager." I laughed, recalling Ruth's words of scarcely a fortnight ago.

"If only she hadn't gotten so abnormal, and queer!" Edith sighed. "Perhaps this stroke of good luck will make her a little more like the rest of us. We must all look out and not let Ruth do anything ridiculous with this fortune of hers."

* * * * *

Will and I went over to see Ruth that evening.

"Why, hello!" she called down, surprised, through the tube, in answer to my ring. "Will and you! Really? Come right up."

"She doesn't know," I told Will, pushing open the heavy door and beginning to mount.

"Guess not," agreed my husband. "Here's her evening paper in her box, untouched."

We found Ruth just finishing with the dishes. The maid-of-all-work was out, and Ruth was alone. She called to me to come back and help her, and sang out brightly for Will to amuse himself with the paper. He'd probably find it downstairs in the box.

Five minutes later Ruth slipped off her blue-checked apron, and we joined Will by the low lamp in the living-room. My sister looked very pretty in a loose black velvet smock. Her hair was coiled into a simple little knot in the nape of her neck. There were a few slightly waving strands astray about her face. Her hands, still damp from recent dish-washing, were the color of pink coral.

"I'm tired tonight," she said, sighing audibly, and pulling herself up on the top of the high carved chest. She tucked a dull red pillow behind her head, and leaned back in the corner. "There! This is comfort," she went on. "Read the news out loud to me, Will, while I sit here and luxuriate." She closed her eyes.

"All right," Will agreed. "By the way," he broke off, as unconsciously as possible, a minute or so later, "Have you heard anything from Mrs. Sewall lately?"

There was a slight pause. The lady's name invariably clouded my sister's bright spirit. She opened her eyes. They were wistful.

"No," she replied quietly, "I haven't. She's in England. Why do you ask?"

"Oh, I was just wondering," my husband replied, losing his splendid courage. "I suppose you two got to be pretty good friends."

"Yes, we did," Ruth replied shortly. There was another pause. Then in a low, troubled voice Ruth added, "But not now. We're not friends now. Something happened. All her affection for me has died. I have never been forgiven for something."

"Oh, I wouldn't be so sure," belittled Will, making violent signs to me to announce the news we bore.

I had a clipping in my shopping-bag cut from the morning paper. I took it out of the envelope that contained it.

"Ruth," I began, "here's something I ran across today."

The telephone interrupted sharply.

"Just a minute," she said, and slid down off the chest and went out into the hall. "Hello," I heard her say. "Hello," and then in a changed voice, "Oh, you?" A pause and then, "Really? Tonight?" Another pause, and more gently. "Of course you must. Of course I do," and at last very tenderly, "Yes, I'll be right here. I'll be waiting. Good-by."

I looked at Will, and he lifted his eyebrows. Ruth came back and stood in the doorway. There was a peculiar, shining quality about her expression.

"That was Bob," she said quietly.

"Bob?" I exclaimed.

"Bob Jennings?" ejaculated Will.

Ruth nodded and smiled. Standing there before us, dressed simply in the plain black smock, cheeks flushed, eyes like stars, she reminded me of some rare stone in a velvet case. The bareness of the room, with its few genuine articles, set off the jewel-like brightness of my sister in a startling fashion.

"You don't mean to say old Bob's turned up," commented Will.

"Tell us," bluntly I demanded, "what in the world is Robert Jennings doing around here, Ruth?"

"Bob's been in town for several days," she replied. "He has just telephoned that he is called back on business. His train leaves in a little over an hour. He's dropping in here in ten minutes."

"Why, I didn't know you even wrote to each other," I said.

Ruth came over to the table and sat down in a low chair, stretching out her folded hands arms-length along the table's surface, and leaning toward us.

"I'm going to tell you two about it," she announced with finality. "I wrote to Bob," she confessed, half proud, half apologetic. "I wrote to Bob without any excuse at all, except that I wanted to tell him what I'd found out. I wanted to tell him that I had discovered that this sort of thing," she opened her hands, and made a little gesture that included everything that those few small rooms of Oliver's epitomized, "that this sort of thing," she resumed, "was what most women want more than anything else in the world. Any other activity was simply preparation, or courageous makeshift if this was denied. I made it easy for Bob, in my letter, to answer me in the spirit of friendly argument if he chose, but he didn't. He came on instead. We're going to be married," she said, in a voice as casual as if she were announcing that they were going out for dinner.

"You're going to be married?" I repeated.

"Yes," she nodded. "After all these years! Once," she went on in a triumphant voice, "our fields of vision were so small that our differences of opinion loomed up like insurmountable barriers. Now the differences are mere specks on our broadened outlooks. Oh, I know," she went on as if inspired, "I've been a long journey, simply to come back to Bob again. But it hasn't been in vain. There was no short cut to the perfect understanding that is Bob's and mine today."

"And when," timidly I inquired, "do you intend to be married, Ruth?"

My sister's expression clouded. She smiled, and shook her head. "I don't know," she said, "I wish I did. Years are so precious when one is concealing a little nest of gray hairs behind one's left ear. Bob and I have got to wait. You see Bob wasn't planning for this. He had some idea a career would always satisfy me. He hasn't been saving. He has put about all he has been able to earn into fighting for clean politics. I myself haven't been able to lay by but a paltry thousand. Madge comes home in May. I shall then probably have to look up another job for myself somewhere or other, while Bob's establishing himself and making ready for me out there."

Will cleared his throat and coughed. He had simply stared until now. "I suppose," he said, as if in an attempt to lighten the conversation with a little light humor, "I suppose a legacy of some sort wouldn't prove unwelcome to you and Bob just about now."

It must have struck Ruth as a stereotyped attempt at fun. But she smiled and replied in the same vein, "I think we'd know how to make use of a portion of it." Then she rose. The door bell had rung sharply twice. "There he is," she explained.

"There's Bob now. I'll let him in."

She went out into the hall and pressed the button that released the lock of the door three floors below.

I knew how fleeting every minute of last hours before train-time can be. I motioned to Will, and when Ruth came back to us I said, "We'll just run down the back way, Ruth."

She flashed me an appreciative glance. "You don't need to," she deprecated.

"Still, we will," I assured her, and then I went over and kissed my radiant sister.

Her face was illumined as it used to be years ago when Robert Jennings was on his way to her. The same old tenderness gleamed in her larger-visioned eyes.

"When he comes read this together," I said, and I slipped the envelope, with the clipping inside it, into her hands.

Then Will and I went out through the kitchen, and down the back stairs.

ABOUT THE AUTHOR

Olive Higgins Prouty (January 10, 1882–March 24, 1974) was an American novelist, best known for her pioneering consideration of psychotherapy in Now, Voyager and her feminist melodrama Stella Dallas. The latter was used as the basis for two successful films - the 1937 version was nominated for two Academy Awards - and a radio serial which was broadcast daily for 18 years, despite Prouty's legal efforts (since she had not authorized the sale of the broadcast rights, and was displeased with her characters' portrayals).

Prouty is also known for her philanthropic works, and for her resulting association with Sylvia Plath, whom she encountered as a result of endowing a Smith College scholarship for "promising young writers". She supported Plath financially in the wake of Plath's unsuccesful 1953 suicide attempt; subsequently, Plath used Prouty as the basis of the character of "Philomena Guinea" in her 1963 novel, The Bell Jar.

In 1961, Prouty wrote her memoirs but, as her public profile had diminished, could not find a publisher; she had them printed at her own expense.

Choose from Thousands of 1stWorldLibrary Classics By

A. M. Barnard
Ada Leverson
Adolphus William Ward
Aesop
Agatha Christie
Alexander Aaronsohn
Alexander Kielland
Alexandre Dumas
Alfred Gatty
Alfred Ollivant
Alice Duer Miller
Alice Turner Curtis
Alice Dunbar
Allen Chapman
Alleyne Ireland
Ambrose Bierce
Amelia E. Barr
Amory H. Bradford
Andrew Lang
Andrew McFarland Davis
Andy Adams
Angela Brazil
Anna Alice Chapin
Anna Sewell
Annie Besant
Annie Hamilton Donnell
Annie Payson Call
Annie Roe Carr
Annonaymous
Anton Chekhov
Archibald Lee Fletcher
Arnold Bennett
Arthur C. Benson
Arthur Conan Doyle
Arthur M. Winfield
Arthur Ransome
Arthur Schnitzler
Arthur Train
Atticus
B.H. Baden-Powell
B. M. Bower
B. C. Chatterjee
Baroness Emmuska Orczy
Baroness Orczy
Basil King
Bayard Taylor
Ben Macomber
Bertha Muzzy Bower
Bjornstjerne Bjornson

Booth Tarkington
Boyd Cable
Bram Stoker
C. Collodi
C. E. Orr
C. M. Ingleby
Carolyn Wells
Catherine Parr Traill
Charles A. Eastman
Charles Amory Beach
Charles Dickens
Charles Dudley Warner
Charles Farrar Browne
Charles Ives
Charles Kingsley
Charles Klein
Charles Hanson Towne
Charles Lathrop Pack
Charles Romyn Dake
Charles Whibley
Charles Willing Beale
Charlotte M. Braeme
Charlotte M. Yonge
Charlotte Perkins Stetson
Clair W. Hayes
Clarence Day Jr.
Clarence E. Mulford
Clemence Housman
Confucius
Coningsby Dawson
Cornelis DeWitt Wilcox
Cyril Burleigh
D. H. Lawrence
Daniel Defoe
David Garnett
Dinah Craik
Don Carlos Janes
Donald Keyhoe
Dorothy Kilner
Dougan Clark
Douglas Fairbanks
E. Nesbit
E. P. Roe
E. Phillips Oppenheim
E. S. Brooks
Earl Barnes
Edgar Rice Burroughs
Edith Van Dyne
Edith Wharton

Edward Everett Hale
Edward J. O'Biren
Edward S. Ellis
Edwin L. Arnold
Eleanor Atkins
Eleanor Hallowell Abbott
Eliot Gregory
Elizabeth Gaskell
Elizabeth McCracken
Elizabeth Von Arnim
Ellem Key
Emerson Hough
Emilie F. Carlen
Emily Bronte
Emily Dickinson
Enid Bagnold
Enilor Macartney Lane
Erasmus W. Jones
Ernie Howard Pie
Ethel May Dell
Ethel Turner
Ethel Watts Mumford
Eugene Sue
Eugenie Foa
Eugene Wood
Eustace Hale Ball
Evelyn Everett-green
Everard Cotes
F. H. Cheley
F. J. Cross
F. Marion Crawford
Fannie E. Newberry
Federick Austin Ogg
Ferdinand Ossendowski
Fergus Hume
Florence A. Kilpatrick
Fremont B. Deering
Francis Bacon
Francis Darwin
Frances Hodgson Burnett
Frances Parkinson Keyes
Frank Gee Patchin
Frank Harris
Frank Jewett Mather
Frank L. Packard
Frank V. Webster
Frederic Stewart Isham
Frederick Trevor Hill
Frederick Winslow Taylor

Friedrich Kerst
Friedrich Nietzsche
Fyodor Dostoyevsky
G.A. Henty
G.K. Chesterton
Gabrielle E. Jackson
Garrett P. Serviss
Gaston Leroux
George A. Warren
George Ade
Geroge Bernard Shaw
George Cary Eggleston
George Durston
George Ebers
George Eliot
George Gissing
George MacDonald
George Meredith
George Orwell
George Sylvester Viereck
George Tucker
George W. Cable
George Wharton James
Gertrude Atherton
Gordon Casserly
Grace E. King
Grace Gallatin
Grace Greenwood
Grant Allen
Guillermo A. Sherwell
Gulielma Zollinger
Gustav Flaubert
H. A. Cody
H. B. Irving
H.C. Bailey
H. G. Wells
H. H. Munro
H. Irving Hancock
H. R. Naylor
H. Rider Haggard
H. W. C. Davis
Haldeman Julius
Hall Caine
Hamilton Wright Mabie
Hans Christian Andersen
Harold Avery
Harold McGrath
Harriet Beecher Stowe
Harry Castlemon
Harry Coghill
Harry Houidini

Hayden Carruth
Helent Hunt Jackson
Helen Nicolay
Hendrik Conscience
Hendy David Thoreau
Henri Barbusse
Henrik Ibsen
Henry Adams
Henry Ford
Henry Frost
Henry James
Henry Jones Ford
Henry Seton Merriman
Henry W Longfellow
Herbert A. Giles
Herbert Carter
Herbert N. Casson
Herman Hesse
Hildegard G. Frey
Homer
Honore De Balzac
Horace B. Day
Horace Walpole
Horatio Alger Jr.
Howard Pyle
Howard R. Garis
Hugh Lofting
Hugh Walpole
Humphry Ward
Ian Maclaren
Inez Haynes Gillmore
Irving Bacheller
Isabel Cecilia Williams
Isabel Hornibrook
Israel Abrahams
Ivan Turgenev
J.G.Austin
J. Henri Fabre
J. M. Barrie
J. M. Walsh
J. Macdonald Oxley
J. R. Miller
J. S. Fletcher
J. S. Knowles
J. Storer Clouston
J. W. Duffield
Jack London
Jacob Abbott
James Allen
James Andrews
James Baldwin

James Branch Cabell
James DeMille
James Joyce
James Lane Allen
James Lane Allen
James Oliver Curwood
James Oppenheim
James Otis
James R. Driscoll
Jane Abbott
Jane Austen
Jane L. Stewart
Janet Aldridge
Jens Peter Jacobsen
Jerome K. Jerome
Jessie Graham Flower
John Buchan
John Burroughs
John Cournos
John F. Kennedy
John Gay
John Glasworthy
John Habberton
John Joy Bell
John Kendrick Bangs
John Milton
John Philip Sousa
John Taintor Foote
Jonas Lauritz Idemil Lie
Jonathan Swift
Joseph A. Altsheler
Joseph Carey
Joseph Conrad
Joseph E. Badger Jr
Joseph Hergesheimer
Joseph Jacobs
Jules Vernes
Julian Hawthrone
Julie A Lippmann
Justin Huntly McCarthy
Kakuzo Okakura
Karle Wilson Baker
Kate Chopin
Kenneth Grahame
Kenneth McGaffey
Kate Langley Bosher
Kate Langley Bosher
Katherine Cecil Thurston
Katherine Stokes
L. A. Abbot
L. T. Meade

L. Frank Baum
Latta Griswold
Laura Dent Crane
Laura Lee Hope
Laurence Housman
Lawrence Beasley
Leo Tolstoy
Leonid Andreyev
Lewis Carroll
Lewis Sperry Chafer
Lilian Bell
Lloyd Osbourne
Louis Hughes
Louis Joseph Vance
Louis Tracy
Louisa May Alcott
Lucy Fitch Perkins
Lucy Maud Montgomery
Luther Benson
Lydia Miller Middleton
Lyndon Orr
M. Corvus
M. H. Adams
Margaret E. Sangster
Margret Howth
Margaret Vandercook
Margaret W. Hungerford
Margret Penrose
Maria Edgeworth
Maria Thompson Daviess
Mariano Azuela
Marion Polk Angellotti
Mark Overton
Mark Twain
Mary Austin
Mary Catherine Crowley
Mary Cole
Mary Hastings Bradley
Mary Roberts Rinehart
Mary Rowlandson
M. Wollstonecraft Shelley
Maud Lindsay
Max Beerbohm
Myra Kelly
Nathaniel Hawthrone
Nicolo Machiavelli
O. F. Walton
Oscar Wilde
Owen Johnson
P.G. Wodehouse
Paul and Mabel Thorne

Paul G. Tomlinson
Paul Severing
Percy Brebner
Percy Keese Fitzhugh
Peter B. Kyne
Plato
Quincy Allen
R. Derby Holmes
R. L. Stevenson
R. S. Ball
Rabindranath Tagore
Rahul Alvares
Ralph Bonehill
Ralph Henry Barbour
Ralph Victor
Ralph Waldo Emmerson
Rene Descartes
Ray Cummings
Rex Beach
Rex E. Beach
Richard Harding Davis
Richard Jefferies
Richard Le Gallienne
Robert Barr
Robert Frost
Robert Gordon Anderson
Robert L. Drake
Robert Lansing
Robert Lynd
Robert Michael Ballantyne
Robert W. Chambers
Rosa Nouchette Carey
Rudyard Kipling
Saint Augustine
Samuel B. Allison
Samuel Hopkins Adams
Sarah Bernhardt
Sarah C. Hallowell
Selma Lagerlof
Sherwood Anderson
Sigmund Freud
Standish O'Grady
Stanley Weyman
Stella Benson
Stella M. Francis
Stephen Crane
Stewart Edward White
Stijn Streuvels
Swami Abhedananda
Swami Parmananda
T. S. Ackland

T. S. Arthur
The Princess Der Ling
Thomas A. Janvier
Thomas A Kempis
Thomas Anderton
Thomas Bailey Aldrich
Thomas Bulfinch
Thomas De Quincey
Thomas Dixon
Thomas H. Huxley
Thomas Hardy
Thomas More
Thornton W. Burgess
U. S. Grant
Upton Sinclair
Valentine Williams
Various Authors
Vaughan Kester
Victor Appleton
Victor G. Durham
Victoria Cross
Virginia Woolf
Wadsworth Camp
Walter Camp
Walter Scott
Washington Irving
Wilbur Lawton
Wilkie Collins
Willa Cather
Willard F. Baker
William Dean Howells
William le Queux
W. Makepeace Thackeray
William W. Walter
William Shakespeare
Winston Churchill
Yei Theodora Ozaki
Yogi Ramacharaka
Young E. Allison
Zane Grey